To Ralph,
the very epitome of WWJWD

D1373598

DEADER THAN DISCO

I've taken some ribbing recently about my qualifications as a detective. So let me just establish my deductive props right off the bat, a-iiight?

The moment I stepped out of the locker room, I knew something seismic had happened. A minimum of eight on the Richter scale.

At my health club, they have a bank of televisions recessed in the wall above the exercise machines. Usually people are flailing away like mad as they stare up at the screens. They look like baby ducks chasing after their momma.

But on this afternoon all exercise had stopped. Some people had dismounted, others were simply sitting there, but all of them were staring slack-jawed at the wall. Thought I: The game is afoot, Watson.

Each set has a different feed. At the hour I choose to work out, the choices are invariably CNN, *Dr. Phil*, *Crossing Over with John Edward* and *Days of Our Lives*. (Jesse, who works the juice bar, sets the channels and she's a big *Days* fan.) Walking over, I saw that the same image was on every screen. Another clue for someone with my trained eye.

Bruce Katz was giving a press statement and enjoying the *hell* out of it—just preening for the cameras. His chest puffed up like a quail, his Roman nose high in the air, his hands gesticulating, his white crown of hair flowing, he looked like a symphony conductor driving a big philharmonic through the final movement. Every few seconds he would look down at the forest of microphones arranged in front of him and beam like a kid with a huge basket of chocolate Easter eggs.

I think lawyers must all have been hammy vaudevillians in their previous lives. Nobody delights in being in the spotlight more than they do.

I'm glad to say I don't know the names of many attorneys, but Katz was a legend in the tradition of F. Lee Bailey and Jerry Spence: a shrewd and bombastic criminal lawyer who had a reputation for always getting his clients off—even if they were caught with their hand Super Glued to the cookie jar.

I took a set of headphones off the rack and plugged it into the jack on one of the unused machines to hear what was going on. It's like hooking up your car at a drive-in theater.

Katz was just concluding. "I am confident that once all the facts are known, my client will be cleared of all suspicion in this tragic incident," he said. Boilerplate lawyer lingo. No one's ever guilty. Katz lifted his hand magisterially, like he was Salvador Dali about to board a rocket ship to the moon. He held the pose while a battery of camera flashes went off. Then he walked reluctantly away from all those delicious microphones as the press corps erupted in a cacophony of shouted questions.

The people around me resumed their loco-motion. The four screens reverted to differentiated feeds. My anchor said, "That was Bruce Katz, the attorney for Angel. The pop megastar remains in custody at Los Angeles central booking. As we reported earlier, the singer was arrested just hours ago and charged with murder. According to sources in the sheriff's department . . ."

Now it was my turn to go slack-jawed. This truly blew my mind. For more than fifteen years, Angel had dominated pop culture, selling more CDs than Shania and Britney combined. Angel in the slammer? It was like the cops hauling off Julia Roberts in handcuffs on the evening news. That is, if Julia had spent her entire career parading around in eye-popping lingerie, blurring the line between underwear and outerwear.

Angel's staying power was nothing short of astounding. Because when she first gained attention with "You're My Lolly," she had "one-hit wonder" stenciled all over her. It was a naughty celebration of oral sex. The video, with Angel dressed like a schoolgirl and acting like a hooker, created an enormous controversy—with outraged commentators branding it soft porn.

But Angel was just warming up. I guess you could say she was the most successful strumpet in history—with a string of salacious hit songs and brazen videos. She was such a staple on MTV that one influential music writer suggested they simply rebrand the channel as AngelTV. When the straight sex thing got stale, she threw in a little religious imagery or S&M, but she always managed to shock.

Meanwhile her profligate love life made her a fixture in every tabloid and gossip column on the planet. She had been married twice—for about as long as most people honeymoon. And she had gone out with every Hollywood bad boy, male model and rock star stud worth mentioning. There was a squadron of paparazzi assigned to follow Angel around exclusively.

Her biannual tours were an event. They grew more elaborate and outrageous every time out. Even if you weren't a fan, you went to Angel's stadium shows just for the spectacle.

And I wasn't a fan. First of all, I didn't find her attractive. I know that's an odd admission to make about the woman

who virtually defined sex in the modern era. But she struck
me as cheap and slatternly. With her dark roots, flinty eyes,
gapped teeth and cruel mouth, she looked to me like a re-
form school version of Tatum O'Neal. She'd change her image with every album and people would ooh and aah about
her protean appearance. To me, it always looked like Angel
with a different hairdo. I say it's trailer trash and I say the
hell with it.

Same with her music. The critics praised it endlessly,
fawning over her uncanny knack for always nailing the mer-
curial zeitgeist. I could only assume that she must have sex-
ually serviced every music writer in this country. Because
her CDs sucked.

I got fooled more than once by her glowing notices. "This
is unquestionably her masterpiece," it would read. Or, "Angel has reinvented herself yet again." And I'd go out and buy
it. And every time it was the same crappy mix of vapid dance
tunes and woozy ballads.

It certainly didn't help that Angel's vocals sounded like a
rake being pulled across a blackboard. All the studio wizardry
in the world—and she worked with the best producers—
couldn't change the fact that she was a shrill, one-dimensional
hack without character or heart.

I could understand Angel getting arrested for lewdness or
for defrauding the public by posing as a singer. But murder?
That was definitely a shocker.

I took off the earphones and went on with my workout because I figured this was going to be a media shit storm I
couldn't escape anyway. Her case was undoubtedly going to
monopolize the news cycle for the foreseeable future. NBC
would probably send Stone Phillips door to door to give people updates.

What I didn't imagine was that within a matter of days I
would be responsible for finding the world's most famous
fugitive.

CHAPTER

2

After showering, I had a carrot juice. No matter what I order, Jesse always adds spirulina to the concoction. I don't even know what that is, but she assures me it's good for me. Then I ran some errands, which took me longer than I thought it would. Am I the only guy who goes up and down the aisles of Home Depot just gawking at stuff? All I needed was a measuring tape and I spent twenty-five minutes wandering around like a zombie.

When I got home, I did a double take looking at my answering machine on the counter. I have one of those models that blinks slowly if you have one message and a little faster with each subsequent incoming call. At that moment, the light was popping like a Morse code operator with a stutter.

As I reached for the Play button, the phone rang again. "Hello," I said.

"Jim McNamara?" said a brisk female voice.

"Yes."

"Hold for Lani Ross, please," she said, and, without waiting for a response, parked me in the ether.

Naturally, I recognized the name. Lani was Angel's publicist, and as such was nearly as well known as her client. Lani was quoted in the press at least once a week because every time there was story about Angel, her official spokeswoman was asked to respond.

It was a job Lani handled with remarkable good humor, never getting drawn into the controversy, always maintaining an air of levity. "Angel has never been on the island of Majorca," I recall her dismissing one rumor, "but she would love to visit one day with Mr. DiCaprio. Of course, they would have to actually meet each other before that could happen."

I was only on hold for ten seconds. "There you are," she said, as if I were an old chum who had been mischievously playing hide and seek with her. "How are you?"

"Uh . . . I'm okay," I said, still surprised to be on the phone with her. "What's up?"

She laughed with genuine merriment. "We have a little situation out here we were hoping to get your help with." Lani certainly sounded relaxed. I suppose when you're representing someone like Angel, crisis management becomes old hat. "Can you be here in, say . . . ten minutes?" she asked playfully.

"Look, I'm flattered you thought of me," I said, "but I really don't think I could be of much help. This is a criminal matter."

"And what was that Sheryl stalker thing? A broken fingernail?"

I sighed, loud enough for her to hear. "Listen," she said, and suddenly the tone changed. Her voice grew more serious. The acoustics focused too, as if she had gone from a headset to a handset. "Lenny at Warner Brothers told me you're smart, you're discreet and you know the business.

We're circling the wagons out here and I'd really like to have you aboard."

It wasn't like she had called the wrong guy. I was, after all, the rock 'n roll detective, a curious job category I had drifted into after being booted out of the record business with a bad drug problem. Once I got sober, I gradually started helping musicians—first with their addictions and then with all kinds of personal and felonious matters.

Now it was a full-time job. When the problem I was being hired to look into happened on tour, I was usually retained by an insurance company, since they ended up holding the bag if anything bad happened on the road. If a recording star ran into trouble in the studio or on the home front, my employer was usually the musician's label or management. Once in a while, the call came from the performer. That was rare. Once you've sold a couple million records, you generally cease having to do things for yourself. Someone even stirs your coffee for you.

So it was reasonable for Lani to call me. When the shit hits the fan, I'm your man. But that didn't mean I had to take the job. I'll be more honest with you than I was with Lani. My initial reluctance, in large part, stemmed from the fact that I simply didn't like Angel.

But I'm also a realist and it had occurred to me that Angel could more than afford my services. My rates aren't written down anywhere. Generally I charge whatever the traffic will allow. And in the short time I had been on the phone with Lani, my fee had doubled.

"I haven't even been following this, Lani," I said. "All I saw was the end of Bruce Katz's press conference."

"Turn on your TV," she said. "They'll catch you up in a hurry. The press is in a feeding frenzy."

"Who is she accused of killing?"

"Gentry Jones," Lani said. I whistled.

According to who you talked to, Jones was either every-

8   David Hiltbrand

thing that was wrong with professional sports or he was the most exciting star in the NBA. Growing up in the projects of Roxbury—the same tough Boston neighborhood that produced the Wahlberg brothers, Donny and Mark—Gentry's athletic skills had emerged early. While still in high school, his verve and ball-handling skills on the basketball court were getting national attention and drawing comparisons to Pistol Pete Maravich.

Despite flat-lining on his SAT scores, he was accepted at the University of Florida and earned the school a share of the SEC title in his freshman year. Then he jumped to the pros—a departure that may have been hastened by the campus rape charge hanging over his head. Drafted by his hometown team, the Boston Celtics, the rangy six-five guard lit up the league, averaging nineteen points and eleven assists his first season.

In the same week, Jones was named Rookie of the Year and traded to the Golden State Warriors for a journeyman forward. You have to be *way* more trouble than you're worth to accomplish that. In his second year, his production dropped off considerably, but he did lead the league in fines. He was missing practices, getting in late-night scrapes in bars and, on one occasion, ran into the stands in Philadelphia to spit on a Sixers fan who was giving him a hard time. The heckler ducked and Jones ended up hocking on a twelve-year-old girl. On TV, footage of that ugly incident ran more often than the French army.

On the plus side, Jones was amassing a truly spectacular assortment of tattoos. By all accounts, he knew his way around the Vegas strip a lot better than he did the Warriors' training facility.

Since joining the NBA, Gentry had dated a number of busty starlet/bimbo types, but I hadn't seen any gossip linking him with Angel. For one thing, she was fifteen years older than him.

"I'd rather discuss this with you face-to-face," said Lani.

"You can fly out today, we'll put you up at a nice hotel and if you still feel the same way after we talk, we'll send you home to Connecticut with a nice bonus. How's that?"

"What is it you want me to do, Lani?"

"My client and friend has just been charged with murder. I know in the depths of my soul she's innocent. And I want you to prove it."

"I can't come until tomorrow," I said. At this point, I wasn't playing hard to get. My home group in Winsted was meeting that night and Danny, a guy I was sponsoring, was getting his ninety-day chip. I had told him I would be there and I wasn't going to miss it. Like a lot of guys in the program, Danny had trust issues after growing up with an alcoholic father. I wanted him to know he could count on the people in AA.

"Oooh," said Lani. "I think we already have a first-class ticket for you out of Bradley this afternoon." I guess I was supposed to be impressed by the upgrade and the fact that she knew the name of the Connecticut airport.

"Sorry."

"All right," she said, "how about we compromise? We'll put you on a red-eye tonight. Send a car to pick you up? You can sleep on the plane."

No reason I couldn't leave after the meeting. As I mulled over this scenario, Lani said, "Great. I'll have my assistant iron out the details with you. See you in the morning."

"Lani?" I said. Too late. She had marooned me back in the ozone.

Now I knew what it felt like to be managed.

CHAPTER
3

When I went through rehab my roommate was Kenny Pate, an ophthalmologist and cocaine addict from South Dakota. Smart guy, very cynical. He told me the only thing that made the human condition bearable was the fact that we couldn't remember pain.

I thought of Kenny and his theory as the plane executed a lazy spiral down to LAX. Analgesic amnesia was the only possible explanation for the fact that I ever boarded an airplane.

I'm not one of those people who runs squealing down the aisle, demanding to be let off as soon as the aircraft starts taxiing for takeoff. But I detest every aspect of the experience: airport traffic, lines, security, waiting to board, shuffling along the umbilical corridor from the gate to the plane, overhead bins, the cramped seats, the canned air, the food, the tranquilized voice of the pilot. Every time I disembark, I make the same vow: Never again.

But as I came down the escalator to baggage claim, there was something waiting for me that lifted me right out of my tired, cramped and cranky mood. A guy was standing there scanning the arrivals, holding a hand-lettered sign that read "McNamara."

I'd never been met with a personal placard before. *God,* did I feel important. It was like the Beatles landing at Idlewild. I looked around to see if anyone was impressed by my status. Nothing. They all just hurried by. How can people be so blasé?

I waved to my greeter. This being L.A., the driver was better-looking than me and far better groomed. He quickly took me in hand, spearing my lumpy duffel off the baggage carousel, leading me to his Town Car and asking if I wanted to make any stops on the way to my hotel.

When Lani's assistant had asked me where I wanted to stay, I blurted out, "The Chateau Marmont." I don't know L.A. well and I'm certainly no connoisseur of accommodations. But I didn't want to come off like a dolt, so I named the first joint that came to mind. The only thing I knew about the Marmont is that John Belushi died there. Good enough for me.

My driver Stan escorted me to the registration desk, handed me a card with his beeper number and instructed me to call him when I was ready to go to Ms. Ross's office.

I sacked out for about a couple of hours, then shaved, dressed and went out for breakfast. When I'm staying in a hotel, I try as much as possible to take my meals outside the building. Just to cut down on the whole trapped-in-the-biodome feeling.

I descended from the Marmont complex, which resembles a scale-model Swiss village, and began walking along Sunset Boulevard, looking for a place to eat. Six long blocks later, I found one. Lots of traffic on the streets, but I was the only pedestrian.

I ordered pancakes and they turned out pretty good. Nice and fluffy, not at all cakey, which is the bugaboo of restaurant pancakes. (I think they usually neglect to add a pinch of baking soda to the batter.) Unfortunately, the syrup sucked. Same old story. When the syrup is good, the pancakes aren't. When the pancakes are good, the syrup isn't.

I don't know if this is apocryphal, but I heard that when baseball legend Ted Williams retired, he devoted himself to finding the diner with the best blueberry muffins in the country. And when he found it, he bought a place about three miles down the road. A guy needs a reason to roll out of bed in the morning.

When I hang up the cleats, I'm starting a similar quest for pancakes, beginning in Vermont.

As I walked back to the hotel—still the only soul on the sidewalks—I used my cell to summon Stan. He picked me up under the portico and drove me over to Renegade Records, which occupied an art deco building just off the 101 about five exits north of downtown.

Renegade was the label Angel started about eight years ago, during a brief phase when she was proving to the world that she wasn't just a sex symbol—she was also an astute businesswoman. To most people's surprise, she had an enormous success right off the bat—signing Jenny Boisson.

Jenny was an emotionally candid singer/songwriter, sort of the prototype for Avril Lavigne, Michelle Branch and other of today's young female stars. Her first CD went titanium, or whatever it is they call it when an album goes ten times platinum. It had been downhill since for Jenny, and for Renegade. Since Angel wasn't on her own label—she was signed to a long-term deal on one of the majors—Renegade hadn't had even a moderate hit since.

It was pretty quiet down by Angel's corner office on the top floor. I got the impression she wasn't a regular presence in the building—even when she was under indictment. But down the corridor at Lani's office, things were bustling. I guess the murder charge had resulted in a few media inquiries.

One of her harried assistants, sitting by a phone console that was lit up like a baseball scoreboard, instructed me to go in. Lani was talking to a reporter on her headset, but she acknowledged me with a smile and gestured me to a chair in front of her desk.

I have to admit, I was surprised by her appearance. Based on her position and her voice on the phone, I expected someone matronly. But Lani had to be about Angel's age and she was hot, with pillowy lips and blond hair pulled back severely into a tiny ponytail. I realized I had seen her several times before, in TV footage, standing next to Angel as they entered an awards show or industry event, but I always assumed she was part of the singer's glamour posse.

"No, Rick, I am not shutting you out," she was saying in a placatory tone. "She's not talking to anyone, not the *L.A. Times*, not *People*, not even you. . . . Well, you're going to have to find a way to work with it, because that statement is all you're going to get today, darling. . . . No, I know. All right. 'Bye."

"There he is," she said, taking off the headset and coming around the desk to shake my hand. "I'm so glad you're here."

We chatted for a while, establishing a reservoir of people we knew in common. Even with the phones ringing constantly and assistants flitting about like june bugs, Lani created the impression that she'd be perfectly happy to sit here shooting the breeze all day. And basking in her attention, I felt like a cat lying in a pool of sunlight.

As I would see over and over again, Lani had a remarkable gift for making people feel at ease. She was charming, but I wasn't here to be charmed.

Breaking free of her personality tractor beam, I said, "So, can you bring me up to speed on Angel?"

She picked up her purse as she walked around her desk. "Why don't we talk on the way over to her house?" Lani gave some brief instructions to her staff as we departed. Their faces bore the doomed expressions of martyrs, their eyes begging, *Please don't leave us*. They knew, without Lani there, they were going to get eaten alive by the press.

Down by the building's entrance, a driver waited for us by a Town Car. It wasn't Stan, but another L.A. lackey, handsome enough to star in *The Tab Hunter Story*. It wouldn't be the Valley of the Dolls without an army of Kens.

As we drove to Brentwood, Lani started asking me about a notorious concert promoter in Manhattan who was a mutual acquaintance. I cut her off. "Lani, before I meet Angel, I was hoping you could fill me in on what happened with her and Gentry. If you want me to clear her, I'm going to need some background."

"And I'd love to provide it, sweetie," she said. "But unfortunately I can't."

"Can't?"

"Sorry," she said, sinking back in her seat. "Since Angel was arrested, I really haven't had a chance to talk to her."

"I thought you guys were close."

A look of amusement played over Lani's face. "These are special circumstances."

"Who has she talked to?"

Lani pondered this briefly. "No one that I know of."

"Come on. Not even Bruce Katz?"

Again I saw a hint of smile on Lani's face. "Our girl is being very tight-lipped about this."

"Doesn't that worry you?"

"Absolutely," she said with conviction.

"So I'll have to go right to the horse's mouth."

"I hate to sound like a broken record, Jimmy," she said, "but you can't."

"What?"

"Couple of ground rules we need to get straight before you meet Angel," she said, pulling her knee up onto the seat as she turned to face me. "The most important of which is you cannot address her."

I just stared at her. Finally I said, "You're kidding, right?" She shook her head. "Why don't you take me back to the airport. This is ridiculous."

"Like you've never had to deal with temperamental stars before," she said skeptically.

"Lani, how am I supposed to pursue this case if I can't talk to Angel?"

"It's not like you can't *ever* talk to her. Just not in the beginning. Until she gets used to you. Have you ever had a haughty house cat? She's like that. She takes a while to warm up to people."

"I'm allergic to cats."

"Good," she said. "Then you won't have any trouble keeping your distance."

"How will I know when she's thawed out enough to have a conversation?"

"She'll break the ice—when she's ready."

I thought about this. "Can I look at her?" I asked.

Lani swatted my bicep playfully. "You think that's funny," she said, "but I've had clients who expressly forbid eye contact. Let me tell you, that can make for a very long video shoot."

Exiting the freeway, we pulled up at a traffic light. On our right, a scrawny, discouraged-looking guy stood on the sidewalk holding up a sign that said, "Will Work for Food." On the driver's side, a Mexican in a faded plaid shirt and baggy jeans walked between the line of cars, offering a bag of oranges.

As the car accelerated smoothly away, I asked, "How long has Angel known Gentry . . . I mean, how long had she known him?"

"I'm not sure she did," Lani said. "I certainly never heard of him until . . . you know. The only basketball player I ever saw at her house was Dennis Rodman, and that was a couple of years ago. Although Shaq's really been a pain in the butt about trying to meet her."

"So as far as you know, there was no history between them until the night he died?"

Lani shrugged. "I gave up a long time ago trying to keep

track of the guys in Angel's life. I just ask her to give me a little advance notice if she's planning on marrying one of them."

"Wow. So Gentry shows up at her house and a couple of hours later, he's dead. That's a rough first date."

"They usually are," Lani said. I looked at her questioningly. "I'm only trying to warn you. Meeting Angel can be . . . a challenge. On her good days, she's feisty. And right now, well, she's not in a really good mood."

That turned out to be an understatement.

I can't really describe what Angel's compound looked like. That's because every time I went there over the next couple of days, the place was under siege. A real mob scene.

Starting a block away, you had police impatiently waving traffic on, just trying to keep the drive-by gawkers crawling. Not that they could see anything. The street was lined with bulky TV trucks and vans, a KOA campground for the media. All the TV vehicles had satellite transmitters affixed to their roofs. It looked like a Martian antiaircraft battery.

All along the two sides of the property that fronted the street, people were lined up and clamoring five deep against the tall metal fence. I flashed on footage of the American embassy in Saigon in 1975. But Ho Chi Minh never saw an assembly like this.

There were the hardcore Angel fans holding vigil. Some held up signs proclaiming her innocence. Others clutched the fence, tears on their cheeks, desperate to show their idol that they were here for her in her hour of need. "We love you, Angel!" they shouted weepily.

A knot of transvestites, Angel look-alikes, had staked out a patch of sidewalk and were being very territorial. Numerous floral arrangements were wedged into the fence, some of them quite expensive. At some point, I recalled, the singer had professed a fondness for orchids. Many of the fans were draped in tartan.

That was another thing that really annoyed me about Angel. She was always starting fads: food, clothes, exercise, even religion. You'd swear bhindi mehendi hadn't existed for ten thousand years—that Angel had created the patterned henna tattooing for one of her album covers. How Eastern! How exotic!

Or jogging. She starts loping around the Central Park reservoir—flanked by two bodyguards—and we're all supposed to marvel: "My God, running? Really? As a form of exercise? What a fabulous idea! Why didn't anyone think of this before?"

The kilts were a recent kick. She had dated some hotshot filmmaker from Glasgow who was supposed to be quite iconoclastic (he seemed like a blatant ripoff of Quentin Tarantino to me) and suddenly she was in love with all things Scottish. Even had her very own tartan pattern created and registered with the prestigious Aberdeen haberdasher who had been dressing Scottish royalty since Bonnie Prince Charlie.

Mixing with the Angel acolytes was a contingent of the curious, tourist types mostly, drawn by the TV trucks. Many of them were clutching cameras themselves, excitedly videotaping the spectacle. This beat the scene outside Graceland all to hell.

Sprinkled around the perimeter were the wackjobs who probably weren't even aware whose house they were standing in front of. They had their own agendas. Some of them carried signs, others just barked their warnings out loud every few seconds, like they had prophetic Tourette's. If it wasn't for the transvestites, you'd have to give the lunatics credit for most colorfully dressed. They ranged from Old Testament formal to patriotic red, white and blue spangles.

I wondered how they all got out to Brentwood. Maybe Los Angeles runs a crackpot jitney.

Finally there was the press, who had staked out the best vantage points close to the entrance gates. Even the crazies didn't mess with them. Cameramen, both still and TV variety, have a well-deserved reputation as the attack dogs of journalism. You jostle them and they'll go paparazzi on your ass.

As we inched our way up to the gate, a barrel-chested black man with a shaved head and sunglasses and dressed in a blazer and tie, gestured for the driver to stop and walked over to the side of the car. Lani lowered her tinted window down halfway and immediately shutters began clacking away madly like a plague of cicadas. Several people ran over to see who was in the car and the cameramen, feeling pressure from behind, started throwing elbows like NBA power forwards hoarding a rebound.

The security point man nodded curtly at Lani and said a few words into a walkie-talkie. A handful of hefty men in identical garb emerged on the inside of the gate, which slowly began to crank open. A wild-eyed girl with scarlet streaks in her platinum hair made a kamikaze run, sprinting past the car. One of the guards caught her by the throat with one hand as she tried to rush past them. Her legs went out from underneath her. Lurch-like, he carried her as she gagged and fumed, her feet kicking in the air. Without saying a word, he deposited her back on the sidewalk and returned to his formation.

The car circled up to the front of the house and Lani got out. Gesturing at the imposing Tudor facade, she said airily, "Home, sweet home."

A mousy woman in a classic maid's uniform opened the thick oak front door before we could ring. This struck me as a rather pretentious domestic touch for a pop star, but, as I would learn, Angel found these types of old-fashioned, aristocratic amenities flattering. I suspect she had seen one too many Audrey Hepburn fantasias on Turner Classic Movies.

The house spread out in two wings from the front entrance, with dual curved staircases leading up to the second floor from the tiled foyer. A riot of mix-and-match art adorned the walls, but the entryway was dominated by two large canvases by the same painter. Both featured primitively rendered blue human outlines, their postures suggesting distress and constraint, against thickly applied epoxy-white backgrounds. To my eye, they looked like Keith Haring Meets Edvard Munch.

Straight back beneath the staircases was what looked like a ballroom or dance studio with a gleaming hardwood floor. Beyond that was a dining room with a table massive enough to seat Puff Daddy's whole entourage.

To our right was a library with shelves of imposingly bound books that seemed to be shellacked in place. To the left was a cushy parlor—the only room that looked lived in. From my vantage in the foyer, I couldn't make out what the couches were all arranged to face. I presumed it was either a fireplace or an entertainment center. I could hear voices from that room.

My survey of the surroundings stopped when Angel started yelling from the second floor. "I swear to God, I'm going to kill somebody," she shouted angrily. All other noise in the house stopped abruptly. Even the building seemed to be holding its breath.

It wasn't just that Angel was loud. She was also incredibly penetrating—an adenoidal siren like Fran Drescher's that made even the most neutral observation sound like a complaint. It was the alley-cat voice that you occasionally heard out of Angel in the early part of her career when her hair was darker, her clothes sluttier and her attitude more street.

Over time, her diction had grown lighter and almost risibly refined, like a pretentious Eliza Doolittle. I guess her at-home voice hadn't changed much.

"Don't give me your fucking excuses, Joanna," she screeched, her voice growing louder. "I'm sick of it!" Then she emerged from the master suite on the second floor, heading toward the staircase to my left, two very frightened-looking young women in her wake.

Angel was wearing a crimson crushed-velvet track suit with white trim. Her hair was pulled up, jutting out in tufts, and she had some kind of brown facial cream applied to her face, except on the lips and eyes. She looked like a bad minstrel show.

"Why do I have to do everything around here myself?" she fumed. "I swear, you could screw up a headache." The woman in closest pursuit, who was clutching a notepad, flinched.

"How can you get the time for my book party wrong? Now I'm going to have to call each of those people—" She stopped as she reached the bottom of the stairs, glaring at Lani. "Did you see the invitations?" she asked accusingly.

"Hello, sweetie," Lani said, smiling. Because I was standing right at Lani's shoulder, I was poised to say hello, my mouth already open to speak. But Angel didn't seem to register my presence. She continued on toward the living room, still kvetching. People scurried from every part of the house to join the fretful retinue in her wake. Her querulous voice gradually faded as she streamed out of sight.

I felt like Alice meeting the Queen of Hearts for the first time.

CHAPTER
5

Lani glanced back at me playfully. "Welcome aboard," she said. I was still frozen, my mouth hanging open. I was, in a word, agog. Apparently accustomed to dealing with this reaction, Lani snapped her fingers. I blinked and shook my head, coming back on-line.

"Wow."

"You all right?"

I scrunched up my mouth as I nodded, dishonestly implying that I was unruffled.

"Our girl is a piece of work, isn't she?" Lani said. "Don't worry. You'll get used to her."

"I'm sure I'll be signing up for her fan club in no time. But that's not what got to me. Did she say 'book party'?"

Lani nodded.

"Are you telling me Angel wrote a *book*?"

Lani's merry laughter sounded like a wind chime in the sterile portico. "Depends on how technical you want to get. Her byline is on it, so I guess that makes her the author. But wrote? . . . Come to think of it, she didn't exactly conceive it either." She made a dismissive gesture with her hands. "But let's not get hung up on the details. It's a big beautiful coffee-table book called *Hot Chick* and if you haven't heard of it, then I haven't done a very good job."

"Don't use me as your litmus test. My subscription to *Us* expired a while ago."

"It's an incredible book. Really. Like a wedding of *Life* magazine and *Playboy*. There's a gallery of provocative pictures of Angel and then all these images of sex symbols that have fired her imagination over time."

"Is there any text?"

Lani thought about that for a moment. "Do captions count?" We both laughed. "Look," she said, glancing at her watch, "I have to go deal with the networks."

"I thought I heard you telling that reporter that the press release was all he was getting."

"That was print," she said. "Television is a whole other animal. It can't be put off. I'm telling you, the producers of these network news magazines are like rats—they have to continually gnaw on something or their teeth go up through the roof of their mouth and puncture their brain."

I gestured around the vaulted front entrance, eerily empty since Angel had sucked everyone up in her vortex. "What would you suggest I do?"

"Wander around," she said, reaching up to pinch my cheek. "Get the lay of the land." She winked at me and headed up the stairs.

I walked toward the living room, assuming this was the more populated side of the house. As I entered, I saw the focus was an enormous entertainment center that took up much of the wall to my right. I should have known that fireplaces wouldn't be a common feature in Southern California mansions.

The unit was more imposing than NASA's mission control. The biggest TV screen I had ever seen was flanked by an array of state-of-the-art stereo equipment and speakers as well as DVDs, a satellite controller, a TiVo box and numerous other video gadgets that I couldn't identify.

On the screen, which looked like Imax compared to my set at home, colors pulsed and blended like a light show from an Ecstasy-fueled rave. Lights percolated on some of the stereo equipment, although the sound was muted. In the upper-right corner of the screen, a small picture-within-picture rectangle was showing surveillance footage of the front gate.

Intrigued, I walked over to study how the security system was hooked into the TV. I reached out to shift a box whose function I didn't recognize when I was startled by a peremptory voice.

"Don't touch anything!"

I whipped around guiltily and saw the notebook-bearing girl who recently was serving as Angel's scapegoat. "Please," she continued. "Angel gets very upset if anyone tampers with her setup."

"Sorry," I said, my hands clamped abjectly at my sides. "Joanna, right?"

She nodded. Angel's assistant had stylishly cut platinum blond hair, an angular face and blue eyes. She would have been quite attractive if it weren't for the frightened expression that haunted her face. She had the eyes of a torturee.

"Why aren't you buzzing around the queen bee?" I asked.

She almost smiled. "I've been banished. Which means I have to stay out of her sight for about ten minutes."

"You time it?"

She shook her head. "Don't have to. I get summoned."

I nodded, trying to load my eyes up with sympathy. "Do you know who I am, Joanna?"

"Yeah, Lani's assistant told me you were coming."

"Does Angel know I'm here?"

"Oh, yeah. Kind of hard to tell, huh?" She sat on the arm of one of the couches. "She does that cold shoulder thing to everybody. But I heard her talking to Inga. She said you worked for Mariah. Is that right?"

I nodded.

"God, I love her." There was an unstated wager in that declaration: *Bet Mariah wouldn't scream at me the way Angel does*. I wasn't about to abuse Joanna of that shaky assumption.

"Listen, Joanna, I'm coming into this situation cold. Would you be willing to talk to me? Give me some perspective?" I saw the frightened look reclaim her and I hurried to defuse it. "Not now, of course. But maybe down the road. If you're comfortable with that." She was looking down at her clipboard, nervously picking at the adhesive strip atop her legal pad. "Anyway, think about it."

I took a couple of steps toward the bank of equipment and her eyes immediately came up to monitor me.

"So Angel really keeps track of all the settings on this system?"

She lifted her eyebrows and exhaled a staccato scoff, as if to say, *You don't know the half of it.*

"This is a pretty elaborate setup. I'm surprised she can master it."

Joanna looked furtively toward the interior of the house to make sure her boss wasn't around. Seemed like an unnecessary gesture to me. From what I had seen, you could hear Angel coming all the way from Bakersfield.

"She never used to care about it. But then last year she was watching *The Osbournes* on MTV with a bunch of people?" Joanna's intonation went up inquisitively at the end of the sentence, signaling that she was telling a story. Follow the bouncing voice. "It was like the first episode, I think. Anyway, poor Ozzy couldn't work the TV in his house. It was stuck on like the Weather Channel and he couldn't change it? And he was getting really flustered. And everyone in the room with Angel started laughing really hard.

"The next day she had one of the engineers from Rene-

gade come over and start tutoring her on all the equipment."
Joanna lifted her palm toward the wall. "He was here every
day for like a week. Since then she's been a total freak about
it. She's even got this universal remote that she keeps locked
away and only she can use."

I pointed at the feed from the front gate. "Is this surveillance footage being taped?"

"I have no idea."

"When the police came—"

She was up off the couch and moving toward the far door.
Clearly she didn't want to be labeled a collaborator. "Umm,
I should be getting back into shouting distance."

"Do you mind if I walk part of the way with you? Maybe
you could just explain to me how the house is laid out."

She shrugged, her frown letting me know it was an imposition. I followed her into a room half the size of the living
room, paneled with wood. There were two desks, the larger
one set in the center of the room, a smaller one facing the
wall. There were phone consoles, fax and copy machines
and filing cabinets. The walls were hung with platinum records and framed photos of Angel in chummy two-shots with
celebrities like Jim Carrey and Bono.

"This is Angel's office," Joanna said. "That's my desk
there. Lani keeps another office upstairs. Past this is the rec
room," she said pointing. "Then there's the breakfast room
where the staff eats, the kitchen which connects with the
dining room. Then there's the sunroom, the gym, the yoga
studio, a den that hardly ever gets used, the library which
never gets used and you're back in the front entrance."

I nodded and we walked into the adjoining room. All
manner of pinball machines lined the walls. In one corner
was one of those motorcycle race simulation machines. In
another a vintage wooden Skee-Ball ramp with its concen-
tric wooden target circles. Spaced apart on the floor were
two pool tables, one standard with six pockets and a bumper
pool unit studded with mushroom-shaped rubber baffles.

A middle-aged man was lining up a shot on the tournament table. He had taken off his suit jacket and draped it over one of the high soda fountain chairs interspersed through the room. His sleeves were rolled up and his tie was tucked into his shirt to keep it from dangling on the table.

Behind him Bruce Katz was leaning on a pool cue, like a buckskin settler propped up with his bear rifle. The famed lawyer had on a tan suit and one of those string ties with silver tips. He was gazing up toward the ceiling and smiling broadly. That's because he was engaged in his favorite activity: listening to himself talk.

"And when we got back to chambers, I said, 'Your Honor, I'm cognizant that this conduct may not reflect well on my client's character, but if that constitutes a crime, you're going to have to lock up every man in the state of Montana.'"

Katz's companion straightened up after missing his shot and chuckled appreciatively. I said softly, "Thanks, Joanna. I'll see you later." She departed quickly, relieved to be quit of me.

"Mr. Katz?" He looked over at me. "My name is James McNamara. I just wanted to introduce myself." He bowed his head in acknowledgment.

"I've been brought aboard to assist with the investigation."

"Really?" Katz said, leaning into the word heavily in a way that reminded me of Jack Benny.

"That surprises you?"

"Me? No. I personally believe the more, the merrier." He was carefully chalking his cue stick, an amused smile playing on his lips. "Tell me, Mr. McNamara, have you met Bruno?"

"I don't believe so."

"You would most assuredly remember it if you had," he said, lining up a carom shot. "But don't concern yourself. When he discovers you're in the house, he will find *you*." As he spoke the last word, he struck the cue ball, ricocheting the seven neatly off the cushion and into the side pocket. Then he looked up at me smugly.

I was dying to know what he was talking about with this Bruno business, but I didn't want to give him any more opportunity to toy with me. So I pushed on. "Well, I just arrived and I'm starting from scratch. I was hoping you might be willing to fill me in on what you know of Jones's death."

"That won't take very long," he said, laughing and looking over at his pool partner, who smiled supportively. "This, by the way, is my colleague Wendell Crane." Extending his hand, the man plodded around the table to shake, then trundled back to his place like one of those creatures from a cuckoo clock.

"I know almost nothing of the events that happened on the morning of March second," Katz said, settling his haunch onto a chair, leaving his extended leg braced on the floor.

"LAPD must have had something to arrest Angel."

"Purely circumstantial. Several people were in the house that night, most of them leaving between three and four A.M. None recall seeing my client with Mr. Jones. Apparently they weren't in the same room. They had met in the VIP room at the Momba Club earlier that evening. No one has said there was any hostility evident between them.

"The call came in to 911 shortly before five A.M., a man's voice trying to disguise itself. Used a cell phone to report a stabbing death at this address. When the first cruiser got here, the officers found Jones on the floor in the library and Angel hiding in her room. She made no statement."

"Stabbing?" I asked. "I read several newspaper accounts on the plane ride out here that reported or at least implied that Jones was hanged."

"You need to read a better class of paper," Katz said, flipping his hand dismissively. "That's an old tabloid ploy. If you say the victim was hanged, then it's a short jump to self-asphyxiation. You have yourself another kinky Hollywood sex scandal. That sells papers. Evisceration doesn't. But I assure you, I've seen the body. Jones was gutted like a brook trout."

"What does Angel say?"

"To this point, nothing. She's retained me, but she's keeping her own counsel."

"She hasn't provided you with any account of what happened?"

Katz shook his head, smiling.

"Doesn't that concern you?"

"Not really," he said, crinkling the eyes that journalists, on more than one occasion, had compared to Paul Newman's. "I'd rather she was confiding in me, but it hardly matters."

"Why is that?"

"At this phase, the police are still trying to build a case. The DA in this town gets nervous as a chihuahua when he has to prosecute one of these celebrity murders. Until we get to trial, it's all about projecting an image—something my client is exceedingly good at.

"Once we get to trial—well, that's something I'm exceedingly good at. I've developed a simple credo over the years, Mr. McNamara, one that's served me well: When the facts are against you, argue the law. When the law is against you, argue the facts. And when the facts and the law are against you, wave your arms around and shout a lot!"

Wendell Crane chuckled, although it was obvious he had heard this little nostrum a time or two.

Sounded like sage advice—for a lawyer. But I couldn't see how it was going to help me do my job.

CHAPTER
6

I left the lawyers playing billiards and ventured farther into the house. In the room next door, there was a refectory table and the remains of a lunch buffet on a sideboard. It looked like one of the Craft Services meals they provide on movie sets. There were breaded cutlets in one serving dish, pasta in another and a nourishing-looking vegetarian offering in a third. They were flanked by a tureen of soup, two kinds of salads, a variety of carbs and vegetables, a fruit bowl and some delectable pastries. Your basic light snack. On the ground, a ice-filled cooler was stocked with fruit juices and Calistoga water

Pushing through a swinging door, I found myself in the kitchen. All dressed in white, what would constitute a full restaurant staff looked up from whatever they were doing to check me out. This was a jumpy household. Actually, one head didn't turn. Sitting at the steel prep table in the middle of the room was a guy in his late twenties in a loud tropical shirt with too many buttons undone, blue jeans and flip-flops. He was totally engaged in a handheld gaming console.

I noticed him not only because he alone was oblivious to my entrance but also because he was bald. That makes you stand out in Los Angeles, like being pale in Miami. It was the usual male pattern baldness, except his skin bunched up in wrinkles running back from the crown of his head. I assumed from his dress and his indifference that he was the chef or perhaps Angel's personal nutritionist.

To my right was a butler's pantry where two staffers were stacking dishes. Beyond them I could see a corner of the Citizen Kane table in the big dining room. I continued straight ahead through another set of swinging doors, stepping down into the sunroom, a spacious, glassed-in enclosure looking out onto a lavish garden area with a sculpted fountain at its center.

The tiled room was decorated with colorful Mexican pastels. Flowering plants were everywhere and there was a bracing hint of ozone in the air. At the far end of the room, Angel and a small retinue were lounging on patio furniture. Angel was chatting on a cell phone, handling the unit gingerly to keep from smearing it with her face cream. The tone of her voice was far softer and less abrasive.

"No! Where did you hear that?" The response made her erupt in a loud, braying laugh. "I'll be there. I promise, Chandra . . . I am not under house arrest. No more than usual anyway."

Standing behind Angel and gently massaging her shoulders was a feline-looking woman with short, gleaming black hair, high cheekbones and green eyes.

As I stepped into the room, she trained those emerald lasers on me. I almost took a step backward. She was that intimidating. The look was a territorial warning: *Come between me and Angel and I will slice you to ribbons.* Or sentiments to that effect.

You know how before boxing matches, the fighters, as they're getting instructions from the referee, stand toe to toe at the center of the ring staring each other down? This woman would have most heavyweights cowering.

Ah, the fabulous Inga Saffron. I recognized her immediately even though I'm not a devoted reader of the gossip pages. I had no idea what she did and where she was from. Mostly she was famous for being a lesbian clubgoer.

I suppose if you could attain celebrity status purely on those terms, that was an accomplishment in itself. The key was to attach yourself to bigger names. And she had obviously fastened herself to Angel like a barnacle.

Fanned out behind Angel were various assistants, ready to spring into action should a need arise. They had that permanently tensed aura of the crouched ball boys at a professional tennis match. Among them was Joanna, who was refusing to make eye contact with me.

Spread in front of Angel, some of them stretched out at her feet, were a handful of young people, chatting quietly and laughing among themselves. I assumed from their lithe, muscular bodies, their energetic spirits and their livid makeup that they were dancers, presumably part of the singer's touring troupe. They certainly seemed at ease around Angel, like remora fish gliding alongside a shark.

I stood there for a moment, intrigued by the scene. I'm not certain why, but it made me think of a Renaissance rendering of Salome in her boudoir.

I quickly became uncomfortable, however. Angel was totally ignoring my existence. Her assistants were afraid to engage me. And the dancers were too vain to look up. That left only Inga, and she was staring at me like a bulldog guarding its food bowl. The mixed reception produced an odd sensation, like being invisible and branded at the same time. I crossed the room and exited through the louvered doors to their left. Inga's eyes followed me the whole way.

I stepped into the most magnificent gym I have ever seen. It made my health club, which I had always thought was pretty nice, look like the exercise yard in prison where guys curl coffee cans filled with concrete. Brand-new, gleaming equipment was poised all along the walls, which were lined with mirrors. Some of the machines were designed to exercise muscles I don't even think I have.

To my left was a wooden door, with temperature controls on the wall next to it that marked it as a sauna. It was flanked by swinging doors with full-body silhouettes of a man and woman on them. That struck me as a rather modest touch for a libertine like Angel: gender-specific changing rooms. Maybe it was a remnant of the Catholic school upbringing she always managed to mention in interviews.

As I was peering at one of the machines, trying to figure out where your body was supposed to go, the door to the sauna flew open and out padded a troll, trailing clouds of steam behind him.

He was a short, swarthy man dressed only in a skimpy Day-Glo orange Speedo that was in danger of being swallowed by his rectum. He had starter breasts above a remarkable beer-barrel belly. He was stomping around on the thickest calves I've ever seen. I'm not sure what was making me stare—whether it was the peltlike dark hair that covered every part of his body except his head or the cigar sticking out of the corner of his mouth. Who takes a cigar into a sauna?

He spotted me and padded over purposefully on pool sandals. "Who're you?" he demanded in a voice like a root cellar.

"Uh, Jim McNamara?"

"Aw, shit," he said disgustedly, his lips curling back from the stogie clamped between his teeth. "I told Lani we didn't need you." His eyes narrowed as he closed the gap between us until his gravid stomach was pushing against me. Gross!

Looking up at me menacingly, he said, "Let's get one thing straight, crab cakes. I'm the big dog around here." He emphasized his point by nudging me with his tumescent tummy. "You can dick around as much as you want, but you get in my way even once and I'll put your ass in a sling. Capisce?"

"All right," I said, my ready agreement having the desired effect of getting him to back off a step.

"Good. Then we won't have no trouble." He started toward the dressing room.

"Just one thing," I called after him. "Who are you?"

He turned around quicker than a teacher at the blackboard who gets hit by a spitball. He took the cigar out of his mouth and pointed it precisely at me like a dart player lining up his shot. "Don't fuck with me, kid. It ain't good for your health." Then he stomped off to the men's locker room. The symbol affixed to the door portrayed a body type so unlike his it might have belonged to a different species.

It made me wonder what the pictographs on the bathroom doors looked like in that alien cantina in *Star Wars*.

My assumption was that I had just met Bruno. And he had met me.

Moving on from the gym with nary a backward glance, I entered a bare room with blond wood floors. The walls were decorated with paintings of several Vedic figures in lotus positions, including a creature with a blue elephant's head and a human torso. As I walked toward the far wall, I saw a compact stereo and a number of thin, rolled-up mats. Notching this up as the yoga studio, I proceeded into a rather clubby room furnished with big leather couches, African artifacts on the wall and an impressive globe on a side table. It looked like Thor Heyerdahl's study. This didn't seem Angel's style at all. Maybe she had bought the house furnished.

Passing through, I found myself back in the library by the front entry. Examining the embossed spines, I saw the stacks ran heavily toward complete collections of the big kahunas: Dickens, Twain, Tolstoy, Maugham, Huxley, Melville and the like. The literary greatest hits collection. I was running my fingertips over Thackeray, wondering if Angel had ever read *Vanity Fair* and what she would make of Becky Sharpe when all hell broke loose.

A car horn began blowing insistently from outside. I saw the maid scurry to the front door and peer out one of the flanking windows. I realized that as I toured the house I hadn't seen her once. She must have had some hidden sanctuary under the staircase.

Frowning, she hurried away from me toward the living room. I walked over to the windows in the library and parted the curtains to see who was making all the commotion. Pulled up by the door in the opposite direction from the way the traffic circle indicated was a beautifully restored dark blue 1969 Camaro convertible. Sitting behind the wheel with his idle turned up too high was Cam Akers, Hollywood's biggest hothead and Angel's first husband.

Cam had become a star right out of his teens, playing an addled stoner in a smart high school comedy called *Going Steady*. There followed a handful of powerful and resourceful dramatic performances which had critics calling him the next Brando. He became the most sought-after young actor in town.

But he didn't handle celebrity well. Akers was a belligerent cuss. He had more fights than Roberto Duran ever did—with directors, with people in nightclubs, with parking attendants outside nightclubs and, most of all, with paparazzi. That probably wouldn't have mattered if he kept racking up box office hits. But his judgment in selecting projects was atrocious. He played dark, tortured characters in a series of commercial flops.

At the pinnacle of his fame, before his reputation went south, he had married Angel in a beautiful seaside ceremony in Malibu. Elaborate measures were enacted to keep the wedding private. Even the invited guests—the cream of the film and music worlds—didn't know the location. They were instructed to meet at a tented staging area and then ferried over to the actual site.

But the media ferreted out the setting and an armada of helicopters was hovering noisily over the bluff shooting away with telephoto lenses. The intrusion drove Cam into a frenzy, leading to some memorable images of the groom running across the lawn, shaking his fist at the aerial cameramen and foaming at the mouth as he hurled curses at them.

The marriage only lasted thirteen months and for the last five of those they weren't even living together. But for a while there, they were the modern-day Richard Burton and Liz Taylor, living extravagantly, fighting and reconciling with great brio.

Now Cam was outside Angel's house, leaning on his horn and glaring at the front door. Noticing me in the window, he emphatically gave me the finger with his free hand, biting his lower lip with naked hostility. There was something iconographic about the tableau. Then I realized that photographers had captured Akers in this pose over and over again. It was his signature gesture.

Out by the gate, I could see the press pushing and shoving each other, trying to get more shots of Cam going ballistic.

Inside the house, there was no response. The front hallway remained vacant. Through the window, I saw Angel's chef emerge from the side of the house in his tropical shirt. He jogged over to Cam's muscle car and they had a brief exchange—Akers snarling and the cook trying to placate him.

Then Cam took off, flooring it around the circle. His tires kicked up a hailstorm of gravel that had the poor chef cringing and shielding his eyes with his hands. The actor only got about twenty yards before he had to slam on his brakes and wait for the security detail to open the gate and part the press. Akers gave them quite a show as he edged through the gauntlet, steering with his knees so he could, arms extended, give the finger with both hands. He looked like a rageaholic Jesus.

I stood there for a minute marveling at the hurly-burly I had just witnessed. I was snapped back by the sound of an approaching storm. I walked to the doorway of the library just in time to see Angel making the turn into the living room with her full retinue scrambling to follow.

I almost dove for cover, because she was marching right

toward me and she did not look at all happy. But Angel stopped abruptly just over the threshhold into the hallway. This caused a comical ten-person pileup as the crowd following her ran up each other's backs. She spun around to face them and hissed, "All right, people, I am calling a house meeting."

This announcement was met with obvious dismay. Even the dancers looked worried.

From out of nowhere, Lani was by my side. "I think that's our cue," she said sotto voce, guiding me firmly by the elbow to the front door. Somehow the maid beat us there, anticipating our exit, opening the door for us.

Before you could say "Hand me down my walkin' cane" we were out on the front steps.

CHAPTER
7

"I didn't mean to jerk you out of there," Lani said as her car crunched to a stop in front of us. "But I find it's best to be exposed to Angel in small doses at first."

"Like a toxin," I said as we settled in the back seat.

"I know you're not going to believe this. You probably won't even admit it when it happens, but you're going to end up liking her."

"You're right. I don't believe it."

"I've seen it over and over. It's easy to be put off by the image. But once you get to know her, she's really creative and bright and funny."

"Yeah," I said, watching the guards cordon off a path to the street. "It was practically a comedy club in there. She's like the musical version of Leona Helmsley."

"Believe me, with friends and colleagues, she's a pussycat. She's just a little tough on the people who work for her."

"Umm, Lani? Don't you work for her?"

She smiled. "We get along pretty well."

"That's obviously not the case with Cam Akers. What was the deal there?"

"Hard to say. Half the time he doesn't know what set his ass on fire."

"What did he want?"

"To talk to Angel."

"So?"

"She won't have anything to do with him."

"Why not?"

She turned to give me an are-you-nuts? look. "Did you see him?" I nodded. "Did that look like a guy you could have a rational conversation with?" I conceded her point with a tweak of my head. "Lord, I jumped through hoops for that man! I deserve a shelf full of Nobels for the efforts I made to smooth his path. Can't be done. Cam is at war with the world."

"I don't get it."

"What, sweetie?"

"You've got all this security at the gate. Why let him in if you're just going to make him sit in the driveway?"

She chuckled ruefully. "Every decision with Cam is a question of limiting collateral damage. What is it they say about big stud athletes? You can't stop him; you can only hope to contain him. We discovered the hard way that if you deny him entrance to the grounds, he's going to fight the guards. And if the press starts taking pictures—and they will—he'll go after the photographers. It's a big mess. So we let him drive in, make his ruckus and then zoom off. It's easier on everyone involved."

I digested this information for a moment before asking, "So when they got divorced, did Angel get custody of the cook?"

"You've lost me."

"When he was parked there, her chef came out to talk to him."

"Angel's chef? I very much doubt that."

"Why?"

"Lars is a maniac, but he *never* leaves the kitchen. If the house caught on fire, he'd go down with his cutlery."

"Well, he ducked out this afternoon."

"Tall, distinguished? Looks like a younger version of Max Von Sydow?"

"No! Dumpy, balding guy with a Hawaiian shirt."

Lani considered this for a moment, then she laughed. "You mean Charlie!"

I tossed up my hands to indicate I'd need more information.

"Charlie Chiavone is Angel's brother. The idea of him as a chef made me laugh. Charlie couldn't fix a Pop-Tart. But he does hang out in the kitchen all the time, so I can see how you made that assumption."

"What is Charlie's role in the house?"

"Technically, he's her choreographer. But that's really an inside joke. Angel gave him that title because he was always chasing after the dancers, trying to hump them. She keeps him on the payroll out of loyalty, I suppose—and to remind herself why she never wants to go home."

Looking out the window for a moment, I saw a city bus go by plastered with a poster for a John Travolta film that had closed two weeks ago. "And that hairy ogre who was using the sauna, I assume that was Bruno?"

"Bruno was using the sauna?" she said with revulsion. "Remind me never to go in there again. Ucch!"

"Tell me a little about him."

"Bruno Volpe is something of a legend in L.A.," she said. "At least he'd like to be. The official bio is that he came here from Vegas, where he was head of security at one of the casinos. The alternate version—which I find a lot more plausible—is that he was a gate guard at one of the studios here in town. They say he made himself indispensable to an actor who is a notorious lush. Then he started doing favors for other entertainers with messy lives. Bruno is a fixer. You come to him with a problem, he makes it go away. Totally unscrupulous, of course."

I had a moment of recognition. "He's the guy who was always hanging around Michael Jackson."

Lani nodded. "He was practically on retainer from Michael." She threw up a hand. "Please don't ask me to explain that relationship."

I had seen Bruno just over Jacko's shoulder in dozens of pictures. His sauna garb—or lack thereof—had thrown me off. I was used to seeing him in his trademark Borsalino with the brim pulled down low on his forehead. No cigar in the pictures, though. Maybe Michael didn't let him smoke in his presence.

"Anyway, that's how Bruno got his cloven foot into the music business. As far as I can tell, before Michael he worked exclusively for actors. Bruno's specialty is extortion. If a celebrity is getting squeezed, they bring in Bruno. He locates the source of the threat and goes after them full-bore. He makes life so miserable for them, they usually forget all about blackmail."

"You should see him nude. He's full boor all right."

"Please stop planting that image in my head. I want to have sex again sometime this decade."

I glanced out the window. We were streaming north on the 101, headed back to Lani's office.

"So if Bruno's on board, does that mean Angel is being blackmailed?"

"What? Sorry." She had been looking at the messages on her PDA. "No. I would have told you that. Bruno was hired by Emmett Langdon, the president of EMI, Angel's label. Emmett is also my boss. But I don't like relying on Bruno. So I brought you in."

"Why?"

"Pardon?"

"Why did you hire me?"

She looked at me quizzically, as if she was surprised we

were having this conversation. "I want you to find out who killed Gentry Jones."

"You're sure it wasn't Angel? From what I've seen, the lady has quite a temper."

"Let's proceed under the assumption that Angel didn't do it," she said with a touch of frostiness.

"Usually when someone is arrested for a murder they didn't commit, they're pretty outspoken about their innocence," I pointed out. "She's not making a peep."

Slipping off her blue sunglasses, she trained her attention on me. "Look, I've known Angel her entire career. She's someone who pulled herself out of some tough circumstances and made herself into a superstar. In a business where three hit albums is unusual, she's had seventeen. She's taken some hard personal and professional shots along the way and never thought about quitting. I've never heard her feel sorry for herself. She's never played the victim and she's not going to start now."

I started to protest, but Lani put up a finger to hold me off. "She's not talking about what happened that night. I'm sure there's a very good reason for that. And I want you to find out what it is, as well as who killed that poor kid."

"I'm not sure I can work for a client who won't speak to me, Lani."

"Give it a few days. Please. I promise the channels of communication will open up. Accomplish what you can by working around it in the meantime."

I could see the Renegade building about a block away, so I asked the question I had been sitting on.

"Does Angel have a bodyguard?"

"Oh, yeah. Cliff Johnson."

"Why wasn't he there today?"

She sighed. "While the house is under siege, we hired Allied Security to set up a twenty-four-hour perimeter. There are at least fifteen guys guarding the grounds at all times. So Cliff gets a couple of unscheduled days off. If Angel plans to leave the house, he'll come over to accompany her. Ah, we're there." Indeed, we were pulling up to her office entry. I could see Stan standing at attention by my car. Guess I wasn't coming up with Lani.

"Could you put me in touch with Cliff?"

"He wasn't there when Jones was killed."

"Indulge me," I said.

She raised an eyebrow at me. "I'll have his number left at your hotel. Anything else you need?"

"Yeah," I wanted to tell her. "A client who will level with me." But I knew that was about as likely as a Guns n' Roses reunion.

Ever listen to music from the seventies? The Thompson Twins, Boston, Duran Duran, all that crap? It sounds so stale and tinny, like it was recorded in a bomb shelter. But not the Risen Angels. Their music is still fresh and original thirty years later. My AA sponsor, Chris Towle, founded that group.

I called him when I got back to my hotel.

"No kidding? Angel? You can really pick 'em, babe."

"That's not the way it works, Chris. You can pick your sponsor. But you can't pick your clients. They pick you."

"The kids were joking about her arrest after group today," he said. "One of them said her next CD would be titled *Live from San Quentin*."

Chris is now a counselor in the adolescent wing of a highly regarded rehab center in rural Pennsylvania. Risen Angels is a lifetime ago. I flattered myself to think that my job let him keep a vicarious hand in the rock 'n roll rodeo. But the truth is he wouldn't care if I worked in a gas station as long as I went to meetings.

"Angel singing chain-gang music . . . it would have to be an improvement over the dreck she usually puts out."

"Here we go."

"What's that mean?"

"Why do you never like your clients? Is that some cynical job requirement?"

"What are you talking about? I like my clients."

"Really? Who?"

"Plenty of them . . . Chris Martin from Coldplay."

"Whom you called a 'pretentious twat.' And you said you would probably have nightmares about Gwyneth Paltrow for the rest of your life."

"Boy, was I right on that score. Let's see . . . Sheryl Crow?"

" 'Vain' and 'self-absorbed' I believe were the words you used to describe her."

"So I have issues with the people who hire me. It's because we're usually working at cross-purposes. But that doesn't mean I don't respect and admire them."

"And what's the problem with Angel?"

"Oh, God, she's awful. The most nasty, angry, shrill creature on the face of the planet. She is so repulsive. I'm telling you, I wouldn't—"

"Whoa, whoa," Chris interrupted my tirade. "Gotta stop you there, buddy. Repulsive? I've always thought of her as the modern Mae West. Someone who wielded her sexuality to beat society at its own hypocritical game."

"Thank you, Jacques Derrida."

"At the very least you're getting to spend time with a certified legend. This is a story you'll be able to tell your grandchildren."

"Sure, right after Peter Cottontail, I'll tell them all about the woman who revolutionized fellatio."

"Have it your way, you pissy bastard. I just find it curious that you always have to adopt an adversarial relationship with the people you work for."

"I like to think it helps me stay objective. If I get all starry-eyed, then I can't tell when they're lying to me. And that's dangerous in my line of work."

"You may not like her. But ten million people think Angel is a goddess."

"Yeah, and people sleep outside for three days to get Creed tickets. What does that prove?"

"You know you might want to consider taking that sour disposition of yours to a meeting. Remind me to give you my friend Whitey's number before we get off. He's quite a character. And he knows every meeting from Oxnard down to old Mexico."

"Okay. Hopefully I'm not going to be here long enough to learn local geography."

"Why is that?"

"This should be an easy case. I just need to win Angel's trust. She tells me what happened that night, and oingo boingo, I'm all done."

"I don't think it's going to be that simple, bud. Not by a long shot. I've been at fabulous Hollywood parties after a night of club-hopping. In fact, unless I'm mistaken, I've been at a few right in that neighborhood where Angel lives. Of course, back when I was active, most of the musicians lived out in Laurel Canyon. Oh, man, I just remembered this wild time out at David Crosby's house. Janis was performing that night at the Whiskey Au Go Go. This was like three weeks before she died. And the Grateful Dead were in town—at least Jerry and Pigpen were—and we ended up . . ."

"What?" I said, urging him to go on.

"Nah, I'm not telling that story. I still have to remind myself sometimes not to romanticize the old days."

"I thought you were trying not to speak ill of the Dead."

"Anyway, the point I was trying to make is that these crazy late-night bashes in L.A. are like Caligula's palace. All is permitted. And you reach a certain tipping point. Everything gets murky and fluid and fast-moving. You get this sensation like you're underwater and nothing can hurt you.

"And then something terrible happens. Maybe right in front of you or in a back bedroom. There's an overdose or a shooting or a rape. Suddenly the vibe goes all raw and bad. But it doesn't seem real either.

"The next day, people don't remember what happened. Or else they have reasons for lying. Either to protect themselves or someone else. And the truth becomes like a jigsaw puzzle—shattered into a thousand pieces. You may get a version of what happened that night. More likely several versions. But even if you had a video camera running, you may not ever find out what really happened."

"Aren't you the optimist."

"How did the guy get killed, by the way?"

"Angel's party mix is made up of all her own songs. This poor sap was sitting by the speaker. Head exploded."

Chris's voice took on the exasperated tone he sometimes gets with me. I suspect he uses it at work too, when the kids in his group are acting like jerks. "I can tell you think that's funny. But you really should restrain yourself from repeating it in front of Angel or her people, because they will definitely not be amused."

We chatted for a while and he gave me Whitey's number before signing off. I turned on my computer to check my e-mail. There were three valid personal messages buried amid more than sixty spam entries. Remember when e-mail used to seem so miraculous and convenient? The process has become so arduous and time-consuming, it's hardly worth it. Like weeding a garden with an out-of-control thistle problem.

It's frightening how many appeals I get on a daily basis to increase my penis size. If there are this many resources devoted to this cause, this many cons beating the bushes, they must be making money. And that worries me. I'd rather live in a world where I was constantly being dunned with bogus offers to boost my IQ.

While I was stripping out junk mail, I watched the local news. Empty speculation about Angel took up about half the broadcast. Authorities would neither confirm nor deny . . . blah, blah, blah. But they aired some great footage of Cam roaring as he exited the property. Showed that particular clip over and over. Cam's aversion to the media was definitely not mutual.

Still on-line, I came up with a dream quinella: a Mexican cantina within hiking distance of the Marmont that got high ratings in the restaurant guide. And it was only a few blocks away from a Step meeting that started at eight. My evening had come together nicely.

I didn't expect the meeting to be an improvement over my home group. I had been to a lot of AA in Los Angeles before. You got some good recovery; you also got a lot of people who really liked to hear themselves talk. But I knew the Mexican food in California was appreciably better than on the East Coast.

Before I went out I called the number Lani had given me for Cliff Johnson. He was a little wary during my long-winded introduction, but he warmed up enough to agree to meet the next day, giving me explicit directions to the USC campus.

Turned out the school, like a lot of inner-city universities, was a spectacular and august vision set down in a dismal, decaying neighborhood, Emerald City twinkling in a charnel field. Cliff's instructions took me to a guardhouse just outside the Trojans' immense football stadium. When I asked for Cliff, the guard pointed me through the gates.

I walked through a nearly deserted parking lot and down a concrete ramp wide and tall enough for two trucks to pass each other. Beneath the building, corridors ran in both directions following the curvature of the stadium bowl. The ramp began to rise again toward a haze of sunlight. I continued on, emerging onto the field near the goalpost behind one end zone.

On both sides of me, the stands rose like canyon walls to towering heights. In front of me, the well-manicured and freshly watered grass shimmered in the morning brightness. The spectacle made my heart swell, I suppose from years of watching helmeted warriors jog onto fields like this ready for battle.

Some time ago my services were retained by Busta Rhymes and I went with him one afternoon to Yankee Stadium, where Busta was "singing" the National Anthem before a game against Cleveland. I got a similar sensation standing at home plate. The feeling, too powerful to be vicarious, is one of treading on hallowed ground.

I took a deep breath and looked around. A couple of joggers loped around the cinder oval circumscribing the field, but neither was substantial enough to qualify as a superstar bodyguard. For that you needed to look like you could throw yourself on a hand grenade and walk away mildly ruffled.

Then off to my left I saw a solitary figure plodding steadily up the stairs near the fifty-yard line toward the top of the stadium. He was a large black man moving at a deliberate pace but nimbly—that is, his knees came up higher than they had to, to run the stairs. His hair was cornrowed and he wore a red T-shirt, soaked through with sweat and burgundy track pants. Had to be Cliff.

As I walked over to the railing by the bottom of his aisle, he reached the last row of seats, touched the wall and began to scamper back down. Though his eyes were trained on his feet, he noticed me approaching. As he neared the field, he looked up, flashed a brilliantly white smile and held up two fingers in a V. Then he touched the rail, turned and began climbing again.

At first I thought he was flashing me the peace sign. Then I realized he was letting me know he had two more circuits left in his routine. At the end of his final descent, he leaped the rail and stood about ten yards away from me where a towel and a sports bag lay on the grass. He stood hunched over, hands on knees, catching his breath.

He reached down, grabbed the towel, ran it over his face and draped it around his neck. It was only when he straightened up that I recognized how big he was.

"You Jim?" he asked, his voice deep and growly like a cartoon bear. I nodded. "You don't mind, I thought we could talk while I work out."

"Sure," I said, resisting the temptation to respond, *No sweat*, because he was flowing like the Amazon Basin.

He picked up his bag and headed for an alcove leading under the stands. I followed. "So you workin' for Angel, huh?" he asked over his shoulder.

"Yeah."

"You poor bastard," he said, his shoulders twitching as he chuckled. A thick roll of what looked like fat ran under his neck, disappearing under the shirt.

"I take it you're speaking from experience."

"For the most part, I stay out of her shit. Just walk her through the crowds, from here to there. Soon as she get there, I fade into the background. Stay incognito."

He turned right in the interior corridor, arriving at a huge, glassed-in weight room. He took an ID card from his bag and swiped it through a reader, which flashed green. Inside, he stashed his bag beneath a bench and grabbed a fresh towel from a pile.

A couple of mammoth Polynesian guys were spotting for each other over in a corner. They looked up when Cliff and I came in and nodded without smiling. He acknowledged them with a flick of his head and began loading plates on an elevated barbell.

"This is a sweet arrangement," I said. "The university lets you work out, huh?"

"I played ball here," he said, sitting behind the apparatus and smoothly beginning to curl more weight than I could press. His body was solid and dense, not cut and angular. His muscles didn't bunch and jump as he lifted. They just seemed to roll.

"Yeah? What position?"

"Offensive line. When they called student body right, I was the body."

"Don't tell me you were a pulling guard for O. J. Simpson?"

He clanked the weights back in the holder and squinted at me skeptically. "How old you think I am? The Juice was retired before I ever put on a pair of shoulder pads. I did my blocking for Delon Washington. I was All-Pac 10 three years running."

"Sorry," I said. "I should of known the math was way off. I guess when I think Trojan running backs, my mind still goes to O.J."

"Shit, when they had him on trial downtown, I was starting my sophomore year here."

"How come you didn't go pro?"

"Wanted to," he said, moving to a squat machine. "But I didn't get drafted until the fourth round. There was a lot of big white boys that year. Looked like prison guards. But the NFL ate them up. I got drafted by Jacksonville. But they lowballed me and wouldn't negotiate." He began lowering down and then smoothly lifting until he was up on his toes. His voice grew staccato with the exertion. "Agent . . . wanted me . . . to go . . . to Canada. . . . I hate . . . cold weather." He finished another set and stepped away from the device. "I tried it. Last game of the season, there was like a blizzard in Ottawa. Couldn't see shit on the field. Some guy crack-blocked me. Ripped up my knee. Never went back."

"How'd you become a bodyguard?"

"Huh," he responded, a life-is-funny grunt. Then he did another set of squats and started to towel off. "Last semester of my senior year, Snoop Dogg asked me to go down to Florida with him for MTV's spring break. We both grew up about a mile from here. Him and my older brother was tight.

"Third night we was down there, we was in a bar right on

the beach and the place is jumpin'. Some guys started getting frisky with Snoop. Happens all the time. Snoop is chill. He's the onliest rapper I ever met who doesn't think he's badder than Ray Lewis. So people think they can fuck with him.

"These boys pushed it a little too far. I ast them nice to step off but they wouldn't. So I clapt them niggas' heads together like I was beatin' chalk off erasers back in third grade. Then I hauled them out and laid them in an alley behind the bar. I guess JT was in the bar that night, but I didn't see him. Or maybe I didn't know who he was back then."

"Justin Timberlake?" I interrupted. He nodded.

"He ast Snoop for my number. Said he liked how I handled that situation. Ast me to go to work for his band, *NSYNC. And that's how I became a bodyguard. Except for the five months I spent in the CFL, I been doing it ever since. It's a real word-of-mouth business."

"So is mine."

He had moved onto an inclined bench press.

"So can we talk about your current employer?" I asked.

"You mean Payback?"

"Payback?"

"Thas what we call Angel."

"You mean because she's vindictive?"

"No doubt. But that's not how she got the nickname. We call her that because payback is a bitch."

After two sets on the bench, Cliff said he was going to hit the showers. "You're welcome to use the facilities," he added.

I glanced over at the Polynesians, who were glowering at me like I had pissed in the poi. "Nah. I'll wait for you out by the guard shack."

I was thinking of forming a search party by the time Cliff finally emerged. Typical jock behavior. After being coddled from an early age because of their physical gifts, athletes think people actually like waiting for them. Making no apologies, he asked, "Wanna get something to eat?"

"Sure."

"You have a car?"

"Unh-unh."

He tilted his head and shut his eyes, a that's-too-bad gesture. "Cars is how we keep score in Angel's camp," he said. "If they didn't give you no driver, then you pretty low on the totem pole."

I didn't tell him I had given Stan the day off. I figured if he thought of us as fellow working stiffs, he might be more forthcoming. So I merely shrugged.

"Thas all right," he said. "We'll go to Claudette's."

As we set off across campus, I said, "Speaking of nicknames, I understand people in the music business have an interesting one for you."

"Yeah. They call me Oops."

"I've heard several versions of how you earned that. What's the real story?"

"After working for JT for a couple of years, I got a better offer from his girlfriend."

"Britney?"

He nodded. "She a sweet kid. But I didn't like her family. They from the Deep South. Them people make me nervous. So when I got a call from Celine Dion's agent, I jumped ship. She from the Far North. Plus I figured the hours would be better anyway. Woulda been an easy gig too, 'cept for this one crazy motherfucka kept pestering her.

"Every time we leave a hotel, climb out a car, open a door, he waiting there with this dopey look on his face, like ain't Celine gonna be surprised to see me? Guy got some kinda skin condition. Got a *ugly* purple stain covering half his face. He smell bad too, like a dog pissed itself.

"Poor little Celine. She scared to death of that boy. Her voice shrink down to four octaves every time he pop up. She went to court for a restraining order. Didn't stop him. I sure didn't miss a chance to discourage him either. Nothing helped. He persistent.

"So she playing three nights at Radio City in Manhattan? Very big deal. The first night, before we leave for the hall, I come out of her hotel suite because I got a bad feeling. Sure enough I look down the corridor and I see that fool's ugly two-tone head duck back onto the service stairs.

"I catch him up quick, give him a good talking-to. Impress on him that Ms. Dion don't need his foolishness right now." Cliff looked at me appraisingly. "You know what he did?"

I shook my head. Adopting a look of astonishment, he said, "He got one of them nerd-ass pocket protectors. He reach down, pull out a Bic and stab me." Cliff touched a spot right over his clavicle. "Right there. Flat pissed me off." Cliff's hand jolted up, miming a claw grip. "I grabbed him and lifted him over the banister. We on the top floor of that hotel, so it's a long drop. Figure that would get his crazy ass to focus on the subject at hand. I ast him to promise me he'll go away and not show his spooky face no more. I could not get that man to agree. Then he hock up some phlegm, like he gettin' ready to spit." Cliff unlocked his hand, turning the palm up.

"Oops?" I ventured. He tilted his head again, a what-are-you-gonna-do? expression.

"There was a big investigation after. Celine had to let me go. But I bought my momma a house with the bonus money Celine's husband, Rene, give me. And I ain't never had to look for work since. Here we go."

We had walked two blocks from USC's campus, but it felt like we had crossed through a portal into another dimension. A row of scarecrow businesses lined the street—a consign-ment store, a tire repair shop without a bay or lift, a ragged laundromat and others. Even the air felt closer and hot-ter. Cliff had stopped in front of the storefront with "CLAUDETTE'S" hand-painted on the front window.

Inside, people were scattered at a couple of the eight booths in the cramped serving area. All of them were con-centrating on their food. An overhead fan tried to keep the air from loitering.

As soon as we walked in the door, a stocky woman hur-ried out from behind the counter demarcating the kitchen. Her hair pushed tight with a net, she walked with a limp that made her rock from side to side. Smiling widely, she said, "Lord, Lord, my baby's here," as she approached Cliff.

After hugging him, she pushed him into a booth. "Sit, sit," she said. "You hungry, baby?"

"I could eat," he said. They laughed at what was apparently a private joke. She cocked her head at me. "How 'bout him?"

"Bring him some chicken, Claudette."

"Coming up," she said, swaying back toward the kitchen.

I sat across from Cliff and looked around to make sure we had a modicum of privacy. The other customers were paying no attention to us. "I was hoping you could tell me about the night of the murder," I said.

"Angel sent me home right after they got back from the club. 'Round two-thirty."

"Was that unusual—to let you go when there were people in the house?"

"Nah. When she partyin' at home, she always tell me to leave. If she's on the road, like in a hotel, she have me wait out in the hall."

"Why?"

"'Cause she don't want me in the room."

"No, I mean why does she send you home?"

"Same reason I got to wait in the hall. She say I got an 'inhibiting influence' on her male friends. Even if I'm just chillin' in the corner, she say the men afraid to act up with her because they worried I'll object."

"You get the sense she wanted Gentry Jones to 'act up' with her?"

An unsmiling teenage boy walked over with a platter and set down napkins, large plastic tumblers, mismatched silverware and a basket of biscuits in front of us. Cliff waited until he had departed to respond.

"Hard to tell who Angel got her eye on. She trickier than most women. But I been with her awhile and I didn't see no signs she was getting ready to jump him. Though he certainly her type."

"Meaning?"

"All fucked up and way too in love with himself. Mostly, though," he said, popping a biscuit in his mouth, "he white-boy crazy."

"I didn't know that was a racial distinction."

"You kiddin'? When it comes to buck-wild crazy-ass shit, you white boys got it all to yourselves."

"What about Dennis Rodman?"

"Dennis ain't black! He ain't even human! He Vesuvian."

The young server returned with the platter, now fully laden, and began surrounding Cliff with heaping platters: macaroni and cheese, collard greens, hush puppies and a heap of fried fish fillets, each on its own plate. Because of the volume of food, I assumed at first it was intended for sharing. But my companion's obvious air of entitlement quickly convinced me I was wrong. He looked around at the Rabelaisian feast, sighed happily, attached a napkin to his shirtfront and tucked in.

Now I understood why the proprietess was so glad to see Cliff. He was her five best customers.

The boy returned and set down a platter in front of me with a couple of pieces of chicken and human portions of all the dishes Cliff was busily decimating.

"Save some room for dessert," he said to me, his mouth full. "Claudette make a killer sweet potato pie."

"So how did Angel and Gentry meet?"

"At the club. They both in the VIP room. He tryin' to act cool, but I could tell from the moment we walked in, he dyin' to meet her. Sure enough, 'bout ten minutes later he slide over, start talkin' 'bout what a big fan he is."

"Did she know who he was?"

Cliff shrugged. "She ignored him. Course she do that to everyone. Didn't seem to bother him none. He started talkin' to one of the dancers. He was happy just bein' in Angel's orbit."

"Was he alone?"

"I believe he was with two brothers. I don't follow the

NBA, 'cept for my nigga Tracy, but they look tall enough to be playas. When we fixin' to leave, he went over to talk to them. They shakin' their heads like he crazy. Maybe they got a game the next night. I can tell that ain't gonna stop this boy. He pile in one of the Suburbans when we leave."

"Tracy McGrady? Is that who you meant? How do you know him?"

"We tight. I met him when I was workin' for Lil Kim. At a party in Orlando."

"So along with Gentry, how many people came back to the house?"

"About ten. The usual entourage. No threats in that group. And I ain't worried about that white boy either. He the type may break some furniture. But I know he ain't gonna hurt Payback."

"How could you be so sure?"

Cliff flicked his head without saying anything, meaning he had made an instinctual assessment of Jones's character. I wrote down the names of everyone who had come back to the house. In some cases, Cliff only knew their circus names, like Flyboy and Shakes.

"Can you see anyone in that crowd stabbing Gentry?"

He shook his head emphatically. "And I know Payback didn't do it neither."

"Explain."

"She mean. And she physical. I seen her pinch some of her assistants, real nasty-like. And she throw things at people, 'specially her brother. But she ain't violent."

I tried to understand Cliff's grading system. Maybe he was working on a curve. "So do you have any theories?" I asked, taking a sip of Claudette's very sweet, not very cold iced tea.

"Impossible to say who showed up after I went home."

"There was no one manning the gate?"

"Not that time of night. Payback believe in safety in numbers," he said, then pointed a fork at my plate. "You gonna finish that chicken?" I pushed the plate over to his side of the table. "You got to understand: She the only pop star I ever seen who watch every dolla. She rather cut off her nose than pay somebody to snooze the night away in that booth."

"So anybody could have walked up to the house?"

Cliff nodded as he worked the chicken breast he was holding. "But she got her brother there. Charlie her last line of defense. And he throw himself in front of a truck for her. Course he would. Angel get hurt, he workin' at Burger King."

"Can you think of any enemies Angel might have?"

It was like an engine trying to turn over in cold weather. Cliff exhaled a single chuckle. Then a couple more. Soon the sound of his laughter, resonant and deep as a bassoon, was filling the room. His whole body shook with mirth like a Buddha.

Eventually he stopped, wiping a tear from his eye. "Angel got enemies? Seem like everyone who know her, hate her."

"Including you?"

The last vestiges of amusement vanished as he squinted at me. "No. She pay me on time. I don't require nothin' else from her."

"No offense, big guy," I said. "So who has it in for her?"

"Shit, every person who have business dealings with her, to start. Those two paintings hanging in the hall? I had to carry Bianco, the guy who painted them, out of the house one time, he so mad. Said Payback stiffed him. She laugh at him. He say he going to kill her. Then he tried to take a knife to his own paintings. Say he destroy them before he let her enjoy them. Called her the enemy of art."

I agreed with Signor Bianco's sentiment. But I put him on the list anyway.

"And that girl on her label?" Cliff continued.

"Jenny Boisson?"

He nodded. "We backstage at one of them music awards shows—seem like there one every week in the springtime.

Anyway, Jenny come at Payback like she gonna scratch her eyes out."

"What was she mad about?"

"What you think? Her money. She say her CD sell eleven million copies and she ain't made a nickel because Payback skimming all the profits."

"That would piss me off too."

"No shit," said Cliff. "They both got lawyers fightin' over that one now. That's Payback. She like to take all the money in the kitty and then dare you to come after her, try to get it back."

"Why do you think she's like that?"

"Don't know. But it seem to run in the family. Her brother Charlie the same way. Small-time shit, mostly." Cliff pointed at me to underscore his next point. "Don't play cards with that motherfucka."

I nodded.

"Bet the repo men out at their trailer every week when they growin' up in Michigan."

"How about Inga?" I asked. "She seems to get along really well with Angel."

"Yeah, for now. But them two going partners on a club that about to open in Miami."

"So?"

"I guarantee you in two months Inga be coming after her with a straight razor."

"Tell me about Cam."

Cliff shook his head with mock rue. "He the original white-boy crazy. Collector's edition." He gestured out the window. "If he grew up in this neighborhood—gettin' in everybody's business the way he do—somebody would have put a cap in his ass before he reach eighth grade."

"Could he have killed Gentry?"

"No tellin' what he might do. But Cam had plenty of chances to go Jason on her ass and he ain't never done it."

"Go Jason on her?"

"You never seen a *Friday the 13th* movie? He the boy with the hockey mask and the machete."

"So Cam is a suspect?"

"Oh, *hell* yes. LAPD doing their job, he the first person they gonna call in, make certain his whereabouts accounted for."

"What do you think?"

"Of Cam? He all right. I had to sit him down hard a few times when he gettin' frisky with Payback in public places. But he never take offense. He always treat me well enough."

"How about her first husband?"

"He some DJ in New York. I never met him. Payback got a big apartment in Manhattan. Even when we there for months at a time, he never come by."

"Any old boyfriends who might still be carrying a grudge?" Cliff sat back, sucked a morsel of food that was caught in his teeth and folded his hands over his stomach. "You wanna go alphabetical or chronological?"

CHAPTER
10

On my way back to the hotel, I passed a big open-air newsstand. It looked like a shrine to Angel, her face was plastered on so many covers. I bought *People,* which carried a grim, unsmiling image of her over the legend "Angel of Death."

One of the many savvy marketing moves my superstar client had made was to shorten her name from Angela Chiavone to simply Angel. It made her a headline writer's darling and a household identity.

It also became a much-imitated strategy in the music business. In fact, you can't find a rapper with a last name because they know it fosters a sense of intimacy and gets them in print more often. Actors, being the perverse creatures they are, keep going in the opposite direction, more and more of them wielding cumbersome hyphenated names. They think it lends them a Merchant-Ivory air of distinction.

Back in my room, I flipped through the cover article. There was a picture of Angel with Gentry Jones taken outside the nightclub on the night of his murder. Turning the page sideways, I read the photo credit in tiny print: "Ron Greshmanick/AutoFocus."

Next I called Lani and asked her to play pulling guard for me. I figured in the professional arena she would be just as effective at removing obstacles as Oops Johnson had been on the football field. If Angel was innocent, then the person who had gutted Gentry Jones had either come to Angel's house looking for her—or else Jones was the intended target all along. It was time to look into that possibility.

I waited about an hour to let Lani's influence marinate and then I called the Golden State Warriors office in Oakland, asking for the head of security. I was informed that Mr. Cooney was traveling with the team, but that he had been informed that I was seeking an appointment.

Luckily for me, there are two basketball franchises in Los Angeles and the NBA doesn't like to schedule visiting teams against them on successive nights. So usually you'll play one at the beginning of a West Coast tour and the other at the end. The Warriors were coming back to town to face the Clippers the following day. Cooney's office called back to say that he would meet me in the lobby of the team's hotel at five P.M.

I called my sponsee Danny back in Winsted. We had a standing agreement that he w~·'-1 call me every day. My sponsor made me do the same thing in my first year. Alcoholism and drug addiction are diseases of isolation, and this pact was a way of getting the newcomer comfortable with picking up the phone and calling someone else in recovery.

But Danny had enough problems at the moment. I didn't want to saddle him with a big long-distance bill, too.

After we talked for about a half hour, I went out by the hotel pool, which was deserted at this hour. I put Robert Palmer's *Pride* CD on my Walkman, lay down on one of the chaise lounges and stared up at where the stars should have been.

I considered having dinner, but Claudette's hush puppies

were still camping in my stomach. In fact, it felt like they had expanded to Jabba the Hutt size. So I went up to my room, put on a Rickie Lee Jones CD and dove back into *Gravity's Rainbow*. I've read Thomas Pynchon's master opus at least five times and would continue to do so merely for the brilliant writing. But I had also discovered that, for whatever reason, the book gave me the most vivid dreams. If I read it just before turning in, Pynchon's prose acted like LSD on my subconscious.

Gravity worked a little too well that night. In my dreams I was sitting in the front row of a carnival. Right in front of me, too close for comfort, Angel and Inga Saffron were riding around and around in the ring, standing on the backs of galloping tigers. Both women were wearing red vinyl short-shorts and mini vests. They were glaring at me with childish looks of sadistic triumph, real neener-neener-neener faces. In the background stood Bruce Katz, taller than in real life, dressed in a ringmaster's evening coat and hat, windmilling his arms.

I woke up with a start and went over to the sink to splash some water on my face. A nacreous light drifted through the window. Outside the air was gray and hazy. The clock by the bed told me it was just after six. I knew I wasn't going back to sleep, so I decided to hit a wake-up meeting. Try to wash that dream out of my head.

The meeting, which I taxied to, was great. I identified myself as an out-of-town visitor and ended up going out to breakfast afterward with a couple of guys. Later, when Stan arrived at the hotel to take me over to Angel's, I asked him to start picking me up on weekday mornings at 6:40 to take me over to La Brea Boulevard. I explained he would have to come back for me an hour or so later.

Stan glanced back at me in the rearview mirror and smiled shyly. "Serenity Group, huh?"

The cool thing about my work situation is that I don't

have to hide the fact that I'm in AA. In fact, most of my clients hire me because I am in recovery.

"You in the program?" I asked.

"No. My mom was. She had fourteen years when she passed away last April."

"Sorry, Stan."

"I used to drive her over to that meeting twice a week. It was one of her favorites."

"Tell me her name. I'll mention to the group that I met her son."

"Sandy." We nodded and smiled at each other's reflections.

The siege at Angel's compound was unabated. I had Stan drop me off about a block from the gate so I could walk up. The crowd was even bigger—more fans, more crazies, more tourists. And they had been joined by an honor guard of right-to-lifers. It wasn't a good mix. Angel's supporters in particular seemed to resent the encroachment of the new-comers, peppering them with insults and whatever objects came to hand.

It struck me that whenever I see a group publicly advocating the sanctity of the fetus, it seems to be composed of people that I hope would have second thoughts about reproducing.

Closer to the gate I spotted a flamboyant free agent: a guy with a pointy goatee, his face painted red, wearing a satin devil's outfit with a high-collared cape. He looked like Perry Farrell from Jane's Addiction. In one hand he carried a toy pitchfork, in the other a sign that read: "Devils are Angels Too." I flinched as he approached me because I suddenly flashed on my dream. I could swear he registered my reaction, because he cackled quietly as he passed.

I wandered up to the knot of camera operators. "Is Ron Greshmanick around?" I asked. I wanted to talk to the photographer who had taken the picture of Angel and Gentry together outside the club. Get his take on the evening.

As soon as I asked for him, all the heads in my vicinity turned to scowl at me. No one spoke. I learned later that the paparazzi close ranks whenever a stranger inquires after one of their guild. That's because it's almost always a process server with a restraining order or a subpoena in his back pocket.

Off on the fringe, I spotted a familiar face. Robin Pratt was a celebrity photographer from Manhattan whom I had first encountered during my most recent stint on MTV's payroll. The previous year, the channel had beefed up security measures for the Video Music Awards. Together with a bunch of law enforcement types, I sat through a week's worth of planning and contingency sessions initiated by a briefing from one of MTV's terminally hip, twenty-five-year-old executives who informed us that "word on the street" was that a major vendetta in the rap world was going to be settled during the telecast.

I wanted to raise my hand and inquire "Isn't that what the Source Awards are for?" But I kept my lip buttoned and took MTV's generous salary. On the night of the awards, I was positioned on the barricades near the arriving limos and armor-plated SUVs outside Lincoln Center with a walkie-talkie and an earpiece. There were no incidents—at least among the hip-hop delegation. There was a scary moment when a rabid fan ducked past the guards and sprinted toward Jack White of the White Stripes, wailing at the top of her lungs like one of the extras in *Braveheart.*

We tackled her at the same time she tackled him and everyone went down in a heap. No harm, no foul, although White looked terribly shaken up. Of course, he always does.

But that's when I met Robin, who was there shooting the arriving stars. As I walked over to her outside Angel's, she was kneeling down, swapping lenses out of black leather bag at her feet.

"Hey, Robin."

She looked up at me and squinted. Robin was mildly

cross-eyed, which made me wonder how she could be a world-class photographer. "Hey, Jim," she said

"Little out of your territory, aren't you?"

"Are you kidding?" she asked, laughing. "This is like one of those Bassmaster tournaments. All the big names flew in for this. You have any idea how much you can get for a good shot of Angel?"

I shook my head. Her attention was back in her camera bag. "A lot," she said.

"Listen, Robin, I'm looking for Ron Greshmanick. Would you point him out to me?"

"Sure," she said, standing up. "But you have to do me a favor too." She put her arm around my shoulder and walked me away from her colleagues. "I hear you're working for Angel," she said softly in my ear. "If you happen to hear she's meeting someone outside these gates, give me a heads-up on my cell." She had released my shoulder and was pressing a business card on me. "I'd definitely owe you."

I shrugged. "If I can." She bobbed her head. Still gazing at me, she yelled, "Ron!"

One of the cameramen turned. The guy I had been standing right next to when I first walked up. "This is Jim," she said, clapping me on the back. "He wants to talk to you." Greshmanick frowned. "Don't be a schmuck, Ron. He's a good guy."

The frown didn't dissipate. I walked over anyway. "Hey, I saw your picture in *People*. Just wanted to ask you a quick question about that night."

"What picture?" he asked, like he was Harry Benson with shots in every issue.

"Oh, sorry," I said, playing along. "The one of Angel and Gentry Jones."

He lifted his chin in acknowledgment.

"Did the two of them seem close as they came out of the club?"

He chuckled. "I don't think she knew he existed until she saw the cameras."

"I don't get it," I said. "Did you pose them together?"

"Didn't have to," he said. "You never have to ask with our Angie. She's automatic." He looked around for corroboration from the other shutterbugs. Heads nodded. "You know how when most celebrities hit the carpet, you can hear us all shouting, 'This way, Gwen. Over here!' Never had to do that with Angie. That girl could give Cindy Crawford lessons in posing. She gives everyone what they need.

"Not like that psycho ex-husband of hers." He turned to his neighbor in the photo fraternity. "Did I tell you what he did outside the club? I could have had two keepers that night if it wasn't for that asshole."

"Wait," I said. "You mean Cam was at the club too?"

"Yeah," he said. "He left not long after Angel came in. He was with that actress from the WB show. I definitely could have sold that shot. No one's seen the two of them together before. But he covered up her face with his jacket just as my flash went off. Bastard. I don't think she appreciated it too much either, judging by her expression when he pushed her in his car."

"What's the actress's name?"

"Oh, shit," he said, searching his memory. "Hey, Sandor, what's the name of that girl from *Ambrosia Street*?"

"Julie Kingston," his neighbor said.

Greshmanick nodded. "Now, Angie would never pull a stunt like that. She's a photographer's wet dream." His voice had gotten louder and more passionate, taking on an evangelical tone. More photographers' heads began nodding. He was preaching to the choir, all right.

"That night at the club was a perfect example. She came out the door with her usual crew and spotted me. She stopped, looked around and scooped up Jones. Because he was young, a pro ball player and a horn dog. Angie can do celebrity calculus in her head faster than anyone I know. She'll always give you the money shot."

"Course it was worth a lot more money after she killed him," said Sandor as he shouldered his video camera.

I thanked Greshmanick and jostled toward the entrance, signaling to the security chief with the shaved head who had been on duty the previous day. He came over to the barricade and I identified myself. He spoke my name into a compact walkie-talkie. I wondered who he was checking with. I hadn't seen anyone inside the house with a similar device. Maybe someone in the booth by the gate was holding a list of approved names.

I must have passed muster because the shift supervisor gestured for me to duck under the barrier. He pointed me toward a recessed wrought-iron gate guarded by a stern-looking behemoth in the company blazer. Though he was regarding me like a store-owner would a notorious shoplifter, the guard stepped aside and opened the gate for me.

As the paparazzi posse I had just been talking to noticed that I was entering the compound, they all began shouting at me. "Hey, come back over here for a minute." "Yo, wait up." And from Greshmanick: "Why didn't you mention you worked for her?"

Obviously I didn't have Angel's knack for keeping the photographers happy.

I crunched up the driveway without looking back.

CHAPTER 11

Damned if she didn't do it again. As I raised my hand to ring the bell, Angel's maid opened the door.

"Ms. Ross is expecting you in the downstairs office."

"What's your name?" I asked.

"Alice, sir."

"How do you do that, Alice?"

"Do what, sir?"

"Open the door before I get there."

As I stepped into the foyer, she closed the door and looked up at me disingenuously. "That's my job."

"But how do you know, Alice?"

"Psychic," she said, and moved off to her sanctuary under the steps. I looked after her as she walked away, her rubber soles making a faint squishy noise. I had assumed from her pinched appearance that she was a woman without a sense of humor. In my life I've misjudged more books than a myopic librarian.

I paused in the hallway, listening for disturbances, trying to gauge the proximity of Hurricane Angel. The chandelier was steady and the paintings weren't shimmying on the walls, so I assumed we were experiencing a lull.

I passed through the media room, resolving an age-old philosophical puzzle in the process: If a Tori Amos CD is playing and there's no one there to hear it, is it really playing? The answer, I am pleased to report, is yes.

In the office, I found Lani on the phone. Flapping her fingers against her palm in greeting, she continued talking. I don't know about you, but I rather enjoy listening to one side of a conversation. Gives me a chance to make up my own rejoinders.

"Well, then maybe I'll have her do it with Larry King," she said.

You wouldn't dare take on that scrofulous old bastard! I shouted in my head.

"I'm not kidding. If Barbara calls me up and starts reading me the riot act, the interview isn't taking place. Part of the deal is you keep Walters off my back."

All right, but you know what that means: You're going to have to give Star Jones a piggyback ride, I responded.

"I don't care how you do it," said Lani. "Just stop Barbara."

Easy for you to say, I said in my imaginary dialogue. *We've thrown acid in that old crone's face. She just towels off and keeps coming.*

"All right, 'bye," Lani said, hanging up.

"What was that about?" I asked aloud.

"I'm setting up a prime-time interview for Angel."

"When?" I asked, the surprise evident in my voice.

"We're going to tape it here Friday afternoon." This was Wednesday.

"What was all that about Barbara Walters?"

"Angel is obviously the biggest get of the year and ABC's interview queens have both been coming after me with the full-court press." Her cell and desk phone were ringing at the same time. The cell quietly played the hook from Angel's most recent hit, "Bliss Me, Kiss Me." I liked the instrumental ring tone version better than I did the single with Angel's vocals.

"Damn that Roone Arledge." I thought for a moment the legendary ABC executive had come back from the dead and was pestering Lani with constant calls. But she was making a statement. "He set up this star system in their news division and these women just beat each others' brains in to get interviews. It's like Rollerball." That was the third time I had heard Lani use a sports analogy. It made me think she had grown up around several brothers.

"Anyway, we're going with Carla." Walters's younger, more glamorous in-house rival was Carla Finn. "You'd think it would end there, but nooooo. After you choose one, the other one starts in with the threats and recrimination. They keep after you right up until the cameras start rolling. They're more persistent than Algerian street beggars."

"So you told Finn's camp to make Barbara cease and desist. Will that work?"

"Probably not. But if they're fighting with each other, maybe they won't have as much time to badger me." It occurred to me I had never seen a badger. They must be nasty creatures.

Lani was ignoring both phones. The desk set kept going quiet after two rings. Maybe there was an operator down in the basement of the house.

"Why did you choose Finn?"

"For the same reason Michael Jackson and Whitney Houston did."

"She's sympathetic to music stars?"

"No, she's brain-dead. Barbara has this annoying habit of actually listening to what you're saying and calling you on it. Not Carla. There's never any follow-up. You could say you committed some heinous crime because Smokey the Bear told you to. She'd nod her head and go right on to the next question on the teleprompter."

"Katz was in favor of Angel going on TV?"

"He doesn't care. The pretrial interview is a pretty standard strategy for celebrity crimes. You get to make your case directly to the public, drum up some sympathy. Plus it's a great opportunity for Angel to promote her book."

"Right. Who cares about murder charges when there's product to sell?" I said.

"Don't be so cynical, Jim. This is a preemptive strike. She goes on TV and sets the agenda for this case. It forces the prosecutor to play catch-up. And she'll be well coached. Bruce will go over all the likely questions with her Friday morning."

I shrugged. "You have time to answer a few of my questions?"

"Sure, but no follow-ups, okay?" she said, smiling.

I went through the list of Angel's companions on the night of the murder: Flyboy, Shakes and the rest of the flying reindeer. Lani gave me rather detailed backgrounds on all of them. Not a single suspect in the pack. It's not unheard of for someone to commit a brutally violent act out of the blue. But it's extremely rare. There's almost always a cloud hanging over them, a history of rage and poor impulse control. A pot that's been sitting at room temperature all day doesn't suddenly boil over.

Angel's party crew all sounded too fey to suddenly go on a killing spree. By the sounds of it, they'd have trouble cutting a sandwich in half, much less impaling a human being. Especially a large one with good athletic skills.

"Is it true that Angel and Inga are opening a club together in Miami?" I asked.

Lani's eyebrows did a skeptical push-up. "So I've been told."

"Where does Inga's money come from?"

"There are a couple of stories in circulation. One is that she had a brief and very lucrative marriage to the heir of a sugar fortune. Another is that her brother is a major figure in the import business down in Florida."

"Imports?" I repeated, wondering if that meant what I thought it did.

Lani flexed her eyebrows again, signaling me to draw my own conclusions. Then, in a quieter, confidential voice she said, "I don't like talking about Inga in the house because she always ends up walking in the room right in the middle of it. It freaks me out a little bit." She resumed her normal tone. "So what have you been up to? Making any progress?"

"Not too much. Still going through the elimination process. Of course, the easiest route through this would be for Angel to simply talk to me."

"Be patient. We're getting there. Anything else I can help you with?"

"Do you think it would be worth it to speak with Cam?"

She widened her eyes with alarm. "Oh, dear. I don't think Cam has a publicist at the moment. He goes through them like tissues. But I can put you in touch with his manager."

"I take it you don't think that would be productive."

"According to Bruno Volpe, Cam has a solid alibi for the night of the murder."

"Julie Kingston?"

"Hmmm, you are getting informed," she said, her voice registering approval. "Apparently she went clubbing with him and then to a party in Malibu. She left, but several people have vouched that he was there until almost dawn."

"Can you put me in touch with Ms. Kingston?"

"I think so. Were you able to reach the guy from the Warriors you asked me to call?"

"Yes, thank you. I'm meeting him in . . ." I glanced at my watch. "About an hour."

Lani nodded. "So where were you yesterday? I didn't see you all day."

I was about to tell her about my lunch with Oops when the sound of Angel's angry, rapidly approaching voice reached us, cutting through the air like a fire engine siren. She was berating someone on the fly.

"I ought to call the police and have you thrown in jail, you piece of shit," she yelled. "No, I should kick your worthless ass and then have you thrown in jail." Angel stormed into the room with her brother following sheepishly behind. He had the same slovenly tropical motif going. Different loud colors, though. Joanna and another assistant brought up the rear.

I pictured a cheery family tableau with the squabbling siblings in adjoining cells. If anyplace would have coed prisons, it would be California.

"Good. You're here, Lani," Angel said. I was obviously still invisible. "I want you to hear this." She dialed up the volume, holding her fists at her sides and staring at the ceiling. "I want everyone in this fucking house to hear this!"

Oh, we were all ears. What choice did we have? Except Charlie, who stood there, slumped and downcast, looking at the floor.

"From now on, this cretin's word and signature mean nothing. Anything he does has to be approved by me. I want him stripped of all financial responsibility, is that understood? He can't even order a pizza from now on unless I say so."

There was something familiar about Angel's strident tone and posture. Then I realized what it was: She reminded me of Lucy from *Peanuts* throwing a hissy fit.

"You know what he did? My piece-of-crap brother? Remember the BMW Paramount gave me for doing that James Bond theme song? He took it out of storage and sold it. Spent the money on a weekend in Vegas.

"Know how I found out?" She was biting her lower lip with anger. Over her shoulder, I could see Alice in the doorway. She was trying to get Angel's attention. The maid opened her mouth a few times to announce something. Then a mischievous smile crossed her face like a cloud moving over the landscape and she walked away. I was starting to like her.

"The Hard Rock called me to settle Mr. Chiavone's outstanding line of credit. Not only did he blow through all the money he made off my car, he left owing the casino eighteen thousand dollars. Mr. Big Shot, playing blackjack at five hundred a hand."

At this point, Charlie clearly wanted to say something in his own defense, but Angel was a hard woman to interrupt. "I am so sick of all the dead weight around here. If any of you actually had to go out and make a living instead of sponging off me. . . ." A handsome figure was standing in the doorway. With his long, lustrous dark hair and loose-fitting poplin shirt, he looked like a young, radiant version of Yanni.

The beatific smile on his face changed to concern and consternation as he entered Angel's rant zone. "You are such a worthless sack of shit. You wouldn't last five minutes without me there to prop up your sorry ass. I should do the world a gigantic favor and just strangle you. I swear to—"

At this juncture, she noticed the man in the doorway. I have never seen such instantaneous change in a person. The stormy look on Angel's face vanished as completely and quickly as a shaken Etch-A-Sketch, replaced by an expression of absolute calm and compassion as she turned to face the stranger, bowing her head.

"I'm so glad you're here," she said. Gliding over and taking him gently by the arm, then leading him back toward the entry.

"How *are* you, Angel?" I heard him ask with a subtle note of censure. I couldn't make out her response because her voice had downshifted to a gentle whisper.

"Who the hell was that?" I asked Lani.

"Uli Baba."

"Uli who?"

"You seriously don't recognize him?" Lani was looking at me like I had just crawled out from under a rock with spider-webs clinging to my hair. So were Joanna and the other assistant. Clearly I had just committed a major faux pas.

"Sorry," I said. "Who is he?"

"He's only like the Tom Cruise of yoga," said the backup assistant, as if she were explaining gravity to the village idiot.

"You've never seen his videos?" asked Lani. She plowed past my shaking head. "Or his books, or his PBS specials?"

"I don't own a yoga mat," I said.

"That town in Connecticut you come from," said Lani. "Exactly how far from civilization is that?"

I considered telling them that I couldn't pick Deepak Chopra out of a lineup either, but I decided not to throw lighter fluid on this fire. "I take it Uli is a very big deal."

Both Joanna and her colleague made plosive scoffing noises. "Yeah," said Lani condescendingly. "There's like a two-year wait to get a spot in his studio. And he doesn't even teach those classes. He does private sessions with exactly three clients: Steven Spielberg's wife, Sandra Bullock and Angel."

"Wow," I said, trying to sound suitably impressed. The women were nodding vigorously, urging me to get a clue. "I have to get going to meet the guy from the Warriors. Would you please try to hook me up with Julie Kingston?"

Lani nodded and I beat a hasty retreat. I knew there was no recovering from my Uli gaffe. Alice was holding open the door for me as I hit the foyer.

Outside a gleaming new C-class Mercedes sedan was parked in the turnaround with vanity plates that read "PRANA." Apparently this yoga racket paid pretty well.

CHAPTER 12

Stan drove me over to the Regent Beverly Wilshire. As we approached the palm-lined entrance, I reflected that this establishment fit better with my fantasy of swank Hollywood living. Swimming pools, movie stars. I put the name of the hotel away in my mental lockbox for the next time someone's assistant called and asked me where I preferred to stay.

In the cathedrallike lobby, I saw a few Warrior players ambling past. They looked like stilt-walkers. It's disorienting to be around pro basketball players. I remembered one time crossing paths with Dikembe Mutombo and some of his teammates in the Denver airport. I felt like I had been transported to *Gulliver's Travels*.

But the NBA is living large in every way. When the league was young, the players used to travel on commercial flights with their knees up by their chins. They stayed in dank hotels with steam heat and beds so small that they literally slept with their feet out in the hall. Now they're regal millionaires flying in chartered jets and staying in deluxe hotels. These are good times to be able to dribble a ball. Except for Gentry Jones, obviously.

I asked at the concierge desk for Jack Cooney and was pointed to a guy sitting in one of a pair of high-backed chairs across the lobby. I had been expecting a distinguished ex-FBI type with silver temples. Jack looked more like a guy sitting at the end of the counter late at night at a Dunkin' Donuts. Hair cut stubble-length. Pockmarked skin on a doughy face. It wasn't so much that he was nondescript. It was more like he repulsed your attention.

Except for those eyes. He regarded me as I walked toward him. I've had X-rays that were less penetrating. We made introductions and he gestured me to the facing chair. He was polite enough, although he neither shook hands nor rose to meet me.

"How can I help you?" he asked, leaning forward, his forearms resting on his knees.

"I'm working for Angel. Trying to gather facts about the night of Gentry Jones's death."

"I talked to Volpe. On the phone," he said, making it clear that this face-to-face interview was an imposition.

"Sorry for the duplication," I said. "Bruno and I are working independently of each other."

Cooney cleared his throat disapprovingly.

"This won't take long," I said. A smirk played at the corner of his lips, a tug of amusement that said, *You're damn right it won't.*

"I was hoping you might share with me your take on Gentry's death."

"Well . . ." he said, pausing as a slick young business-type threw himself on the couch across from us and pulled out his BlackBerry. Cooney stared at him. The guy glanced up and twisted his face into a *What? You think you own the lobby or something?* look.

This was the weird part. It appeared to me that Cooney merely narrowed his eyes, but the impact was startling. The guy's expression shifted from defiance to fear. The blood drained from his face as he scrambled off the couch and backed away from us, his eyes fixed on Cooney as if he were staring into a clammy nightmare.

"Where were we?" Cooney asked, still focused on the retreating interloper. Then he turned to me. He had dialed back the intensity from flee-for-your-life to his usual armor-piercing gaze. That struck me as a neat parlor trick, particularly if you walked into a crowded waiting room at the dentist's office.

"Gentry's death?"

"I'll tell you one thing: He died happy."

"Pardon?"

"That was a little strong. Getting gutted is a nasty fucking way to go. What I meant was if Gentry could have picked the circumstances of his death, it would have been his dream to go out in the bedroom of the country's biggest sex symbol."

"My understanding is he died in the front entrance by the library."

"Yeah, okay, Colonel Mustard. The guy's gone. You mind if I dress up his legend a little?"

I just stared at him. Cooney was hard to read. Ugly and opaque is a rare combination.

His attention was elsewhere. His eyes kept sliding across the lobby to an impossibly lanky young player with cornrows and a flaming red athletic suit. I couldn't remember the kid's name. He was a forward who had come out for the draft after his freshman season at Oklahoma State. People were calling him the next Chris Webber.

At the moment, he was talking animatedly to a pair of heavyset guys in leather jackets, crisp jeans and immaculate Timberland boots. I realized our meeting had been arranged so Cooney could conduct surveillance.

"Were you surprised when you found out about Gentry's death?"

"Very," he said, his eyes returning to mine.

"Why?"

"Because that kid could talk his way out of anything. You grow up white in a predominantly black neighborhood with mad basketball skills, you learn early how to defuse a situation. People always wanted to kick his ass, sometimes just on principle. But usually he did something to antagonize them."

"Like what?"

Cooney shrugged. "Shooting his mouth off. Hitting on their girlfriends. And like I say, he had a cocky attitude that just generally seemed to fire people up. White, black, Hispanic, Asian—Jones rubbed everyone the wrong way. It was a gift."

"Sounds like you had your hands full keeping your eye on him."

The security director was staring across the lobby. "Actually I never worried much about him. Not after a while anyway. I just accepted the fact that I couldn't control him. He was going to go out carousing, and short of handcuffing him to his bed, there was nothing I could say or do to stop that.

"Some nights I didn't even wait up to see if he made curfew. I'd just mark him down as missing and go to bed. But I didn't worry about him. He was a magnet for trouble, but somehow he always found a way to skate out of it. The kid lived on thin ice. Built a fucking palace out there. So, yeah, I was surprised when he I heard someone killed him."

"Do you think he could have been defending Angel?"

Cooney gave a staccato snort. Not a pretty sound. "I *seriously* doubt it."

"Why?"

"First of all, Jones didn't have a chivalrous bone in his body. And second, he was a coward. If someone was menacing Angel, he wouldn't jump up to defend her honor. More likely you'd find him running out of the room. In fact, some of the guys on the team called him Scooby, because of how fast he would scoot away at the first sign of danger."

"So you think it's more likely that whoever stabbed Jones was specifically after him?"

"Didn't say that." Cooney shook his head slowly. "He did stupid shit all the time. Stirred people up. But the kid had this goofy sweetness at his core. It was hard to hold a decent grudge against him."

"Still, you piss off the wrong guy . . ." I was thinking of someone like Cam who was prone to spontaneous combustion.

"It's possible," Cooney conceded. "But my guess is Jones was just in the wrong place at the wrong time." He reached down for a device at his side that must have been set on vibrate, because I never heard it go off. After reading the message, he said, "I have to take off. But I'll tell you something I didn't tell Volpe: If I was you, I'd be looking for a guy who did time."

"Why is that?" I had to admit, I was intrigued.

"You see those bangers hanging with Dante?" Of course. That was the rookie's name: Dante Abernathy. I looked across the lobby to where he was having a raucous time with his two visitors. They were all laughing paroxysmally and sharing ritualized hand grips and shoulder bumps. "Both those guys are strapped. That's not unusual in the least. Street toughs today carry guns the way most people carry cell phones. When a fight breaks out at a hip-hop club, it's like a Wild West saloon. All firepower.

"No one carries knives anymore. Except for graduates of our prison system, who tend to have a fetish about blades because that's the only weapon you can make and carry on the inside."

He was already up and moving. "Hope you find the guy. I liked Gentry."

On the way back to the Chateau (I decided that that phrase alone made my hotel worth staying at), I had Stan drop me at a chicken shack down the street.

You'd think with me being an alcoholic and drug addict,

I'd be intimately acquainted with the mechanics of craving. But I'm like a cartoon version of a pregnant lady. Wait, scratch that. I've never hankered for Rocky Road ice cream and pickles. But there are times when only broiled chicken will do. Or a hot dog with sauerkraut. Or even—dare I say it?—beets. And I can't reset my desktop until that urge is satisfied.

So I started walking back with my sack of chicken, stopping at a quickie mart to load up on bottles of Snapple peach iced tea. I passed a GNC store, which, as usual, was well lit and empty. There are a lot of retail situations that bewilder me, but this vitamin chain had to be near the top of the list.

The stores are everywhere and I never see a customer in one—even in crowded malls. The only thing I could figure is that they must have an astronomical markup that allows them to get by on one sale a month and still make their nut— rent, payroll, the works. Either that or nutritional supplement buyers all shop really early in the morning.

Back at the hotel, I had a message from Julie Kingston's rep telling me the actress would meet with me the following morning on the set. I had also called Cam Akers's flack, but I wasn't holding my breath on that one. His publicist had sounded really furtive and jumpy, like someone working a weak, amateurish phone scam. I got the impression she didn't have much success getting Cam to respond to requests.

I called my sponsor. He had just gotten in after a long day at the rehab. They had had to boot some poor thirteen-year-old because the grounds crew found him down in the paint locker huffing solvent. Chris had to stay late until the kid's very pissed-off stepfather had driven down from Binghamton, New York, to pick him up.

We talked for a while about how deplorably early the disease sinks its fangs into most people. *Remember your first kiss? Nah, I was in a blackout.*

Afterward Chris asked me for a progress report on Angel.

"Do you know Uli Baba?" I asked.

"The yogi master? Sure."

"Am I the only person in the world who's never heard of the guy?"

"My local PBS station sent me one of his tapes after I pledged money last year."

"You respond to pledge drives? Those things are worse than the Jerry Lewis telethon."

"Are you kidding? I consider that a sacred duty—supporting public television. It's putting my finger in the dike against the flood of idiocy on the tube."

I told him about Angel's private yoga lesson, about her brother Charlie fencing her BMW, my session with Cooney and the plans for the prime-time interview.

"Maybe that's why she's refused to discuss with any of us what happened that night," I mused. "She's been waiting for the opportunity to tell the whole world."

"I doubt that," said Chris. "Unless I miss my guess, this will be a carefully choreographed fan dance for Angel where she promises to come clean and ends up revealing nothing."

"Well, I for one am sick of being ignored. And I'm going to tell Angel that I'm really pissed off . . . if she ever lets me talk to her."

"I'm serious, Jim. I've been thinking about this," Chris said. "Why do you think Angel isn't telling the police or her lawyer or you what happened that night?"

"Because she's an arrogant, self-absorbed pain in the ass?"

"I don't think that's it. Not when she's facing a murder rap. The stakes are too high. I feel like she would have protested her innocence by now unless something really scary was hanging over her head. I'm convinced that the only reason she's keeping quiet is because she's afraid."

"Wouldn't it be great, though, if the world's biggest pop star confessed to murder on network television?"

"Yeah, I would tune in to see that."

"You mean theoretically, right?" I said. "You probably have that night blocked out for watching the seventh installment of a documentary on Byzantine mosaic art."

"Hey, I only said I contributed to PBS. I never said I watched the stuff."

You mean *specifically* Cam? I suppose you probably
got the right church but you're reading the wrong row.
A red chameleon on a Hawaiian shirt.
Orange tang, and I wondered if . . . "Who're you with?"

CHAPTER
13

After Stan drove me to the morning meeting, I had him
swing back a couple of hours later to take me to the
Warner Brothers studio in Burbank to talk with the actress
who had been out with Cam Akers on the night of the murder.

I thought that was impressive—being dropped off right at
the studio gate in a chauffeured car. But the guards treated
me like I had just jumped out of the back of a banged-up,
badly smoking delivery van.

They were only deferential to the producers and stars who
drove up the guard booth in a string of incredible luxury
cars. There was a clearly demarcated hierarchy at work.
Anyone making less than $100,000 a day had to park in the
big garage across the boulevard and walk onto the lot.

For a visitor like me, the security measures were stifling.
U.S. customs agents aren't this demanding on passengers
coming off direct flights from Afghanistan. They did everything but take a blood sample. First I had to fill out a two-page
form of personal data. Then they asked for my driver's license and made a copy. I waited in a plastic chair in a bunga-

low just outside the gate while someone took away my documents for verification. I spent the time flipping through a *Los Angeles Times* someone had left behind. It may be the only big-city newspaper in the country that I find totally flavorless.

Fifteen minutes later a guard came in and called my name. I found that a little strange since I was the only one in the room, but I was relieved the wait was over.

It wasn't. He had merely come in to tell me my identity had been confirmed. They were now going to call the publicist for *Ambrosia Street,* who would have to come vouch for me and accompany me into the studio.

Still, I suppose such stringent security measures are necessary. Must be a lot of disgruntled *According to Jim* viewers out there.

I was starting to think about lunch when a harried-looking woman with frizzy dirty-blond hair and big eyes scurried into the room. "Are you Jim?" I nodded and rose from my chair. She walked over, shifting a sheaf of papers to her other arm so she could offer me a handshake. "I'm Rosemary Sloan, the publicist for *Ambrosia Street.* Sorry it took me a while to get over here. This has been an insane morning."

I didn't doubt that for a minute.

We walked out of the bungalow and up to the pedestrian gate. Showing her photo ID, Rosemary explained that she was taking me inside. The guard handed her a clipboard and she signed next to a space where my name was printed on a label. He gave me a laminated visitor's pass to wear like a necklace around my neck and cautioned me to keep it visible at all times.

Once we entered the lot, I couldn't understand what all the fuss was about. It looked like a giant army base to me. The narrow avenues ran alongside row after row of outsized Quonset huts. They resembled giant airport hangars, each one the dimension of a city block. Rosemary told me these were the soundstages.

Trailers for the actors were lined up in the alleyways between the buildings like so many Monopoly houses. Around the perimeter of the lot were modest two-story bungalows which served as offices for writers and producers. Self-important people whizzed by us on golf carts. We walked.

Our route took us past a permanent outdoor set designed to look like a generic city street. "You've probably seen this a thousand times without recognizing it—in movies, TV shows, commercials and music videos."

"Isn't this the street you always saw on *Seinfeld*?"

"That's right," she said. "Good eye."

We crossed a town square with a gazebo. "This is where they shoot *Gilmore Girls*. Do you watch that? You're standing in Stars Hollow."

I shook my head, feeling guilty because it's the only series that I know of ostensibly set in my home state of Connecticut. I could have gone for bonus points with Rosemary by telling her I recognized this same village green from *The Music Man* with Robert Preston. But I had already discovered that impressing her didn't feel that good.

"Here we are," she said as we strolled up to one of the big barracks marked Stage 19. For some reason, my eye transposed that to Stalag 17. "Oops, we have to wait," she said, pointing to a revolving red light over the entry door. "They're shooting."

A knot of people gradually gathered around us, most of them looking like blue-collar support staff. When the light was extinguished, we all piled inside the windowless building. In an underlit murk, Rosemary led me on a circuitous path around tall, free-standing walls. It was like a maze constructed to thwart giraffes. I followed a little closer on her heels because I knew I'd never find the way out of there on my own.

Eventually we arrived at a bustling, brightly lit set fitted out like a suburban kitchen. Or at least three walls of a suburban kitchen. All the interior sets, I realized, were built like box canyons, with the cameras, lights and crew all arrayed around the opening, peering in at the actors.

"Wait here," Rosemary said, and scuttled off to talk with a sturdy olive-skinned brunette wearing a headset. After a quick conference, she returned. "After they finish this take, they have to break to rearrange the lights. Julie can talk to you then."

"Cool," I said.

"We can watch from over here," she said, leading me to a double row of canvas-backed chairs set up a few feet behind the director, who was peering into a pair of video monitors. Take away the Cubs baseball cap, twenty years and twice that many pounds, and I recognized him as the guy who played Eric on the sitcom *Head of the Class* with Howard Hesseman. As Steven Wright once noted: It's a small world, but I wouldn't want to have to paint it. For the life of me, I couldn't remember his name, and it wasn't written on the back of his director's chair.

For the next forty-five minutes, they ran through the same brief scene over and over again. I'd never seen *Ambrosia Street,* but I surmised that Julie Kingston was the blonde with the Botticelli curls and the pleading eyes. She was having what seemed to be an innocuous conversation with a woman I took to be her mother about her plans for the weekend. But I detected a certain tension between them. We all felt it. Something unresolved.

Julie's character, whose name was I believe Siobhan, had a friend in the kitchen with her. When Siobhan's mother reminded her that she was taking the real estate licensing exam Friday night, the two teens exchanged a meaningful look. I call them teens, but both actresses were clearly closer to twenty-five.

Every take looked exactly the same to me—same lines delivered with the same inflection, same expressions on the actresses' faces. But the director clearly had a more discerning eye. He continued to call for resets. Curiously, no one seemed to mind. Except me. By the seventh take, I was ready to strangle him.

Finally, after a run-through that looked precisely like all the others, he shouted, "That's a wrap. Check the gate." The crew began scurrying around and three less glamorous women in blue jeans stepped in to stand where the actresses had been. They were resetting the lights and camera to reshoot the same scene from a different perspective. All for what would eventually be twenty seconds of screen time.

So much for the glamour of showbiz. Working in a tollbooth on the turnpike would be less tedious.

Julie headed off the set but was intercepted by the woman with the headset. They huddled briefly and the actress pulled another selection from her repertoire of meaningful looks, rolling her eyes in a way that shouted, *Can you believe the crap I have to put up with?*

Then she glanced over at me darkly, nodded her head, whipped back her hair and marched toward me with the cocked hips of a runway model. I wondered if she knew the cameras were no longer running. Maybe for actors, they always are.

As she approached, Rosemary tried to make introductions. "Julie, this is—" but Kingston moved right past her. Coming to a halt right in front of me, she struck a statuesque pose, offered a limp hand to shake and said, "Hey, you mind if we do this outside?"

I gestured in the direction I hoped led toward the exit. And she was off, with me trotting briskly behind. Rosemary remained on the set.

"This will have to be quick," Julie said without glancing back. She just assumed I was obediently following.

"Yeah, no problem. I just wanted to ask you about your date with Cam Akers."

She scoffed. "That was no date. He held me hostage for an evening."

Outside the door, she turned left toward the line of trailers. Stopping at the first one, she sat on the top step of the corrugated steel steps pushed up against the trailer door like those old-fashioned ramps people once used to board airplanes from the tarmac.

"You have a cigarette?" she asked petulantly as if I should have anticipated her need.

I shook my head and was about to tell her I didn't smoke when a scene from a Barbara Stanwyck movie broke out. Hands suddenly appeared from all directions, eagerly proffering packs of cigarettes toward her. And they say chivalry is dead. I looked around at the pack of guys surrounding us.

Julie looked at the nicotine bouquet and picked one with a white paper filter. Immediately a gaggle of cigarette lighters began to jostle with each other. It looked like a Punch and Judy show put on by pyromaniacs. Pulling her curly tresses behind her ear, Julie leaned into the nearest flame.

Curiously, she seemed to take this dutiful service as her due. Actresse oblige. In fact, during the time we talked, a steady stream of crew members passed by, all offering hopeful variations on "Hi, Julie."

She ignored all of them. At first I thought she was oblivious. But then a guy in an expensive suit came out the exit and she lit up like the Rockefeller Center Christmas tree. "Hey, Bobby," she sang out. Obviously she had a selective recognition system.

He waved. "Thank you so *much* for getting me out of that promo appearance last weekend," she said, then put on a pouty expression. "I hope you don't think of me as a prima donna."

The suit coughed, clearly not wanting to go anywhere near that issue. "Everybody loved your scene with Ramsey," he said, trying to recover. "Fantastic work, Julie." He smiled tightly and walked on.

Julie frowned and muttered, "Network sphincter." Shaving the ash off her cigarette against the top step, she asked, "What was the question again?"

I prompted her. "You were saying your evening with Cam Akers wasn't a 'date' date."

"Strictly business," she said. "His camp called mine. Believe me, he needs me a lot more than I need him."

"Would you walk me through the evening?"

She sighed. "I don't know how I got talked into that one. We go to a screening of his buddy Ed Norton's new movie. That guy is so fucking overrated, if you ask me. All you have to do in this town is grimace a lot and people think you're so intense."

She was sitting hunched over, her chest pressed against her thighs. "I'm supposed to be Cam's date coming down the red carpet, act all cozy for *Access Hollywood* and *ET*. Except he picked me up in a convertible. You believe that? So my hair was a mess. I'm not going to get photographed looking like one of Marge Simpson's sisters. So I basically ran into the theater without him. We've known each other a grand total of fifty minutes and neither of us is talking to the other." She inhaled, tilted her head back and blew the smoke straight up in the air. She looked like a fountain naiad.

"I assumed he would take me straight home afterwards. But he drives over to the Momba Club."

"Did things improve there?"

"Oh yeah," she said sarcastically. "It was the type of romantic evening a girl can only dream of."

"Were you at least talking at this point?"

"Barely. He gets a table and orders a bottle of champagne."

"On the floor or in the VIP room?"

"VIP. So, I tell him I'm going to freshen up. I spend a few minutes in the ladies' room desperately trying to rescue my hair. Like twenty minutes tops. Just as I'm finishing up, Cam comes bursting in—to the women's room! And he says we're leaving right away. Grabs me by the arm and pulls me out of there."

"Was he upset about something?"

"The guy only has two moods: pissed off and enraged."

"Did you see Angel?"

"No, I barely had time to grab my purse. But a friend of mine told me Angel came in a few minutes after me and Cam did. I've always wanted to meet her. She's like my idol. I have such a talent crush on her."

I was dying to take a swing at that statement, but I gave myself the take signal.

"Did you see Gentry Jones?"

"The guy who got killed? I wouldn't know him if I was handcuffed to him."

"Umm, very tall . . ." I suggested, trying to jog her memory. She shrugged. "So then what happened?"

"We leave the club and there's some photographers by the door. And I'm thinking, Well, at least I'll get a little publicity out of this wasted evening." Her voice began to grow incredulous. "And just as they start to shoot, my charm-school date throws a jacket over my head! Like I'm some Megan's Law felon leaving a courtroom."

I assumed there had to have been an incident like that in a recent episode of *Ambrosia Street* for her to have that simile at her fingertips.

"He hustles me into his car, still wrapped in a windbreaker. And he peels out."

"Why did he try to conceal you from the cameras?"

"I don't know. He's like allergic to photographers or something. But I had just finally gotten my hair right. I could have killed him."

"He didn't explain himself?"

"No, he didn't pay any attention to me. I think the guy's been ragged on by experts, because I was giving it to him good and he tuned me out completely." She thought about Cam's disregard for a moment as she stubbed out the cigarette. "That might have had something to do with his temper. He was steaming over something. Smoke was like literally coming out of his ears."

I notched that up to exaggeration—and to a belief that

Julie didn't know the meaning of the word "literally." "So what happened then?" I asked, prodding her along.

"He was driving like a maniac. I'm used to reckless driving because my brother is like insane. But I want to tell you, I was scared in that car with Cam." I nodded encouragingly. "So we get a few miles away from Mambo. I think he's headed for Santa Monica. But suddenly he pulls over to the curb, slams on his brakes and yanks out his cell phone."

"You know who he called?"

"No. As soon as he said, 'It's me,' he got out of the car and walked down the sidewalk. He was on the phone for like five minutes, real worked up, flinging his arms around. But I couldn't hear what he was saying."

"I thought it was a convertible."

"Yeah, but his exhaust has like an amplifier instead of a muffler."

"Sorry. Didn't mean to interrupt."

She exhaled heavily. "Anyway, when he comes back to the car, he's in a much better mood. He's even smiling. I ask if he remembers where I live and he pulls a U-turn on the street, tires squealing. He says we're going to a party in Malibu. And I'm like 'Oh, no, we're not.' And he's like, 'Sorry, the evening's been such a drag so far, but we can have fun,' blah blah."

"So you went?"

"Well, I wasn't up to wrestling control of the steering wheel away from him. I told him he was an asshole and left it at that. He was trying to be amusing on the drive out, telling me stories from different movie locations. I just ignored him. But the party wasn't bad. I knew a few people there. It was chill."

"What time did Cam take you home?"

"He didn't."

"Sorry?"

"We walked into the party and that was the last time I saw him. He went into a back room with some of his friends."

She mentioned the names of a few Hollywood bad boys from Cam's coterie, a group the press usually referred to as the Young Lions. "I think they were getting wasted. I stayed out by the pool, talking to people. I left around two-thirty. I had an early call here at the studio."

"How'd you get home?"

"Called a car. The studio has a twenty-four-hour service so its starlets don't show up on the set with bags the size of donuts under their eyes. His car was still there when I left."

The girl with the headset emerged from the studio. "Julie," she called, "they need you." The actress stood up and dusted off her derriere.

"You didn't see Cam again?"

"No," she said, walking away. "I guarantee that's the last time I go out with that asshole."

Obviously I couldn't speak for Cam, but I would be willing to wager the feeling was mutual.

CHAPTER 14

After I turned in my visitor's pass, I walked outside the gate to call Stan on my cell. He had told me studio security was really adamant about not letting cars park on the broad expanse of Burbank Boulevard. Can't give those damn Nielsen terrorists an inch. He had told me he'd wait in a Safeway lot about a mile away.

So I was surprised to see a black Chevy Tahoe with tinted windows sitting twenty-five yards to my left directly under a sign that shouted "NO STOPPING AT ANY TIME." As I looked at the guy behind the wheel, he tugged the brim of his Borsalino lower on his fat face. Bruno Volpe. What a pleasant surprise.

The fact that he seemed to have immunity from the studio's Draconian parking regulations, that he could idle there without anyone rousting him, would seem to lend credence to Lani's story that he had spent time as a gate guard.

As I strolled over toward his vehicle, the frown on Bruno's face grew more and more pronounced until he looked like a constipated gargoyle. Just before I stepped off the curb to approach his window, he mashed his accelerator, roaring out onto the street. A bright yellow Humvee slammed on its brakes to avoid being sideswiped by Bruno. The driver blew her horn angrily. I think it was the maid from *Will & Grace*.

Stan swung by a couple of minutes later to transport me back to the Chateau. I asked him how long it would take to drive from Malibu to Brentwood.

"That's a long trip," he said. "Maybe forty-five minutes."

I had noticed that Angelenos as a rule of thumb underestimate the travel time between any two points in their sprawling, congested metro area to be a flat twenty-five minutes. I suppose minimizing their intolerable driving time is the only way they can rationalize living in this smoggy circle of hell.

I translated Stan's information to mean that the trip took well over an hour. So if Cam had been in Malibu at two-thirty, that didn't let him off the hook for a murder committed shortly before five A.M. Of course, you'd have to be demented to drive over to kill someone in such a distinctive, easily recognizable vehicle as Cam's classic muscle convertible. That would be like pulling a payroll heist using the Oscar Meyer wiener mobile as your getaway car.

But then Cam didn't strike me as the judicious, carefully premeditated type. There was an old-timer in my home group who referred to a particularly reckless sponsee as "Ready, Fire, Aim." That would be an apt description of Cam as well.

Speak of the daredevil, and up he pops. As we pulled up to my hotel entrance, Cam was lolling behind the wheel of his Camaro. His head was tilted back, one arm thrown over the seatback, the other, holding a cigarette, braced on the car door. Consciously or not, his pose evoked James Dean contemplating the world from the front seat of his Cadillac in *Giant*.

"I think you've got company," Stan said, glancing over his shoulder. After repeated requests, I had broken him of the habit of getting out to open the door for me. I'm not sure why, but it made me feel uncomfortable to be treated like the belle of the ball.

Climbing out of the car, I walked back to Cam's vehicle. He still seemed unaware of my arrival, lost in thought. I hesitated to disturb him, thinking of the proverb about sleeping dogs.

"Mr. Akers? Were you looking for me?"

His head swung around and he winced, as if upset that he had been caught in an unguarded moment. His face, a handsome mix of Irish and Slavic features, took on its usual flinty, belligerent cast.

"Get in," he said, pushing his fingers through his hair and checking himself in the rearview mirror.

"You don't mind," I said, "I'm expecting a phone call. Could we talk in my room?" I wasn't looking to antagonize him. I just didn't want to try to conduct a conversation while he was tearing around the streets.

"Unless I'm mistaken," he said in that cranky tone I knew so well from his movie roles, "you asked to talk to me. This is your shot, pal." I walked around to the passenger door and let myself in. Out of reflex, I was about to fasten my seat belt, but I noticed with some relief that he wasn't reaching for the ignition key.

"So?" he asked.

"Uh, I've been retained by Angel's record company to—"

He was flicking his hand, erasing what I was saying. "No, no. I know what your job is. I'm asking who *you* are. I like to know who I'm talking to."

"All right. My name is James McNamara. I live on the East Coast. I help people—usually people in the music industry—with legal and confidential problems. I'm a detective."

He had been waiting for me to make that claim. "Yeah? You licensed?" he asked challengingly. I shook my head. "Because I've played detectives . . . many times," he continued. "That certificate is the only thing that halfway legit-imizes them."

"It's not like a pilot's license," I said. "In most states all it signifies is that you spent five hundred hours fetching coffee for an already licensed detective. That's a pretty tedious qualification process. And since I'm not seeking to carry a firearm, I never bothered to go through it."

"Ever work law enforcement? Or as an MP in the ser-vice?" Again I shook my head. "Then all you really are is a rinky-dink investigator, right?"

Remember what I told you right up front? Everyone is al-ways trying to sweat my bona fides.

"Whatever," I said. "Is this really what you came over here to debate?"

"I also hear you're a holy roller."

"What?"

"One of those AA apostles. You can't have fun anymore, so you try to make sure no one else does either."

Now he was beginning to piss me off. "I'm a recovering alcoholic and drug addict," I said. "But I've never tried to convert anyone. You want to drink or shoot dope? That's your goddamn business."

I was glad my sponsor couldn't hear that last statement. My petulant response wasn't really in keeping with the idea of AA being a program of attraction. It made Cam smile, however. I realized that he had been trying since I sat down to get under my skin.

"So who have you worked for?"

"I treat all my clients with confidentiality."

He nodded his head approvingly. "I spoke to Flea about you. He said you're all right. I was just busting your chops, man."

I found the endorsement a little odd. I'd never spoken to the bass player for the Red Hot Chili Peppers or worked for any-one in his band. But I was glad to have his seal of approval.

"So can we talk about the late Gentry Jones?"

Cam was tapping an unfiltered cigarette against the steering wheel. Now he lit it and inhaled deeply. Spitting out a shred of tobacco, he said, "That's why I'm here. Fire away, snoop."

"Did you know Gentry?"

"Saw him play a few times his rookie year with Boston. Hell of a ball handler."

"Ever meet him off the court?"

"Nope."

"Not even that night at Momba?"

"Nope."

"That VIP room is about the size of a two-car garage and you didn't notice a guy who was six-foot-seven and covered with tattoos?"

"Didn't say I didn't notice him. Only said we didn't talk."

"Why not?"

Now it was his turn to get annoyed. "Because I'm not a jock sniffer, all right? Can we move this along?"

"Why did you leave the club so abruptly?"

"Because my ex showed up. All right? 'Nuf said?"

"I would imagine, Cam, in the circles you two run in, you must bump into each other all the time. Do you always storm out as soon as you see her?"

"Depends on what kind of mood I'm in."

"What kind of mood were you in that night?"

He half closed his eyes into slits. "You keep pushing it, you're going to find out."

I paused, considering a safer tack to proceed along.

"You're working for Angel, right? What do *you* think of her?" he asked.

"I haven't gotten a chance to know her yet. I don't know what she's usually like, but at the moment, she's pretty guarded."

"She hasn't spoken word one to you, right?" he said gleefully.

"Not yet," I conceded. Still smiling, he was about to launch into an explication of Angel when one of the hotel doormen came trotting up to his side of the car.

"Excuse me, Mr. Akers?" he said deferentially. "Would you mind moving your vehicle over to the other side of the entryway?" I glanced in the side mirror and saw that a squat airport shuttle bus was having trouble making the turn into the driveway.

I don't know if you've ever seen junkies in that moment when the narcotic hits their bloodstream. They just melt. Cam went through a similarly dramatic transformation when the hotel employee spoke to him. Only his drug was anger.

His jaw set; his face turned red. The skin on his forehead seemed to shrink and the skull plate beneath jumped out. He twisted out of his seat to bring his face closer to the doorman's. I thought for a moment that Akers was going to bite him.

"Unless you want to spend the next few months eating your dinner through a straw, I suggest you get out of my face right now," he snarled.

The man blanched and backed away. He started to jog back to the hotel entrance, then spun around and, making a wide detour around Cam's car, ran over to redirect the bus.

It was as if an explosion had gone off in the front seat. And I suppose in a very real sense, one had. We sat there, Cam seething, me looking through the windshield with my mouth open.

"Wow," I finally said.

"Don't you fucking start," he said without looking over at me.

There was something pathological about Cam's overreaction. His flashpoint was way too close to the surface. It was as if the moment he encountered a challenge or contradiction, it mushroomed into a feeling of being harshly criticized, bullied and trapped. And he immediately tried to blast his way out.

"I'm just saying . . ."

"Don't!"

". . . you could get help. Anger management."

"Oh yeah," he scoffed. "Like you're the first person to suggest that!"

"I'm serious, man. That's a crappy way to live—losing it because a guy asks you to move your car."

"Look, no offense, but you're hardly in a position to be handing out advice. Recovering or no, in my book you're still a guy who couln't handle his booze." I let that nasty little zinger sit between us in the rumble seat for a while. "Are we done here?" he asked restlessly.

"Just a few more questions."

He sputtered as he exhaled, letting me know his willingness to cooperate was drawing to a close.

"What was it that set you off that night at Momba?"

"I don't remember," he said snarkily.

"Julie Kingston told me that you made a long phone call right after you left the club."

"Cunt!"

"Who were you calling?"

"None of your fucking business."

"How late did you stay at the Malibu party?"

"I've answered all these questions. Stabbing death in Brentwood. Boyfriend killed. You don't think LAPD had an O.J. flashback? They locked on me first thing—the ex who had some issues with his former old lady. I was questioned at length. And guess what? I'm alibied up the wazoo." He flashed me a self-satisfied smile. "Three friends say I was with them until six o'clock in the morning. Forty miles away from the murder. And there were a dozen other people at that party who'll swear I never left that house. I'm no longer a suspect. Ask the cops. They've moved on. You should too, bro."

"Why were you at Angel's house a couple of days ago? What did you want to talk to her about?"

The signs of Cam's rage began to surface. His face flushed and his forehead flattened. A white triangle emerged on his reddening forehead. Carefully enunciating, he said, "Get . . . out!"

I did as I was bid. Before the car door had fully shut, Cam was blasting around the hotel's half-oval entry, tires bellowing. Bellmen and customers jumped back in alarm.

As I walked into the lobby I decided I'd have to arrange a drag race between Cam and Bruno. Speaking of which, I marveled at what a busy day this had been for unexpected visitors.

Seemed like everybody knew exactly where to find me. But how?

Then I thought of how Lani always seemed to know my itinerary too—except for the morning I went to speak to Oops Johnson. The only time I had taken a taxi.

It would appear that Stan was working both sides of the street—a treacherous way to drive.

CHAPTER 15

It had been like looking at a ghost. The obdurate cast of Cam's face, the way the anger consumed him, his surly isolation—it all reminded me of my father. Most of the time Francis X. McNamara was a fairly charming guy and a pleasure to be around. But he had moods that were darker than a mine shaft. As with Cam, you could see the anger transform him. It was like watching Bruce Banner turn into the Hulk. My old man was truly scary when he was mad.

From a very early age, I learned to evacuate the premises at the first warning signs of his rage. If we were at home, I'd slip out the door as soon as I noticed his eyes begin to focus inward, his jaw clench or his cheeks start to flare. If we were in public, I'd just cower and start to say "Hail Marys" as fast as I could spit out the words. I'm not sure what survival tricks my mother developed. In my house, you fended for yourself.

It took a toll on my father too. He died of a massive coronary at age forty-four. At a rotary, in the middle of a traffic argument with some guy. When my mom and I went to identify him at the hospital, they pulled back the sheet and his face was still locked in a rictus of anger. Live by the sore, die by the sore.

Later, the mortician put a smile on his face, but it wasn't fooling anyone who knew my old man.

Anyway, when I got back to my room, I found myself in the mood for some Gaelic music. Maybe it was thinking about my pops. He was always big on all that Blarney claptrap. Of course, I have better taste in music than my father did. He went for the sentimental tenors and their "Danny Boy" hymns. Sit in the parlor and dab away a tear.

I dug out a CD by Paddy Keenan and Tommy O'Sullivan. Brilliant musicians. No mawkish lyrics. The sprightly sad music hit my sweet spot like a hot bowl of soup on a raw, cold afternoon. Listening to it, I considered adding one of their jigs to my final set list. I have a confession: I spend a ridiculous amount of time working on the precise order of the songs I want played at my funeral. I know it sounds morbid, but it's the last chance you have to make a statement—and I want to make mine with music.

I picture row after row of friends gathered in the pews of an acoustically perfect church. I suppose I'm laid out in a coffin by the altar, but I never think of that—just the glorious selection of tunes and its impact on the assembled multitude.

Stirred by the sounds, one guy wipes away a tear and says, "Jaysus, Jimmy was a grand lad, wasn't he?" (Apparently, some of my mourners are from Galway.) Another, sitting there as if poleaxed, says, "My God, I never realized how beautiful this song is." Someone else, no longer able to contain himself, shouts, "That guy had the *best* taste in music! Somewhere up in heaven, I bet God has a new DJ." The candle-scented air fills with murmurs of assent.

The current list was spectacularly eclectic, kicking off with a solo piano interlude from a Keith Jarrett concert in Bremen, then "Reflections of My Life" by Marmalade, an obscure Ennio Morricone composition from the soundtrack of *State of Grace* and then a flashy kicker: "Big New Prinz" by the Fall. In the end I rejected the Irish jigs because I couldn't figure out a way to fit them in the flow of my memorial service.

But Keenan and O'Sullivan's medley, "O'Rourke's/The Spike Island Lassies/Lord McDonald's," had enough merit that I added it to the little notepad I keep for just such a purpose. It could always resurface. After all, I revised the selections top to bottom at least once a month. Today, Joan Armatrading. Tomorrow, the Foo Fighters. The list of my final set is always under construction.

I tried calling my sponsee and my sponsor, but neither was home. I chatted for a moment with Danny's wife. She was still pretty tentative around me. Of course, she had been through a lot with Danny's drinking and was understandably unwilling to trust that the war was over. I'm convinced that the spouses and children of alcoholics suffer far more than the drunk does. There's a lot of spillage with this disease.

Still, I wanted her take on Danny's progress. She said he was at a meeting—always a good sign—and that things were generally going well with, I deduced, a few rocky episodes.

When I was first getting sober, there was an old-timer named Butch at the Perry Street clubhouse in Greenwich Village. An outgoing former Merchant Marine with snow-white hair, Butch used to ask me how I was doing. Before I could get out the lie that I was fine, he would say, "Aw, what am I asking you for anyway? If I really wanted to know how you was doing, I'd ask your girlfriend."

It took me a few years to understand how accurate an observation that was. Most guys can put on a calm and reasonable face at AA meetings and around people from the program. But it's how you act at home that is the true barometer of recovery. So I was glad to hear Danny's wife gaining confidence.

Afterward I was still in the mood to listen to music—or rather I wasn't in the mood to watch TV, not on a Wednesday night, not since NBC destroyed *West Wing*. So I went on-line to peruse the nightlife in Los Angeles. Christina Aguilera at the Staples Center. Wild horses couldn't drag me to that one. I had seen the skank queen. I wouldn't be going back.

An array of cockrock bands at the clubs on Sunset Strip. Los Angeles's only contribution to modern music was big-hair metal, and I guess the city hadn't tired of it yet. Then I saw that Kenny Wayne Shepherd, a young blues guitarist from Louisiana, was playing just up the street at the House of Blues. Yahtzee!

I had a long shower, made a fitful attempt to meditate and took myself to the House. Walking up the street—once again the only pedestrian in L.A.—I stopped for a burger, fries and a vanilla Coke at a Formica-and-glass diner. The ketchup was the best part of the meal.

The bad news started before I even got inside the club. The building's exterior was a grotesquely busy attempt to ape the voodoo vibe of New Orleans. In my experience, the fancier the venue, the worse the music. If you ever go to Chicago, check out some of the blues dives on the South Side. They're funky as hell, but the spartan backdrop enhances the sound.

Overdecorated joints like the House of Blues and the Hard Rock are travesties. They are to nightclubs what TGIFridays is to cuisine. Hang enough crap on the walls and maybe people won't notice how crass and empty you are at the core. It's the Great Gatsby school of distinction.

This wasn't the right setting for Shepherd. His chops were awesome, but they were also derivative. The whole show was like an homage to Stevie Ray Vaughan.

I've only seen two guitar geniuses in my life: Stevie Ray and Jimi Hendrix. Honorable mention goes out to Jeff Beck, Duane Allman and Richard Thompson. A lot of guys are in the running for the bronze. But Vaughan and Hendrix were category busters. You try to pattern yourself on one of their styles—as Shepherd was doing—and no matter how talented or flashy you are, you're going to come off as a shabby imitation.

Still I stayed for two sets, even though they were charging me $4 for every ginger ale I tossed back. I'm sure they were unmercifully soaking the clientele who were pounding down the real drinks. But that's the thing about booze: After a few pops, the price ceases to matter. The cash in your pocket might as well be Monopoly money. When you're sober, you never stop wincing while you're being ripped off.

Anyway, I hung in there because the music was loud and raucous and because I kept hoping for a celebrity sighting. This was L.A., right? At some point in the evening, Uma Thurman would have to sit down and wiggle her eyebrows suggestively at me, or Reese and Ryan would take the adjoining table and beckon for me to join their party. Maybe they were all backstage at Christina's show. Serve them right.

As I sidled out of there, I considered taking a taxi over to Momba, but I figured looking at the club's layout wouldn't be all that helpful in terms of finding out what happened to Gentry Jones. So I headed back to the Chateau, thinking I'd have a quiet night—that is, once Shepherd's searing solos stopped echoing in my head.

But as soon as I let myself in my room, I could see the place had been ransacked. My clothes had been pulled out of the drawers and tossed all around. The mattress had been flipped over and only one corner of it was still resting on the box springs. My laptop was turned on and someone had poured the contents of the ice bucket over the keyboard, frying the circuits. Renegade Records was going to buy me a new one, because that was definitely going on my expense account.

My CD case was emptied and jewel boxes had been Frisbee'd all around the room. I noted with a pang of sadness that my disc of Dave Mason's *Alone Together* lay mashed and broken on the floor.

It looked like Linkin Park and Insane Clown Posse had engaged in a spirited tag team match of hotel-room trashing. And this little display of vandalism was about as pointless as a rock star's wanton demolition of his accommodations.

No one involved in Angel's case—from either side of the aisle—could have tossed my room thinking they would find anything significant. It was manifestly obvious that at this point I was stumbling around in the dark. I knew nothing that could help or hurt Angel.

So I assumed whomever had done this wasn't on a mission of discovery. He or she had broken into my room and scattered my shit just to prove I could be gotten to. Okay, message received: I'm vulnerable.

That part didn't anger me, not at first. But the Dave Mason CD? That scorched my ass.

My mood got steadily worse as I set about tidying up the room. When it comes to nursing a grudge, alcoholics are regular Florence Nightingales. I started out merely annoyed, but by the time I had restored order, I was feeling totally violated.

I knew I wasn't going to fall asleep anytime soon, so I fished out the number Chris had given me for his pal Whitey. Maybe he would know the location of an insomniac's AA meeting I could go to.

"Hello," a voice said after picking up on the fourth ring.

"Hey, Whitey? This is Jim McNamara. I'm a friend of Chris Towle's. I'm really sorry to be calling you this late—"

"Hey, Jimbo," he said warmly. His tone was deep, resonant and ingratiating like a radio DJ's. "It's not a problem, man. I don't spend a lot of time hibernating."

"Then you're exactly the right man for me to be talking to. Do you know of any AA meetings at this hour?"

"You okay? You having a booze crisis?" There was no judgment in his question, only concern.

"No, nothing like that," I said. "I'm just worked up." I explained to him the state I had found my hotel room in.

"You know who did it?" he asked.

"No idea," I said, although in my mind's eye I was picturing a hairy troll pawing through my stuff wearing only Speedos and a Borsalino. Yuuch! As James Taylor sang, "Gotta stop thinkin' 'bout that."

"Well, there are no meetings scheduled for another couple of hours," Whitey said thoughtfully. "But I know something that'll do almost as good. Where you staying?"

"The Marmont."

"I'll be there in twenty-five minutes. Meet me out front."

Before I could tell him not to bother—I really hadn't intended to roust him out of his house in the middle of the night—he had hung up.

I was outside, breathing in the night air, which seemed oddly fragrant and intoxicating for such a smoggy city, when Whitey's car pulled up off the street about thirty-five minutes later. It was a stately but weathered Olds convertible that floated boatlike above its worn shocks and spiffy whitewalls. It needed muffler and valve work, judging by the noise that preceded it and the smoke that trailed it. But the tan leather upholstery looked to be in excellent shape.

Before I could walk over to the curb, the night desk man came running out of the lobby, a crooked smile on his sour face. A slender man with close-cropped blond hair and a grouchy expression, he hadn't even looked up when I crossed the lobby from the elevators, but suddenly he was perky as hell.

"Hey, Whitey," he called, like he was a homesteader in Apache territory and the cavalry had just ridden up.

"Hey, Pinch," answered the vibrant voice I remembered from the phone. It was hard to tell the age of the man behind the wheel. I would have guessed mid-forties from the middle age spread evident on his torso and face and the silver streaks in his brown, windblown hair. He had on pale tortoiseshell glasses and a thin navy blue windbreaker over what looked like a black bowling shirt. His face wore what I came to call Whitey's birthday expression—like he was being pleasantly surprised over and over again and couldn't believe his good fortune.

"What are you doing out at this hour?" asked the night clerk.

"Picking up a friend," said Whitey, flicking his chin in my direction. "How you hitting them, Pinch?"

"Aww, shit," he said, rubbing his hand over his head. "I'm so snakebit, my cat hides from me when I walk in the door. You got anything for me?"

Whitey leaned across the front seat conspiratorially, a curious gesture, I thought, considering we seemed to be the only three guys awake in Southern California. "Pen Pal in the fifth at Santa Anita."

"Thanks, Whitey. You're a prince," he said, moving back to the lobby, a rapturous look of anticipation on his face.

Whitey waved to me. "Hey, Jim. How's it going, man? Hop in."

The hinges protested as I pulled the door open and sat down. "Thanks for coming out," I said.

Whitey regarded me happily through his thick lenses, patted my shoulder and turned to throw the car in gear. "No problemo," he said in that sonorous voice.

"You play the ponies?"

"Me? No-o-o," he said, amused. "I like gambling far too much to indulge in it. As Oscar Wilde said, 'I can resist anything but temptation.' "

"You don't bet, but you happen to have a tip ready on tomorrow's races?"

"Comes in handy," he said, chuckling. "This is a big gambling town. And I have friends who work at the track."

"So if there are no meetings, where we headed?" I asked. "A clubhouse?"

"In a manner of speaking," he said, his birthday expression returning. "So how's Chris?"

We fell into an easy rapport. Whitey was one of those guys who had a funny anecdote for every topic and he was genuinely interested in what you were saying. Curiosity can be a very magnetic characteristic.

Later I marveled at how easily he drew me out. Five or six innocuous questions and he knew as much about me as most of my relatives. We drove along, chattering like a pair of magpies. The combination of Whitey's energy, his goodwill and his plummy voice was remarkably spellbinding.

With Whitey, I discovered the ideal way to tool around Los Angeles: at the darkest hour of the night in a convertible with sweet jazz playing on the stereo. You feel like you own the city.

"Who's that playing vibes?" I asked.

"Gary Burton. You want me to turn it down?"

"No, it's nice."

"Speaking of vibe players, I once drove Lionel Hampton from here to Las Vegas. With several memorable stops en route." And Whitey was off on another rollicking story. He had taken the streets all the way down to the area around LAX. And just as he and Lionel were barreling into the driveway at the Tropicana, with the jazz great's newly acquired macaw flapping and crapping in the back seat, we were pulling up in front of an all-night diner near the airport rent-a-car lots on a side street wide enough to land an airplane on.

The clientele at the diner was made up mostly of loners sitting glumly over their plates, except for a group of men gathered around a table by the far wall. They hailed Whitey boisterously as soon as we walked in the door. After a round of jocular greetings, he announced, "Boys, this is Jim McNamara. He's a friend of ours." That was code to let them know I was a member of AA.

The five men, dressed casually and sitting over coffee at

four o'clock in the morning, welcomed me as we sat down. Without being bidden, an old Greek in a stained apron brought over a couple more cups and a coffeepot and poured for everyone at the table.

"Hey, Whitey," he muttered in his thickly accented voice.

"Morning, George. Your son get that thing taken care of?"

The waiter nodded. "Thank you," he said quietly, and shuffled off.

Everyone at the table was talking at once. You can find enclaves like this in most cities—the beachcombers of recovery. They're groups of older guys for the most part who have been around the block more than your average number of times, maybe even been hit by a truck or two, but they got the license plate. And they never lost their sense of humor.

Sometime in their sobriety they figured out how to float through life without punching the clock—which explains how they could sit around at all hours, swapping wit and wisdom and laughing their asses off. They're the wise men of AA—or at least the wise guys.

The atmosphere at the table was a cross between a 12-step meeting and the floating craps game in *Guys and Dolls*. After Whitey provided the boys with some of my circumstances, he encouraged me to tell them about the hotel room break-in.

The story got a sympathetic reception. The coffee crew made all the appropriate sounds of commiseration. I told them my conclusion—that my room had been tossed to illustrate to me how easily I could be gotten to. When I was good and done, they hit me with a number of scenarios, some of them sarcastic, some quite sly.

"Maybe it was Angel, searching for her lost innocence," said a heavyset guy named Ivan who bore a strong resemblance to Broderick Crawford.

"It's interesting it happened on the same day you ran into Bruno Volpe," said Sal, a dark-skinned Italian with hooded eyes who looked like a bastard Medici.

"And Cam," pointed out Larry, deeply tanned with a bad comb-over.

"Or it could have been a party you ain't met yet, someone too eager to find out what cards you're holding." That was Ron—balding, big ears and tiny, gapped teeth. He spoke without looking up from his coffee cup, which he cradled with both hands.

"Right, or the other possibility is it had nothing to do with him," said Rusty, a beefy guy with freckled blacksmith's arms, his red hair going pale with age. "Maybe a thief was working the hotel. You should check with the front desk; see if any other break-ins were reported."

"Sometimes when they toss your room," said Ron, looking up to glower at Rusty, "especially when they're extra messy about it, it's a cover-up for something else. You should check the phone in your room when you get back. See if they planted a bug." I got the impression Rusty and Ron argued a lot.

They say confession is good for the soul. Like so many of the practices in AA, I don't know exactly why or how sharing works, but I swear it does. You talk freely about a personal struggle or something that's rankling you in front of a group of people at a meeting—or in this case, at an all-night diner—and it lifts you out of solitary confinement. Every time.

There's no question that as I walked back out to Whitey's car with a piece of paper in my pocket with all those guys' phone numbers on it, I felt decompressed.

"So you want to hit a real meeting?" said Whitey, settling behind the wheel. "I know a good sunrise group in Hollywood."

"Sure."

Traffic on the street was already picking up, even though it wasn't six A.M. yet. After a few blocks, Whitey pulled into a gas station. We were at a self-serve island, but a turbaned guy with dusky, almost purple skin came running out of the office. "Hello, Whitey," he shouted in a melodious voice, smiling radiantly.

"Udai, how are you?" Whitey said, climbing out of the car. As Udai pumped gas into the Olds, Whitey quizzed him about his wife's headaches.

There's a very old, very long guy-walks-into-a-bar joke with the refrain, "I'm Bob Parsons from Odessa, Texas, I know everybody and everybody knows me."

Well, Whitey was the real Bob Parsons. As I would see over the next few days, his universal familiarity was even more pronounced at AA meetings. Wherever we went, the whole room would hail him as soon as he walked in the door. If sobriety were a popularity contest, Whitey would be the straightest man in L.A.

"Is there anyone you don't know?" I asked when he pulled back out on the street.

"Well, pardner. I don't know who broke into your hotel room. But I'm determined to make his acquaintance."

CHAPTER 17

The scene at Angel's estate the next morning was chaos cubed. ABC's news division had showed up early and in force. There was a fleet of satellite trucks, equipment transports and support vans parked in the driveway. People were streaming in and out of the house's open front door.

All that traffic inside the gates had driven the crowd of fence-hangers into a fevered state. Maybe they thought they were all going to be on television.

The hardcore Angel fans were more vocal than they had ever been. The usual tearful barrage of "We love you, Angel" cries pierced the air, but the tone was more desperate. And they were serenading their idol as well. The fans were conducting a noisy but oddly euphonious singalong of "Believe in Me," one of Angel's signature ballads. As they stood there singing, swaying, clinging to the bars of the fence, it reminded me of a prison scene in a musical.

The charged mood had also galvanized the unaffiliated crazies. Or maybe they had neglected to take their medication that morning. But it was a bad day in bedlam. The cuckoo crew was jostling around the perimeter at double speed, many of them with their eyes strikingly wide open, like day-care kids who realize they're not going to make it to the bathroom in time.

The marginal demonstrators, pleading causes that only they cared about or understood, were waving their placards with rapid, herky-jerky motions. The costumed emissaries were so desperate for attention, they were performing their little pantomimes for each other. A handful of street schizos were stomping around, screaming incomprehensibly. It was like a frenzied, apocalyptic mosh pit on the sidewalk.

It took longer to clear security than it had on previous days. In large part that was because every time they started to crank open the gate, a few free radicals would surge out of the crowd and streak past the car to storm the opening. The guards would tackle them and drag them to the back of the throng. Then we would repeat the catch-and-release process.

Just when I thought they were going to have to resort to tear gas or rubber bullets, a solution was arrived at. The security team formed a cordon around the back of the car and slowly retreated as we rolled inside. The burly guards standing there shoulder to shoulder in their matching blazers looked like the offensive line from Nebraska attending a formal sports banquet together.

"Wow," said Stan as he pulled up to the door, "this is nuttier than Oscar night." I hadn't brought up the fact that he seemed to be telling everyone in Southern California my business and I didn't intend to. I figured at some point I might be able to twist his perfidy to my advantage. Use the motor-mole to spread some disinformation. But I wondered if Lani had assigned him to drive for me knowing he would inform her of my whereabouts, or if he had volunteered to act as a Lo-Jack.

I wished I had a camera as I walked inside. There, standing side by side under the staircase, were Oops Johnson and Alice. Would have made a great snapshot—the bodyguard and the maid with their arms folded over their chests, frowning at the antlike procession moving in and out of the door, the TV people who were making their jobs impossible. They looked like a supremely mismatched pair of bookends.

Banks of lights and sail-sized reflector panels were set up in the library to my right, forming a parabola around a pair of Queen Anne chairs that faced each other from a distance of just under five feet. Cables snaked out of the room in every direction.

Angel and Carla Finn were nowhere to be seen, but as I walked around the ground floor, I saw that representatives of the two camps were already skirmishing. The first battle had been over the location of the interview. The TV people, after scouting the layout, had opted for the sunroom at the rear of the house. Sunny and splashy, it bespoke Hollywood. Angel insisted on the library, which conveyed seriousness and substance. Obviously that set went to Angel.

In Angel's downstairs office, Bruce Katz was arguing with a chunky senior producer with pale-rimmed glasses and frizzy yellow hair chopped off just below her ears. They were wrangling over the scope of the interview. "You can't ask her about Gentry Jones's death," Katz insisted.

"Oh, please, Bruce," she responded dismissively. "What the hell do you think we're here for?"

"You can characterize the situation any way you want in the setup, but you can't ask Angel about the case. This is an ongoing criminal investigation."

"Oh, we're going to ask," she insisted. "And she can respond in whatever nebulous fashion we both know you've already tutored her to say."

Two doors down in the breakfast room, Lani was sparring with Carla's executive producer over some ground rules. Expensively dressed, the woman had shiny black hair streaked with gray bracketing a broad, rather featureless face that was shaped like a cello—narrow at the eyes but bulging at the forehead and chin.

They were contending about some finer points of editing and postproduction that I didn't really understand. The e.p. wasn't giving an inch, especially when Lani told her it would be a single run-through. "No wiggle room on this one, Sandy," Lani said to the producer. "Barring technical holdups, it's one hour of questions and then Angel is out of there. No b-roll footage. You pack up and go."

The woman merely looked at Lani as if they both knew this idea was ludicrous. "We're shooting exteriors. We're shooting that insane crowd out there," she said, pointing toward the street. "And Carla gets all the time she needs for reaction shots."

As I would shortly see, a prime-time tête-à-tête like this one had two chapters. After the interview was over, a network-hired double sat in for the celebrity or politico or thieving CEO, and they ran through the entire thing again. Only this time all the cameras were focused on the news star, who was bathed in far more flattering light. That explained the shimmering Doris Day haze that always engulfed Carla Finn.

Prompted by their producers, the correspondent repeated the questions, which were often framed more intelligently now that the answers were known. Then they were cued to run through a gamut of silent emotions—skepticism, indignation, curiosity, wonder—as if they were listening intently to the statements of the interviewee. These more dramatic facial responses were then spliced into the broadcast.

Finn's specialty was a reaction of overwhelming sympathy, as if her heart were breaking from all this person had to endure, as if she would do anything in her power to rectify the situation. *Let's start a fund drive immediately to help you,* her dreadfully concerned face seemed to say. *I'll donate my thirteen-million-dollar salary.* At any moment, you felt, her luscious lips would begin to tremble and her crystalline blue eyes would begin to puddle with tears.

Obviously, her producer was going to fight tooth and nail to protect Carla's emotional signature. That was the franchise.

It turned out Lani was a pretty canny negotiator. She had threatened to cut out Finn's empathy orgy in order to extract a concession of her own: The broadcast segment would include a prominent mention and display of Angel's racy photo book, *Hot Chick*, which by the time this program aired would be available in a bookstore near you. "It's already number three on Amazon," said Lani, "and it won't even be published for another five days."

I wandered into the dining room. Previously this space had seemed immense, but now that it was serving as command central, it felt almost cramped. Equipment and papers covered the table. The mahogany surface had been covered with a plain white linen cloth. Two banks of video monitors had been set up, one near the entryway to the library, the other at the opposite end of the table.

A middle-aged man sprawled in one of the folding chairs by the far monitors. He was barking impatiently into a headset. An assistant stood next to him, holding a waiting cell phone for whenever he was free to talk. That had to be the director. What clinched it for me was the New York Yankees cap pulled down over his baggy face.

At the other end of the table sat Charlie Chiavone. He seemed discomfited, compulsively snapping the faceplate on his cell phone open and shut, open and shut.

A few chairs away Inga Saffron was typing intently but with a notable lack of speed on her laptop. She was wearing a puffy blue shoulderless top without any visible means of support. From my vantage behind her, I could see a remarkably vivid tattoo of a stemload of cherries just above her left shoulder blade. It looked like the paybar on a slot machine. She had four windows open on her screen and was instant-messaging on all of them.

Based on my hurry-up-and-wait experience on the set of *Ambrosia Street*, I assumed we were hours away from getting this show on track. But the process coalesced with astonishing precision. Lani, Bruce Katz and a sampling of Angel's entourage swept in through the same door I had just used as if summoned. At the same time, a number of ABC producers and technicians piled into the room through the library entrance.

"Okay, people," shouted the director, hunkering in his chair, "let's make some magic."

Lani gestured to me to take the seat next to her directly in front of the monitors. Bruce Katz and Charlie were in the seats to her left. A sound engineer walked over, offering us each a set of the wireless headphones she had draped over her arm. Inga took a pair and returned to her computer.

The audio wasn't turned on yet, but on the screen we could see Angel and Carla meeting under the lights in the library. Both had come directly from lengthy sessions in hair and makeup and it showed.

Angel had gone respectable. All the punky elements were gone. Her hair was swept up in an elegant chignon, showing off her neck and the demure gray silk collared blouse she was wearing. The makeup was quite subtle, with an overall etiolating effect. All she needed was a string of pearls and she would have looked like a PTA mom.

Carla had gone sexy. Her lank, lustrous golden hair was parted in the middle, folding back in on her shoulders. She had on a light charcoal turtleneck sweater that accentuated her breasts. Most daringly, her famously sensuous lips were gleaming electric red.

A guy in my home group, John H., used to be news director at the NBC flagship station in Manhattan. After his third rehab, he quit the business and moved up to my rural corner of Connecticut before the stress and the booze killed him. Now that he was sober and pastoral, he only had to worry about four ex-wives.

He once told me that in the post–Jane Pauley era, every female anchor in the news business, from Portland to Pawtucket, was hired on the BJ scale. Forget credibility or reporting experience. Could she make male viewers fantasize about blow jobs each time she opened her mouth? As John pointed out, Carla Finn was the poster girl for this oral methodology. She was a solid 10 on the BJ scale.

On the monitor, you could see Angel and Carla brazenly appraising each other as they walked up to briefly and stiffly shake hands. Both of their smiles faded toward a slight smirk, as if they had met the enemy and victory was already assured. That seemed odd to me, because they had both adopted the other's image for this interview.

They sat down facing each other, both of them getting quick cosmetic checks from their seconds. Then they spent a few minutes fastidiously arranging their seated poses, craning their necks, tugging at their clothes, checking the monitors.

Suddenly the audio kicked in.

". . . tells me Botox horror stories that would make your hair stand on end," said Finn.

"I hear they're getting remarkable results down in Brazil with an extract taken from a frog that lives only in the Amazon," replied Angel.

"The lady who does my follicles in New York—she's Hungarian—she says—" Finn halted. The director was addressing her on her earpiece. Evidently she couldn't talk and listen at the same time.

Even though we were in the same room with the director, we couldn't make out what he was saying to her. Their communication was on a separate channel. On the monitor, Carla nodded. "Are you ready to get started?" she asked Angel.

"If you are."

Despite the muffling headphones, we could hear the director shout, "We're rolling, people." This was followed by several voices on the audio feed echoing, "Rolling."

Finn's face puckered to a strained, myopic expression, like she was trying to read an eye chart through frosted glass. This was her serious newswoman's face.

"A whole new generation of young pop stars has come along with you as their primary influence," said Finn. "So how is it you are still able to be so original, so shocking?"

Obviously they had elected to start with the easy questions—her career, her personal life. Soften her up a little before delving into the murder rap. As Angel launched into a platitudinous soliloquy about how she had always relied on her instincts as a performer, I thought my ears were playing tricks on me. I even touched one of the earphones to check if my reception was distorted.

But then, as Angel responded to Finn's second query— "At this point, what do you have left to prove?"—there it was again, even more pronounced. I leaned over and nudged Lani. We both slipped the cushioning pads off our contiguous ears. "Is she speaking with a British accent?" I asked incredulously. Lani nodded. "Why?" I asked.

"She usually reserves it for award acceptance speeches," Lani whispered. "She thinks it makes her sound classy." It makes her sound completely balmy, I thought, as we slipped our earphones back on.

I missed big swatches of Angel's answers because my giggles would upgrade to laughs and even guffaws whenever she would try a particularly clubby phrase. The rain in Spain, and all that Tommyrot. My reactions were primarily muscle spasms because I muted myself so as not to disrupt the taping. But Lani, Katz and Charlie were clearly annoyed by my quiet hilarity.

I couldn't help it. I found Angel's phony accent funnier than Peter Sellers doing Inspector Clouseau.

You probably saw the interview. It got the highest ratings for a prime-time one-on-one since Monica Lewinsky was interrogated by Barbara. And yet not one commentator or critic—at least none that I caught—found it worth mentioning that America's biggest slut, the laureate of lowbrow, was trying to sound like Margaret Rutherford.

It's possible I was chortling from a position of ignorance. After all, I had spent most of the last decade studiously disregarding Angel. Maybe she had been slipping into this affectation for so long that people now just accepted it as a quirk. But come on! This was something that deserved to be mocked at every opportunity.

Finn rattled through about twenty minutes of Nerf ball questions ("Does your biological clock ever get noisy?" "What inspired you to write *Hot Chick*?") before getting to the point. A couple of times, I turned around and saw Inga trying valiantly to provide a transcript, but she looked like a closed-caption provider on heavy sinus medicine.

Ever notice who gets the most garbled closed captioning? Kids' shows and talk-is-cheap platforms like *Maury* and *Ricki*. You read the captioning, it looks like it's being translated from Bulgarian. I think they assign the really zonked-out typists to these genres.

"We are now sitting," Finn essayed, "less than five yards from where Gentry Jones, a promising NBA star, was brutally killed less than two weeks ago. You have been charged with his murder. What can you tell us about this shocking incident?"

Finn's senior editor had been right when she surmised that Katz had coached Angel thoroughly for this line of questioning. "I wish I could clear this up, Carla," she said. "But because it is the subject of an ongoing criminal investigation, I have been advised not to comment. But my thoughts and prayers go out to the Jones family. I'm sorry for their terrible loss."

For her part, Finn lived up to her reputation of never deviating from the scripted questions, even when Angel's statements seemed to beg for a follow-up. For instance, asked how well she knew Gentry, Angel replied, "Not at all." It didn't occur to Finn to inquire, "Then what was he doing at your house at five in the morning?" And when Angel volunteered, "I would never harm another human being. That is against the most basic precepts of my religion," Carla might well have asked, "What religion is that?" since Angel moved from faith to faith like it was the reception line at a wedding.

Why wasn't the director screaming in Finn's ear to ask for clarification? I can only imagine it was because he had learned through painful experience that to ask her to do more than read from the monitor was to invite a meltdown. Carla Finn was a pretty circus pony that ABC was content to have trot around and around the ring without ever requiring her to change her gait.

For her final question, Finn asked Angel what she would plead when this came to trial. I noticed Katz lean forward eagerly. "Not guilty," said Angel. "Definitely not guilty, Carla." Katz gave a full-body jerk of bitter disappointment. He looked like a baseball manager whose slugger has just struck out with the bases loaded.

"I think that's it," said Finn, after peering into the teleprompter. Her head tilted sideways as one of the producers reminded her of something in her earpiece. "Oh . . . stay seated for one second, Angel." A network still photographer sprinted into the room, his equipment clanking. The audio feed went dead as he walked around snapping pictures of the two women in their chairs.

I was the only one in the dining room, it seemed, who didn't jump out of his chair. Everyone else pulled off their earphones and got busy. Charlie finally received the phone call he had been eagerly expecting. Good timing. "Yo, yo, yo," he said into the mouth perforation. He answered the phone so fast I couldn't hear his entire ring tone, but I think it was some John Mellencamp song.

"Yeah, it just ended," he said, walking quickly out of hearing range into the pantry that separated the dining room from the breakfast area.

Katz was in a confab with the heavyset producer confirming what time Carla and the camera crew would be at his office. I should have known he would extract some airtime out of this situation.

Lani was having a heated discussion with Inga. They were keeping their voices down, but both of them looked angry.

I just sat there, cynically projecting how all this would play out. The network would rush out a fifteen-second teaser for the special, probably by the end of the day. "In an exclusive interview with Carla Finn, pop superstar Angel speaks out about the night that could land her in prison for the rest of her life!" ABC would air this enticing spot during every other commercial break for the next week and a half, fully aware that it was an empty promise.

It would be followed with a clip of Finn saying as if she were narrating a ghost story, "We are now sitting less than five yards from where Gentry Jones was brutally killed. You have been charged with his murder. What can you tell us about this shocking incident?" The implication of course was that Angel was about to spill the beans. The truth was that the interview contained no revelations at all—only another famous miscreant tap-dancing around the charges.

When is false advertising not false advertising? When it's promotion.

On the monitor, the photographer took some shots of Carla and Angel standing together. As soon as the flash stopped popping, so did their smiles. They shook hands and Carla gestured impatiently to one of her assistants, who rushed over with a pen and a business card. Carla scribbled something on the back and handed it to the singer. Then Angel crossed the frame toward the front entrance with Oops right behind her.

Out in the breakfast room, Lani was pouring herself a cup of tea from an ornate urn, frowning down at her cup. "Something wrong?" I asked as I approached.

She glanced at me and made a *tsk* sound with her tongue. "Ah, Inga has arranged a little celebratory night out for Angel now that—in her words—'the worst part of the ordeal is over.' "

"I take it you don't approve?"

"I'm sure Angel is anxious to get out of the house. But I'd rather her first public appearance be at her book party tomorrow, not out sipping champagne at a nightclub."

"You mean it's all right to appear on television but not to go out with friends?"

"That's right. We can control the message in an interview but not in paparazzi shots. If everyone sees pictures of her out partying, it makes it appear as if she isn't taking the death of that man and her role in it seriously."

"Why don't you put your foot down?"

"Oh, you dear boy," she said condescendingly. "As if I could keep Angel from doing what she wants to do. No, my job is never to prevent these messes from happening. It's to tidy up after they do." As she poured a packet of Equal into her cup, she said, "At least they're going to Spider, which is a private club. So the press exposure should be minimal." She glanced over at me. "Do you want to go?"

"To Spider?"

"Umm-hum."

"I thought you said it was a private club."

"I can put you on Angel's list. Members can bring guests."

"Is she going to speak to me?"

Lani made a face that said: *Afraid not, kid.* She took a sip of her tea. "Honestly, I think you're still two or three encounters away from a conversation."

"Then I don't see any point in going tonight. They probably don't even leave the house until well after midnight. I'd just be a fifth wheel—a flat one."

"You'd be one meeting closer to becoming friends with Angel," she said with a playful rising intonation.

"Couldn't you just parade me past her now? Accomplish the same thing."

Lani smiled. "For what it's worth, I think she likes you."

"You picked up on that too?" I said.

"I'm not kidding. I've seen the way she looks at you."

"Lani, she hasn't even glanced in my direction."

"You'll see," Lani said in a singsong voice.

"So how do you think the interview went?" I asked.

"Fantastic. Couldn't have been better."

"Really," I said with surprise. "You think it helped her with Gentry's murder?"

"Oh, I don't know about that," Lani said. "But it's going to sell a ton of books."

CHAPTER
18

A ngel and Inga were closeted away upstairs. Carla Finn shot a brief standup in front of the house. Then they reversed the angle so you could see the roiling crowd behind her. Then she and most of the ABC army packed up and left. Lani departed for her office and Katz for his. I elected to join the exodus and had Stan drive me back to the hotel.

We stopped at a computer store on the way, where I replaced my drowned laptop with a new one with WiFi capacity. We also stopped at a sporting goods store, where I bought a basketball and some sneakers. I had to get some exercise. It only takes three days in a hotel before I start to feel like one of those carmelized ducks you see hanging in the windows in Chinatown.

I know, I know. I could have been doing laps in the Chateau's pool. But swimming has always seemed like a survival skill to me. As exercise, it's sheer drudgery, a near neighbor on the activity scale to bailing water out of a boat.

I had seen a court in pretty good shape during my hike up to the House of Blues. There were even nets on the rims. Before I left, I dialed the number my photographer friend Robin Pratt had given me. Always a good idea to keep the Fourth Estate appeased.

"Hello," she said sourly. People were shouting around her and I heard a chorus of "Believe in Me." If she had been listening to that song over and over for the past five hours, I couldn't blame her for being in a bad mood.

"Hey, it's Jim McNamara. I have something for you."

"Hold on a minute," she said. After about fifteen seconds she came back on. "Yeah, Jim." The background noise had diminished greatly. I assumed she had walked across the street for privacy.

"Angel is going to party at the club Spider tonight. You know where that is?"

"No, but you can bet your ass I'll find it. You think her publicist is going to leak this?"

"I'm sure she isn't. She doesn't think Angel should be seen clubbing while the charges are hanging over her head. You should have the field to yourself."

"Ooh," she squealed with excitement. "I could kiss you." Then she was gone.

I dribbled along the sidewalk uphill to the court, getting loose, putting a little grit on the shiny new ball. All right, I was no Gentry Jones, but the Voit felt good in my hands. I shot around for a while, mostly pounding in bank shots from about sixteen feet out on the right side of the basket. Once I had the range, I started taking shots, moving counterclockwise around the court. I found myself singing that old Carl Perkins chant, "I been told when a boy meets a girl/ Take a trip around the world, hey, hey."

A skinny guy with a goatee, a baggy green T-shirt draped over clothes-hanger shoulders, wandered up and asked if I minded. We followed universal shooting etiquette, taking turns except if the other guy hit. Then he got a bounce pass back for the bonus shot.

As we were shooting around, getting to know each other

without talking, I heard the sound of another ball bouncing. Three black guys came walking up the fence by the park, dribbled in and started playing at the other basket.

The sound of a basketball is like a siren song for guys. People drifted into the park from nowhere, first two, then three. We soon got up a full-court five-on-five game. It was a pretty good run. Playing to fifteen, my team won two out of three, in large measure because my goateed friend was raining baskets from the corner. His shot looked awkward, with his elbows akimbo, but he was automatic.

Afterward, as I dribbled away, I gave him a head bob, which he returned. "Take it easy," I said. They were the only words we exchanged. It was the most satisfying relationship I had during my time in Los Angeles.

I did a few quick sets on the weight machine at the hotel fitness center, took a shower and went back to the Mexican restaurant I had previously patronized. Hey, addicts are ipso facto creatures of habit.

Afterward, I spent some time installing stuff on my new computer and then stayed up to watch *The Daily Show* with Jon Stewart, turning it off when he brought out Charlie Sheen for the interview segment. There was nothing I wanted to hear that guy say.

I'm pretty sure I didn't read *Gravity's Rainbow* that night, but my dream was quite vivid nonetheless. Maybe it was the salsa.

Anyway, I'm in this towering health club, and it's closing time, or maybe just afterward, and I'm about to leave when I realize I've left my stuff in a locker, which is like five levels below. A pumped-up guy in a tight-fitting LaCoste shirt—he's got personal trainer written all over him—explains that the elevators are already turned off. Only the service corridors are open if I want to retrieve my stuff.

He offers a very explicit and very involved route I must take to the basement, including the names of the guys on various levels who will point me to the right unmarked doors. Now I'm worried, because I know myself. When someone gives me directions, I stop listening after the second turn. Oh, I nod like I'm carefully taking it all in, but I know I'll never remember it all. So I resign myself to taking the initial suggestions and then stopping to ask someone else for directions.

Same with social or business situations. If someone is introducing me to a group of people in one fell swoop, I nod and say hello, but I stop paying attention after the first one. My thinking, based on exhaustive fieldwork, is that I can focus on the first, and at least go one for five, or I can try to retain all the names and end up remembering none. Like Aesop's fable of the fox and the grapes.

So with some trepidation off I go to the bowels of the building. Most of it is like a massive boiler room with insulated pipes running along the downward-sloping path. One level is like a mall or a subway promenade with all the shops shuttered. Blank-eyed commuters buzz past me, intent on getting somewhere. I'm starting to feel like George Orwell in Wonderland.

Corridors branch off every which way, but I'm actually doing pretty good when the phone rings, waking me from my pilgrimage. Groggy, I reached around in the dark for the phone. I knew it couldn't be six A.M. yet because that's the time I had the alarm set to wake me up for the Serenity meeting.

"Hello," I croaked.

"Jim, this Sandy Hirsh, Danny's wife." She gave me all the information I needed to identify her, but it still took me a second to put her in context. It wasn't a pleasant one.

When a sponsee's spouse calls, it usually means only one thing. And it's not an invitation to dinner.

CHAPTER
19

"I know it's early out there, but I didn't know who else to call," Sandy said. "Danny had your hotel number written down by the phone."

"What's up?"

"Remember the other night when you called and I said he was at a meeting?"

"Yeah."

"Well, I don't think he was. Anyway, he never came home. Not yesterday either. I called the dealership. He didn't make it to work. I thought for sure he'd show up last night, but he didn't."

"I'm so sorry, Sandy. What do you think has happened to him?" As if I didn't know.

"I think he's out drinking."

"You check with his mom? His sister? His buddies?"

"Yeah. Nobody's heard from him." I could hear one of their kids crying in the background.

"You check the hospital? The police?"

"Yeah. Yeah. Look, I know his patterns, all right? He's sitting someplace right now shit-faced, afraid to come home. . . . He should be afraid."

"Okay, Sandy," I said. "I'll get there as soon as I can and look for Danny. What are his usual haunts?"

I jotted down the names and locations of the bars as she ticked them off.

I assured Sandy things would be all right—a promise that sounded empty even to me—and told her I would be in touch as soon as I found anything out.

After I hung up, I showered, packed and called the concierge, asking him to call me a cab and please get me on the next flight to Connecticut. No, I wasn't checking out, just taking what I hoped would be a quick trip East.

It was still too early to call Lani, but I figured Whitey was fair game. He picked up the phone on the fifth ring. "Hello?" he said, sounding flustered.

"Hey, Whitey. It's Jim."

"How's my favorite detective?"

"I'm fine. You all right?"

"Got a little shampoo in my hair."

"Sorry. I rousted you out of the shower?"

"Don't worry about it. If you hadn't called, someone else would have. I haven't taken an uninterrupted shower in seventeen years."

"You want me to call back?"

"No, no. What's up?"

"I have to go home for a little bit. I have a sponsee who fell off the wagon pretty hard."

"That's rough. Anything I can do?"

"Matter of fact, there is. I'd like to put you on retainer. Thought you could do a little investigating for me while I'm gone. You know this town better than anyone I know."

"You're deputizing me?"

"I guess."

"Cool."

I filled him in about the night Gentry was killed, how angry Cam Akers got when he saw his ex with the basketball player in that nightclub and how he had called someone on his cell phone as soon as he got outside. I also explained Cam's very public Malibu alibi.

"I'm convinced that whatever happened that night was set in motion by Cam's phone call."

"Okay."

"So I want you to sniff around Cam's story a little bit. Maybe talk to other people who were at the party. Find out when he got there, who he was hanging with, that sort of thing."

"Right."

"Of course, if you could find out who he called right after he saw Angel with Gentry, that would be very helpful too."

"I'll give it a shot."

"You haven't asked me how much you're getting paid, Whitey."

"I don't care about that. Just do me a favor. From now on, don't call Whitey. Address me as Super Snoop."

I laughed. "You got it, Snoop."

"How do I get in touch with you?" he asked.

"You on-line?"

"Aren't we all?"

I gave him my e-mail address and my home number in Connecticut, then we said our farewells.

"Good luck with your friend. There's nothing worse than having a head full of AA and a belly full of booze."

CHAPTER
20

I know I should spend these long flights doing something enriching like catching up on my reading, but I did what I often do—hung by the back galley, pestering the flight attendants, drinking bad coffee and counting the minutes.

On the ground at Bradley, I rented a Mitsubishi sedan that smelled of cigarettes and headed for Winsted. It was night already, so I made a circuit of all the bars Sandy had mentioned. No sign of Danny.

I started driving around, pulling into every grubby tavern I passed. I figured Danny was unlikely to be camped in some high-class establishment. He was probably looking to stay stinking drunk as cheaply as possible, and that meant the dingy joints where the odor from the men's room permeated the whole room and nobody cared.

It was an odd, eye-opening pilgrimage for me. Although I had lived in Winsted going on five years, I moved there sober and thus had no familiarity with its watering holes. From what I saw that night, I wasn't missing much.

In nearly every place I stopped, the bartender knew

Danny or else knew his father, Danny Hirsh, Sr., a notorious
drunk whose loud and messy exploits were still the stuff of
local legend.

Funny how on TV the town drunk is always a sweet, gentle soul like Otis on *The Andy Griffith Show*. In fact these
characters tend to be extremely toxic louts who sow disappointment and pain everywhere they go.

I gave up the hunt sometime after midnight and headed
home. Lani was furious when I called her. "Where the hell
are you?" she said. "I've spent the entire day trying to get
hold of you."

I explained the situation. "Couldn't this have waited?" she
asked.

"I didn't fly all the way back here on a whim, Lani."

"So this guy is drinking again. Angel is charged with murder. Where are your priorities?"

I took a long, calming breath before answering. "You
may think I'm exaggerating, Lani, but I'm not. When an
alcoholic goes out on a binge, it's a matter of life and
death."

She blew an exasperated breath through clenched teeth.
"Fine. So when will you be back?"

"Soon as I can. As soon as I find him and get him settled,
I'll fly right back."

"Make sure you do. I didn't think this situation could get
any crazier, but it is."

"Did something happen today?"

"Just get back as fast as you can, Jim," she said, hanging up.

I thought I'd fall asleep as soon as my head hit the pillow,
but I spent hours worrying about where Danny was spending
the night.

Thank God for small towns. Try as you will, you can't
hide in one. When I went to my customary God As I Understand Him meeting the next morning, one of the other regulars, Ray, approached me by the coffee urn.

"You sponsor that kid Danny?" he asked. Ray worked for

the county on a road crew, driving a plow during the winter. He wasn't big on conversation, rarely shared at meetings. But he was serious about his program.

"Yeah," I said. "I have been. But I think he went out a couple of days ago."

Ray nodded. "I think I saw his truck parked over in Calvary Cemetery this morning."

"Thanks," I said, as the chairwoman banged the gavel to start the meeting. I begged off going out to breakfast afterward with my Sunday morning cronies and drove over to the cemetery instead.

Generally when you go on one of these 12-step calls—that is, going to meet with a drunk—you're supposed to bring someone else from the program with you to ride shotgun. But I figured Danny was going to have a hard enough time talking to me. I didn't want to overwhelm him.

Sure enough, I found his truck parked in the back corner of the plot, over the rise and down by the creek. I don't know how Ray spotted it. I pulled up next to it and got out. No sign of Danny.

Until I walked up to the side of the cabin. He was hunched up awkwardly in the back seat, passed out. On the floor was an empty whiskey bottle, lying on a pile of vanquished beer cans. I tapped on the window.

Danny startled awake as if emerging from a bad dream, blinking painfully and rubbing his temple. He sat for a moment, blankly, not looking at me. I didn't rush him.

Eventually he clambered out. I could smell the booze as soon as he opened the door. He stood there for a moment, leaning against the hood, folding his arms across his chest. He still wasn't looking me in the eye.

"What's going on?" he asked, and coughed.

"You tell me."

"I fucked up," he said neutrally.

"Did something happen, Danny? Something that made you want to take a drink?"

He was scuffing his foot against a rock that was half submerged in the tire path.

"Not really."

"Nothing at work? Maybe an argument with the wife?"

He shook his head. I bet that hurt. "I was driving home from work and out of nowhere I had this thought: 'I want a beer. No, I fucking deserve a beer.'" Now he looked up at me, daring me to find fault with that logic. "You know?"

"So now what? You going to keep drinking?"

He winced. "I don't know. I feel like shit." The usual reaction is defiance. I figured he must feel really bad.

"What are you doing parked out here?"

"That's my dad's grave over there," he said, jerking his thumb toward a headstone behind him. "Everybody knows how I felt about him. Shit, I didn't even go to the asshole's funeral. I figured this would be the last place anybody would look for me."

"You got any money left?"

"Nah," he said, and patted his pants pockets as if to prove it.

"Come on. I'll buy you a cup of coffee."

He glanced around at his truck. "Just leave it here for now," I said. "We'll come back and get it."

He climbed into my car. "Where'd you get this piece of shit?"

"It's a rental," I said, starting it up and rolling slowly toward the cemetery gate. "Your wife is worried about you."

He whipped his head as if I had slapped him and looked out the window.

"You remember what I said when you asked me to sponsor you, Danny?"

"You said a lot of shit."

"Yeah, well, one of them was that we'd try to make it a day at a time, but if you slipped, you had to go to a rehab."

"I can't go away for four weeks," he said as if the idea were patently ludicrous. Never fails. I've yet to meet the alcoholic who can spare time from his busy drinking schedule to go save his life.

"That was the deal, bud." He spent the rest of the drive explaining why it was impossible. Then we sat in a booth at a diner off Route 8 while I dismantled his arguments one by one. I prevailed on him to eat a couple of eggs too.

Then I called Sandy from a pay phone by the cigarette machine. I couldn't believe how much a pack cost. You need a bank loan to smoke nowadays.

Sandy wanted to talk to Danny. I explained my plan to check him into a detox down in Torrington. I told her it might be better if she met us down there and brought some clothes and a razor for Danny.

I was keeping an eye on the booth in case Danny decided to bolt. A lot of drunks, when they feel the clammy grip of commitment closing in on them, try to run for it.

I asked her if Danny's insurance from work would pay for rehab. "Yeah," she said. "I checked into it a few months ago before he started going to those meetings of yours, when his drinking was getting real bad. He's covered."

"Can you get along without him for a few weeks?"

"What's the alternative? He blows his paycheck and doesn't come home all weekend? Yeah, I think we can get by."

"All right. I'm going to call the hospital. If you don't hear back from me right away, that means they can admit him. I'll meet you down there in an hour. Detox is on the sixth floor."

The unit had a bed. In fact, Dawn Petersen, a counselor I know, was on duty, so I was sure Danny would be taken care of.

I bought him a couple of packs of Tylenol at the diner's cash register as I paid the check, just to cushion the blow. Then I drove him down to Torrington, keeping the conversation light the whole way. Even got him to laugh once when I described going from bar to bar looking for him.

The only time he bucked was inside the hospital when he

spotted his wife near the nurses' station. The way she was looking at him would have stopped me in my tracks too. All in all, he went to his salvation rather meekly.

After he had gone through the admittance interview, had been searched and was being escorted to his room, I gave him a goodbye hug.

"You're doing the right thing. I'll talk to you soon," I said, smiling.

He stared at me glumly and walked away.

I drove home and booked a late-night flight back to Los Angeles. That left me with a few hours before I had to leave for the airport. I started in on some overdue domestic maintenance, piling loads of laundry into the washer and then the dryer. As they were done, I carried hampers of still-warm clothes into the living room, folding in front of the TV. The Spurs were dismantling the Warriors. Maybe Golden State missed Gentry Jones. But there wasn't much anyone could do to stop Tim Duncan when he was on his game like this. The guy was a machine. With ten minutes to go in the fourth, it was a lost cause and both coaches were sending in subs. Just before the final buzzer sounded, the phone rang.

"Hey, Jim. It's Whitey," he said enthusiastically. "I found some stuff I thought you'd want to hear."

"Wow. I gotta give it to you, Super Snoop. You're fast. You've been on the case like, what? Thirty-six hours?"

"Once I found someone with the inside track on Cam, it all came together pretty quick."

"So what'd you find?"

"Well, Cam runs with a pack of actors. At least that's what they call themselves. I've never heard of any of 'em. Acting must be a better gig than I realized, because some of these guys work about once every two years. Anyway, Cam is by far the most celebrated of the bunch. Basically they're just a bunch of sycophants feeding off his fame. But in Hollywood, that's an accepted job category.

"Anyway, that's who he hooked up with at the party. All

the usual suspects. What's interesting is who wasn't there." Whitey paused in his delivery like Hideo Nomo. I got the impression he was enjoying the presentation.

"Who might that be, Snoop?"

"His name's Mike Rouse. They call him Mouse. Apparently he and Cam have been inseparable for more than a year. Joined at the hip. But Mouse wasn't there that night. Which made me think maybe he was off doing things he shouldn't have been doing.

"So I started looking into his background. A couple of Cam's crowd fancy themselves hardasses. But Mouse is the only one who gets the merit badge," Whitey said, and chuckled. "Or whatever the opposite of that would be.

"You don't get the criminal vibe off him right away. A handful of arrests. One drunk and disorderly, one car theft, dismissed, one making terroristic threats to a guy who apparently owed him money, and a bunch of domestic disturbance calls with no actions taken. Reading between the lines, I'd say Mouse has a history of knocking around his girlfriends, but none of them have pressed charges.

"None of that would really separate him from the rest of Cam's posse. Apparently your acting résumé's not complete without a few months in county. But when you start digging through Mouse's past—oh, boy. He's got a juvie record that would make your skin crawl.

"Grew up in the foster system down near San Diego. Guess he got bounced around a lot as a kid. The usual nightmare. And it obviously took a toll. He was a scary kid. Always carried a knife. Tortured animals. Tortured other kids. Took a box cutter to some poor security guard when he was thirteen. Left him with eighty-five stitches. The system didn't know what to do with him. He escaped twice from juvenile correctional facilities before he was fifteen.

"Then he just dropped off the map. There's a couple of years unaccounted for there. I think he left California for a while, but I don't know where he went."

"His history with a knife makes him good for Gentry's death," I said. "How did he hook up with Cam?"

"A few years ago he became drinking buddies with a couple of stunt men from Covina. That got him on film sets. Cam apparently took an instant shine to him, encouraged Mouse to get a SAG card, and got him bit parts in a few of his films. They're real tight. I'd bet you dollars to donuts when Cam made that phone call on the night of the murder, Mouse was on the other end."

"Wow. You did great, Whitey. Thank you."

"No problem. Anything else?"

"Yeah, why do they call him Mouse?"

"Well, it rhymes with Rouse, but mostly it's because he has a reputation from the time he was a kid as some kind of Houdini. He could get into or out of anything."

"He definitely could be our man. What does he look like?"

"I've got a picture of him. The one his agent sends to casting directors. You want me to send it to you?"

"Drop it by the front desk at the Marmont. I'm flying back in a few hours."

"You want me to pick you up at the airport?"

"Nah, I have to call Lani anyway. I'll have the driver meet me."

"So what are we going to do now?"

I liked the way he had put himself on the team.

"Tomorrow I think we'll ask the police to take a close look at Mouse. He sounds too nasty to confront without official firepower."

"How'd it go with your friend?"

"He's in a rehab."

"That's about the best outcome you could hope for."

"You might have a hard time convincing Danny of that. But yeah, I think so too."

"All right, so I'll talk to you tomorrow."

"Good. And thanks again, Super Snoop."

I called Lani and gave her my itinerary, but I didn't share the information about Rouse. I didn't want to open a can of worms if I wasn't there to watch the rascals crawl away.

I paid some bills, raked my yard by porchlight and wolfed down a dinner of Chinese takeout from the place in town while watching *The Simpsons*. A little later I drove my rental car back to the airport.

It seemed like my investigation into Gentry's murder was coming together neatly.

I should have known all hell was about to bust loose.

CHAPTER
21

Stan had a pretty laid-back demeanor. But he was practically pogoing in place as I walked toward him at the LAX security gate.

"I have to get you out to Angel's house right away," he said, grabbing my carry-on and trotting for the luggage carousel.

"Why? What's happened?" I asked when I caught up to him.

"I don't know," he said. "Lani just said to get you out there pronto. All I know is that there's police all over the place."

That turned out to be an understatement, as I discovered after a high-speed trip to Brentwood that had me clenching the hand strap in the back seat. The sun was barely up, but martial law was in full effect.

Angel's security team had been told to stand down. LAPD was manning the gate at Angel's place and they weren't letting us in.

The driveway was filled with black and white units and unmarked blue Chevy sedans. Too early for the pedestrian mob, but the media was out in droves. And the police contingent had the press foaming at the mouth. Lenses poked through the fence, pointing at the house, filming everything that moved. A pack of rabid reporters surrounded every vehicle that rolled up to the gate. Through the sedan's moonroof, I counted four helicopters hovering above the property.

"What now?" We were parked about twenty yards away from the gate. The tinted windows had gradually discouraged even the most determined media leech. I had asked the question of myself, but Stan had the answer.

"Call Lani on her cell. Here," he said, passing me back his sleek, impossibly tiny phone, which was already connecting. He had Lani on speed dial. What a surprise.

"Hello?" said a hectored voice. You could hear a brittle edge of hope in the tone, the thin possibility that this call might finally offer help in the middle of her ordeal. Sorry. It ain't me, babe.

"Lani? It's Jim McNamara."

"Where are you?" she asked. "Why don't you get a cell phone like everyone else on the planet?"

"I'm outside the gates. The cops won't let me in."

"I'll send Wendell out to vouch for you. Wait by the pedestrian entrance."

I passed the phone back to Stan, thanked him and slipped out the driver's side of the car. As I sidled through the crowd, I pasted a depraved look on my face to blend in with the reporters. A uniformed officer stood behind the side gate, staring out impassively. I lingered a few feet away, trying to be unobtrusive.

Over the policeman's shoulder, I saw Wendell Crane, Bruce Katz's associate, trundle over. He peered out at the sidewalk. I gave him a little wave on the downlow and he nodded. He spoke a few words to the cop and gestured for me to approach.

The cop pushed the gate open as I neared and I walked inside without anyone noticing. Sanctuary. It was creepy on the sidewalk. The press were prowling around so ravenously it felt like *Dawn of the Dead* outside there.

The mood wasn't a whole lot better inside.

"What's going on, Wendell?" I asked as we weaved through the police cars.

"It's a bit of a madhouse, I'm afraid," he said.

"But what happened?"

"Let's get inside, shall we?"

As we passed through the entrance, I saw police activity was centered in the media room to our left.

"This way," said Wendell, gesturing toward the library. "We're down this way."

A jowly detective with a bad haircut was standing under the staircase talking on a cell phone. He noticed me peering around as I was being led off by Wendell.

"Ruben," he yelled at a uniform by the door. Then he pointed at me. "Get his goddamn information."

The officer walked over and politely asked my name, affiliation and contact numbers, jotting down the data in a notebook. Then he thanked me and walked away.

I followed Wendell through the library, the study, the yoga room, the gym and eventually onto the sunporch, where I saw Lani, Oops, Bruce Katz, Joanna, and a handful of other very worried-looking people gathered.

"What's going on, Lani?" I asked.

"We're still trying to figure that out, Jim," she said, frowning. "Angel has disappeared."

Before I could ask what that meant, Katz interjected, "*Please* don't say that. At this point, we don't know what has happened to Angel. And until we do, the party line is we don't know her whereabouts and are worried to death for her safety. Is everyone in this room clear on that?" Wendell was the only one nodding, but he was really putting his chin into it.

"What happened?" I continued. It felt like I had been asking variations on this same question since I landed, without getting a shred of enlightenment.

"Angel went to a club with some friends last night," Katz

said. "She returned home around four. We don't know where she is now."

"Who was with her?"

"Inga and three of the dancers," said Lani.

"How about you, Oops? Were you there?"

He nodded glumly. "I drove one car, Annette drove the other." He gestured at one of Angel's assistants standing next to Joanna. "I went into the club with them. And I brought Angel back here after. She was in the front room, dancing to the Black Eyed Peas, when I went home."

"So what happened? And why is the place crawling with cops?"

"The guard at the gate said the Suburban came in at four-oh-nine with Oops driving and Angel in the front seat," Lani explained. "He said Oops left eleven minutes later. And at four-thirty the Suburban drove back out with Angel behind the wheel. She never drives. I don't even think she has a license."

"Let's agree not to share that detail with the authorities, shall we?" said Katz.

"How did the police get involved?" I was just full of questions.

"A patrol car found the Suburban with two wheels up on the curb in a No Standing zone in front of the bus station downtown," said Katz. "The engine was running and the front door was wide open."

"They ran the plates and sent a unit out here," continued Lani. "When the guard told them Angel was driving that car, all the red flags went up. They're treating her as a fugitive."

"Which is of course a flagrant presumption of guilt," thundered Katz in his courtroom voice.

"Has anyone heard from Angel since she drove out the gate"—I glanced at my Swatch—"two and half hours ago?"

"I've been trying her cell every two minutes, but I just get a recording."

"You can stop trying," said a voice to my left. Inga Saffron stood shimmering in the doorway to the kitchen in shiny black trousers and a clingy black sleeveless blouse. She was magnificent-looking, like a cross between Gina Gershon and Cleopatra. How did you go out clubbing all night, get woken up an hour later and still look that good?

Everyone stared at her, and it wasn't because of her exotic beauty. "She threw her cell phone away."

Several voices clamored for answers. "How do you know that?" Katz boomed over the chorus.

"Because she just called me from a pay phone and told me so," said Inga.

"Where is she? What did she say?" asked Lani.

"Not much," Inga said, walking toward us. "She told me she didn't want to involve me in this mess. She wanted everyone to know she's sorry for the commotion this is going to cause." A couple of people started to interject questions, but Inga calmly continued relaying her message. "But she told me she's going to have to disappear for a while."

At that point there was no restraining our crowd. The room suddenly sounded like a frazzled henhouse as everyone burst out with expressions of alarm and bewilderment. I think the basic sentiment could be captured in two words: *Say what?*

Inga stood there inscrutable and indifferent as we strafed her with questions. When we finally quieted down, she said, "Angel said it's very important that no effort be made to locate her. For your safety and for hers."

A voice boomed out, "Fuck that," behind us. Another country heard from. Everyone turned at the sound. This whole scene was becoming like an Edwardian drawing room farce.

It was Bruno Volpe standing in the entrance from the gym. At least this time he had his clothes on. With a leather jacket and his wide-brimmed hat. There was a diffident, owlish man behind him. "I'll locate her inside a week and we'll get this whole deal straightened out," said Volpe.

Then he saw me and rushed into the room at me. However, he misjudged the step down and stumbled as he advanced. It gave him the appearance of a charging bull. Righting himself, he yelled, "What the fuck are you doing here?"

I wasn't sure how to respond to that. He turned his ire on Lani. "You called him before you called me?"

One thing you could say about Team Angel: At least we had our priorities straight.

CHAPTER
22

Lani peeled Volpe off me by making a show of introducing me to the man who had entered the room behind El Torito. Turned out he was Emmett Langdon, the president of Angel's record label. The man was something of a legend in the music business. He had started out as a writer of pop hits in the late sixties under the name Ernie Lang. Then, working with a variety of artists, he produced some of the only good songs to come out of the plague era known as disco. Shortly thereafter, he founded his own label, Mercy, enjoying a remarkable run of commercial success with a diverse bunch of acts, from screaming punks to sensitive singer-songwriters.

Popular music is a boom-and-bust enterprise and Langdon had his fair share of both in the intervening years, but he was still respected for his unerring ear for talent and his keen business sense. Above all, he was treasured for his loyalty. He had been able to build and nurture careers for recording artists when most of his peers were only interested in milking them dry. Why he was working with Angel, I had no idea.

As he lightly shook my hand and looked at me through his thick horn-rimmed lenses, I felt momentarily disoriented. I know this sounds odd, but standing there, I had this acute atemporal sense that he was a renowned Roman prelate and I was an acolyte unexpectedly invited into his presence. That's a pretty strong aura to project. I stifled the urge to bow.

"Mr. McNamara," he said with a calm, hushed voice that made me lean in closer. "I've heard many good things about you." I doubted that was true, but I wanted it to be. I wanted to earn this man's admiration. "I'm sorry we're meeting under such trying circumstances. I know that after the events of last night there hasn't been time to arrive at the best strategy to aide Angel. But I'm grateful you'll be helping. And if there's anything I can do to help—anything at all—I hope you won't hesitate to call on me."

"I may take you up on that."

"Please do." He handed me his business card and looked over at Lani. "If you'll excuse me, I need to speak with Mr. Katz for a moment, and then we should probably hammer out a statement for the press before they storm the building." Langdon nodded to me, a gesture I returned, then he walked over toward Katz, who at the moment seemed to be haranguing Inga.

"Is the guy in charge of the security detail here?" I asked Lani.

"Gus Harris? He should be in the dining room. That's where the police were interrogating his guys."

"How did Mr. Harris get over here so quick?"

"His crew called him as soon as the first police car arrived."

"And Inga?"

"She came back with Annette, Angel's assistant, after dropping off the dancers. Angel had already gone. Please, Jim, you have to find her."

"All right, I want to talk to the security guys briefly," I said. "I'll be back in a minute." I took a couple of steps and turned back. "By the way, where is Angel's brother, Charlie?"

Lani seemed to search her mind for a second or two. "I don't know." Then she loudly addressed the whole room. "Has anyone seen Charlie?"

Joanna, Angel's girl Friday, was standing with two other women I placed as lesser assistants. They looked at each questioningly. Then they all shook their heads. Lani turned to me and shrugged.

"When I get back, I'd like to talk to everyone who was in the house at four this morning, even if they were sleeping."

My path took me past Oops, who was sitting slumped over by himself.

"What do you think happened, Oops?"

He looked up at me from under his eyebrows without taking his forearms off his thighs. "Damned if I know."

"Was she acting funny?"

"Nah, she seemed happy, 'specially after a few glasses of Cristal."

"How about when you got back here?"

"She worked the radio all the way home, singing and laughing. When we got inside, she turned on the stereo and told me I could go home—'less I wanted to dance. Didn't take her up on it. Startin' to wish I did."

"Was anyone up in the house?"

He thought for a moment. "'Cept for the guard out front, I didn't see nobody."

As I left, I squeezed his shoulder in consolation. At least I tried to. It was like trying to massage a rock.

The chef wasn't in the kitchen, but a pair of white-garbed workers was busily whipping up breakfast victuals. As I walked into the adjoining room, a gaggle of uniformed cops—ten or so—looked at me expectantly as I came through the door, then turned away disappointedly. They were milling around, wolfing down the platters of food as soon as they were set out.

In the dining room, three guys in blazers were seated at the table, studying their hands. Behind them, dressed in the same jacket, stood the man with the shaved head whom I had seen supervising the gate on previous days. A knot of detectives gathered at the other end of the table, talking to each other. One was on a cell phone.

"Mr. Harris?" I asked, approaching the security supervisor. He glanced at me without removing the frown from his face or the folded arms from his chest. "May I speak with you a minute, sir?"

We wandered a few feet from where his staff sat. I introduced myself and then asked, "How many men were working last night?"

He pointed with his chin at the seated trio. "We work three shifts at Allied: eight A.M. until four, four to midnight and midnight to eight. The graveyard shift is by far the smallest."

"Where were your men positioned?"

"One was in the booth at all times. Another does periodic checks inside the perimeter. The third is posted by the front door of the house." I thought about that coverage for a moment, a silence he seemed to take for criticism. "Obviously we would have had a larger presence if we thought there was a real or immediate threat of attack. But our client never indicated that. We were here strictly to keep out the press and the looky-loos. And," he added, "she had her bodyguard with her."

"Would you run me through the chain of events?"

"At approximately twelve-thirty, two vehicles went out the gate. Ms. Chiavone's bodyguard Cliff Johnson was behind the wheel of one. Her assistant Ms. Ruffio was behind the wheel of the other."

"Ms. Ruffio?"

"Annette Ruffio. I'm told she often serves as a designated driver on these late-night outings." I nodded. "Ms. Chiavone was in the vehicle with Mr. Johnson, as was Ms. Saffron.

Three individuals in the car with Ms. Ruffio. At approximately four-ten, Ms. Chiavone returned with Mr. Johnson. My guard got a good look inside and he's certain there was no one else in the vehicle. The man at the door confirms they were the only two to enter the house. A short time later Mr. Johnson departed by himself in his Explorer. At approximately four-thirty, Ms. Chiavone drove out again in the Suburban. This time she was alone."

"Did the guard notice if she seemed agitated or nervous?"

"Negative. He saw the client only in profile. She didn't engage him in conversation or roll down her window. Just waited for the gate to open."

"How about the man at the door? Did he get a look at her when she came out?"

"She rushed past him. He never even saw her face." He paused as if wondering if he should volunteer anything further. "None of this was unusual. No one on my detail, including me, has had any kind of dealings with Ms Chiavone. No chitchat, no eye contact. Nothing."

I nodded. "Please continue."

"At approximately four-forty-five, Ms. Ruffio returned with Ms. Saffron. The first police car arrived about fifteen minutes later. Officers relieved my men of duty at five-twelve. They've been questioned and are now waiting to be released."

"Did your guards notice anything out of the ordinary in the interval before Ms. Chiavone left the house for a second time?"

"Negative," he said, frowning.

"Not even the man by the front door?"

"He heard music playing. Very muffled. The residence is very well insulated. There can be raised voices in the vestibule that won't be audible on the threshold until the front door is opened."

"Any other traffic during their shift?"

"The client's brother, Mr. Chiavone, went out on his motorcycle just after one A.M. That's it."

"Did he return?"

"Not to my knowledge. Not before the police arrived anyway."

"You have any theories about what Ms. Chiavone is up to?" I asked, adopting his formality.

He squinted at me. "No, not really. I don't know the client well enough to venture a guess."

"Other than the traffic you described, did your men report anything unusual happening last night?"

"Negative."

"Could someone have snuck onto the property?"

He considered the idea. "I suppose so. There are no motion detectors set up, so someone could have scaled the gate. The police have searched the house and the grounds."

"If there was an intruder who broke into the house, wouldn't they have set off an alarm?"

"The system was deactivated."

"By whom?"

"Could have been anyone who knows the code."

"When was it turned off?"

"Sometime earlier in the evening. There is a console in the guard shack at the gate that indicates whether the system in the house is on or off. Mr. Grant, who was posted at the gate, reports that the system was off when he came on duty at midnight."

The man sitting farthest from us looked over at the mention of his name and confirmed what his supervisor was saying with a nod.

"Was that unusual?"

"Since we've been retained, the alarm has been on most nights. But Ms. Chiavone had been keeping a low profile since her arrest. Recently, since the TV interview, there's been a lot more nocturnal activity. People going in and out. So no one questioned it."

"How about video surveillance?"

"The police have the tape. They want to study it before

they let my men go. But the camera is focused on the gate area. I'm confident it will show only what I have described to you."

"All right. Thanks for running through all this with me. Where can I reach you later if I have any other questions?"

He reached in his pocket for a card. "Try me at the office. No reason to remain at this property. The hen has fled the coop."

Couldn't have put it better myself.

CHAPTER 23

Lani had jotted down a list of names of the people who had been in the house overnight. It was longer than I expected. Then I realized I had never been upstairs. Since the second floor was just as capacious as the first, I'm sure they could sleep an army up there.

I started with Joanna, the person in the house who seemed most familiar with Angel's comings and goings. She told me she had been sound asleep and hadn't heard anything.

By this time, most of the staff had gathered in the sunroom. Joanna took me around to everyone else on the list and they had the same story: Slept straight through until the police roused them. Didn't hear a thing. All of them seemed quite credible.

Employee bedrooms were at the back of the house. They had their own entrance, up the staircase in the pantry near the dining room. The rooms were walled off from Angel's lavish suite at the front of the house. A couple of the overnighters pointed out that the stereo in the living room could be turned up to pulverizing levels and they wouldn't hear it in their distant quarters.

Katz continued to lecture Angel's employees on the preferred content for all public statements. "Remember," he said, index finger in the air, "we don't know where Angel is. Don't get drawn into any sort of speculation. If a reporter asks if she may have fled to Mexico or Brazil or Timbuktu, you say, 'I don't know.' Just make sure to say that you are very worried for her safety. That's a key talking point. If you get a chance to amplify, say that everyone in the house is terrified that Angel may have been abducted.

"And under no circumstances should anyone breathe a word about her calling here. She has vanished. No one has heard from her. We hope that she is safe and contacts us soon. Is that clear?"

He looked around and apparently registered a few too many blank stares. Sighing, he said, "All right, people. Here's the short version: Angel is missing and we pray she has not been harmed."

When Katz had finished briefing the staff, I corralled him.

"I have to admit I'm a little confused, counselor."

"How so, Mr. McNamara?"

"Your talking points seem pretty flimsy."

"Really?" he said, with his Jack Benny inflection, stretching to his full height and arching one of his snowy eyebrows.

"How do you think that poor-little-Angel-abducted-by-a-maniac story is going to play once people find out she drove out the gate under her own power?"

"It doesn't matter, Mr. McNamara, as long as we get our version out there first. Then we are setting the agenda. Angel is established as a victim, not the perpetrator. Once that seed has taken root it can never be eradicated. In cases like this, where public opinion is crucial, it's all about setting the initial perception."

I wondered if Katz really believed he could get away with feeding the public a steady diet of red herrings. If Hollywood statistics held true, at least one of the people in this room was on the payroll of a tabloid. And that meant everything would be leaked.

The supermarket tabs thrived on sensationalistic crimes like this. And they were incredibly resourceful at reporting them, usually scooping the legit press over and over in cases like Elizabeth Smart, JonBenet Ramsey and Robert Blake.

The challenge, of course, was sorting fact from fiction in their stories. The pieces typically contained a couple of significant details that no one else had, inside information obtained with persistence and a very generous open checkbook. Those nuggets, however, were padded with blatant fabrications. As a result of this purple prose style, everything played out surreally in the tabloids, like a fractured fairy tale.

But I suspected that these rags, not Katz, would be setting the agenda, particularly now that Angel had fled.

"Also, all due respect, Mr. Katz," I continued, "but when you ask us not to tell the police that Angel called, doesn't that fall under the heading of suborning perjury?"

He looked down his nose at me witheringly. "Why don't you let me worry about that, eh? Besides, I only asked people not to volunteer that information. I never told them to lie about it."

I cleared my throat, the passive-aggressive equivalent of barking, *Bullshit!*

"Anything else?" he asked with mock politeness.

"As a matter of fact, yes," I said. "What was it that led the police to charge Angel with Gentry's death? You told me it was circumstantial, but you never told me what it was."

He glanced around. I suspect he was looking to see if he could simply blow me off or if there were people around that I might complain to like Lani or Emmett Langdon, the label president who was paying Katz's lavish bills. The lawyer's cheeks puffed as he blew out an exasperated breath. "Very well. One of the partygoers informed the police that as the evening was winding down, the people remaining were all sitting in this room. Angel got up to leave and Mr. Jones followed her out the door." He gave me a dour look that said, *Satisfied?*

"That's it?" I said skeptically.

"A dancer who had been using the bathroom in the adjoining room," he said, pointing at the gym, "said he saw them walking together toward the front of the house."

"And?"

He leaned toward me, I think more out of dramatic reflex than any real concern for confidentiality. "My sources inside the department tell me that the DA plans to build his case around the fact that when Jones's body was found shortly afterward, Angel was alone with him and no one heard her scream or cry out for help."

"I see."

Katz waved his hand dismissively. "I can shred an argument like that into confetti. It's pure conjecture. There are no witnesses and no murder weapon. My client showed no signs of engaging in a struggle. There was blood all over the floor but none on her clothes or skin. No one is going to convict a figure of Ms. Chiavone's stature based purely on conjecture. And you can rest assured I will provide the jury with numerous plausible scenarios for what may have happened in this house."

"Doesn't her flight amount to an admission of guilt?"

"Not unless she never comes back. And that's where we're counting on you, Mr. McNamara. To find her and bring her home. Please don't let us down."

"One last thing, counselor."

"Make it quick," he said, appraising his watch for emphasis.

"During the interview with Carla Finn, I noticed that you got upset when Angel said she planned to plead not-guilty to all charges. Why would that make you angry?"

"It's not important, really," Katz said. "It's just that I had anticipated that question and coached Ms. Chiavone repeatedly on her response. She was supposed to say, 'I think the question you should be asking, Carla, is: What will I plead *if* it comes to trial.' We wanted to convey that the case against her is very weak. She essentially conceded that there will be a trial. It was merely a wasted opportunity."

"All right. Thank you, counselor."

As we were talking, I noticed Charlie Chiavone enter the room. He bounced around from group to group, talking animatedly, making the same faces of shock and astonishment for each audience. I think he understood instinctively that with his sister and biggest critic out of the picture, his own stature in the house had risen significantly. Ego abhors a vacuum.

I watched him work the room, plotted his path and went to wait in ambush by the kitchen. Sure enough, when he finished with his last constituency, turning back as he walked away to enthuse, "Let's pray that you're right," I was right in his path, forcing him to jolt to a stop.

Either he realized my intent was confrontational or else he simply decided he didn't have to bother to charm me, but Good Time Charlie vanished. He scowled up at me.

"Where have you been, Charlie?"

"None of your fucking business," he protested. "I don't answer to you."

"You know your sister took off."

"Duh," he said. "I thought all these cops were here for a barbecue."

"This strengthens the case against her," I said.

He shrugged.

"You know what's struck me as unbelievable from the very beginning?" He just stared at me. "I find it impossible to believe your sister could have overpowered a big, athletic man like Jones."

He snorted with derision. "She could kick anybody's ass," he said, swiveling his chest as he settled in to tell a story. "When she was fifteen, she put Paul Hennessy, the biggest jock in our town, the captain of the football team, in the hospital. He asked her out, which was a big deal for a sophomore. Then he spread it around the locker room that she was a slut.

"When Angie found out, she jumped Hennessy in the boys' bathroom before assembly. Bashed his head against the sink three times and kicked the living shit out of him. Chipped his two front teeth, broke the thumb on his throwing hand and shattered a bone in his cheek." Charlie's eyes sparked as he told me this story, as if this incident were a source of immense pride to the Chiavone clan.

"He was a big guy too. He couldn't play the rest of the season. Lost his scholarship to Michigan State. She got suspended—for going in the boys' room."

"If the beating was that bad, why didn't he press charges?"

"Because he didn't want to publicize the fact that a chick three years younger than him and a hundred pounds lighter had kicked his ass. That's why. He told people he got jumped by three black guys from another school. Course everyone in town knew the truth. And nobody messed with Angie after that."

"Yeah, but whoever killed Gentry was awfully adept with a blade," I said, testing him. "That doesn't sound like your sister."

"Maybe, maybe not," he said. "She studied fencing for four months for that piece-of-shit action flick she did last year." I hadn't seen the film. Not many people did. It was remembered primarily as the project that brought Angel and the Scottish director together. "And she's taken just about every martial arts discipline there is, including ones that ain't hand-to-hand."

I hoped that Katz wasn't planning on calling Charlie as a witness. His outlook wouldn't do much to bolster the case.

"You know a guy named Mike Rouse?"

His eyes narrowed with suspicion. "I've met him," he said, shrugging. "Friend of Cam's. What about him?"

"Ever see him here at the house?"

"Nope. Anything else?" he asked, pursing his lips to indicate his impatience with this conversation.

"Yeah. You don't mind my saying so, you don't seem to be very worried about your sister," I pointed out.

Charlie executed a standing swagger, to convey the utter confidence he had in his next statement.

"Believe me," he said. "She don't need me or you or anybody else. Angie can take care of herself."

I watched Charlie roll into the kitchen. I wondered how the household would run with Angel gone. Would everyone be laid off? Or would they continue to report to work? I knew which way Charlie would vote. He was probably already eyeing the master bedroom, drafting invitation lists and composing menus in his head.

As I turned back, I saw that Emmett Langdon was gone. Lani was conferring with one of the detectives I had seen in the dining room. When he walked away, Lani caught my eye and flicked her head toward the gym. I made my way across the room to join her there.

"As you might imagine, the police have made locating Angel something of a priority," she said.

LAPD would probably rather have dealt with a full-scale riot than another one of these high-profile celebrity crimes. The pressure on them and the level of scrutiny guaranteed that no matter what they did, it would result in a black eye for the department.

"They've completed their sweep of the building and the surrounding area. No sign of Angel. They've designated it a felony flight. The FBI has been called in."

"Why?"

"Because more than two dozen buses have left the terminal in the past couple of hours, bound for everywhere from Mexico to Las Vegas to Seattle. And there's a shuttle service to LAX every twenty minutes. They're spreading the net wide."

"Did anyone report her buying a ticket or boarding a bus?"

"They wouldn't share that information."

"How about it? Could she have crossed into Mexico?"

"No way. The police confiscated her passport last week. I have all her other photo ID and personal documents in my office safe."

"Why do you keep them?"

"Because I organize her tours and all her international press junkets. There are times we have to go to Europe or Japan on short notice. It's easier if I have everything ready, rather than having her root around for things."

"She's not organized?"

"No, she is. But that's why people like Angel who are creative and successful hire support staffs—so they don't have to be bogged down in details."

And I thought it was so they would always have someone to send to the drive-through window at Wendy's in the middle of the night.

"While we're on the topic of international affairs, why hasn't that Scottish filmmaker flown in to hold Angel's hand while she's on the hot seat?"

"Mordecai? He's shooting a film in Budapest. But they've been talking on the phone."

That spurred my memory. Mordecai MacTavish was the name of this bold auteur.

"I'll need his contact info," I told Lani, who nodded. "Is it possible she had false documentation? Another passport under a phony name?"

She looked at me as if I had just suggested we swim to the Philippines. "She's a pop star, Jim, not a CIA operative."

"Okay, let's examine her options. She left here in a hurry. What could she get her hands on in a hurry that would help her flee?"

"Her wallet is full of credit cards."

I shook my head. "That would be the quickest way to get caught. The cops are sitting on that. If she uses one of her cards at a ticket counter or a restaurant or a department store, she'll be in custody within two minutes. How about . . ." I started to delve into another line of inquiry when I noticed Lani was staring off distractedly.

"Oh, gee," she said spacily.

"What is it, Lani?"

Her straying attention returned. "I just remembered. Angel keeps a stash of what she calls 'mad money.' " With my hand I beckoned her to explain.

"Well, no matter how big Angel got, she always believed it could all end without warning. Although I have to say, I don't think she ever anticipated anything like this happening. But she always said she wasn't going to walk away empty-handed."

"Meaning?"

"Since I've known her, she's always kept a pile of cash hidden away."

"You think she still does?"

"I know she does. It's in the floor safe up in her bedroom."

"Can we check to see if she's emptied it?"

"Yes. I don't have the combination memorized. But I have it saved on my computer at work. Hold on while I call my office."

As she whipped out her cell phone, I asked, "Is there someone there at this hour?"

"Today there is," she said, and then began speaking at an accelerated pace to one of her assistants.

I have to say, Angel's compulsion to salt away cash didn't strike me as odd. My mother did the same thing. Of course, she grew up scarred by the Depression in a big, poor Irish family in Jersey City. And decades later, when she was a widow living a secure life in a house that was bought and paid for outside Providence, she still kept a shoe box in her closet stuffed with money she amassed week by week, bill by bill.

I guess when you've known the sting of poverty and deprivation, you always want to keep a cushion against falling back into it. Angel probably maintained her nest egg for the same reason.

"Okay," Lani said, snapping her phone shut, "let's go."

As we walked toward the front of the house, I asked, "Lani, do you have even a guess about where Angel may be going?"

"I'm sorry, Jim. I'm stumped."

"Think about it. Among all her friends, who would she be most likely to run to for help?"

She shook her head. "Believe me, I've been wracking my brain. I almost think she's too proud to ask anyone for help."

"All right, what's the most likely way she would disguise herself: wig, scarf, sunglasses?"

"Oh, God, who knows? She's a total chameleon."

As we approached the main staircase, the gravy-stained cop who had stopped me on my way in with Wendell assailed us. "Whoa! Where do you two think you're going?"

Lani and I looked at each other. Obviously we couldn't tell him we were going to examine the private personal effects of a fugitive murderess. But we hadn't prepared a cover story. Lani bounced back more quickly than I.

"There's a book-launch party scheduled for this afternoon, Detective," she said. "We need to call people to tell them it's been canceled. The invitation list is in my office upstairs."

"Oh, I think they'll figure out on their own that your boss won't be throwing no parties today," he said smugly.

"Please, Detective," she said sweetly. "This is just a courtesy. Not everyone may see the news this morning. The people on this list are very important and influential. Some of them are flying in to be here. This will just take a minute."

"All right," he said with a sour face, as if he were doing us a huge favor. "Make it snappy."

We hustled up the stairs and into the center doorway. The first room was a museum piece: gray marble floors, Modigliani-like statuary spread around the room, some on pedestals, and a couple of large, livid, Rothko-influenced modern paintings. Both of the paintings hung in recesses, the frames surrounded by red, brocaded curtains.

"Even though Angel isn't here," Lani said, "I'd like to respect her privacy. Would you mind waiting in my office while I open the safe?"

She pointed to a door to our left. Then she proceeded through the double doors at the end of this garish gallery. Ah, Angel's inner sanctum. I regretted that I couldn't join her only because I think I would have found Angel's bra bazaar far more impressive than her art collection.

Lani's office-away-from-office was a well-stocked, efficient module: desktops, faxes, copiers, wooden filing cabinets, the works. The walls were hung with framed copies of posters from various stages of Angel's career, among them the live HBO concert from Montreal that marked her arrival as a diva, the lavish Heaven Can't Wait tour and the cover of her first greatest hits package, *Sanctified*.

There were two phones on the desk and on the waist-high shelf along the facing wall that served as a second writing/typing surface. One phone had multiple lines, all of which were flashing, though the ringers were quieted to murmurs. There was also a vintage pink Princess phone.

I assumed that was the hotline, reserved exclusively for when P Diddy called to convene a meeting of the League of Pop Superstars. Would you please settle down, Cher, so that Justin can read the minutes?

At the end of the shelf an open Sony laptop was recharging. I recognized it as the machine I had seen Inga Saffron typing away at during the Carla Finn interview. Walking over, I saw her AOL sign-on page was on the screen.

The user name was filled in: Sappho1. The Password box was empty. I tried a couple of wild guesses, first "Inga" then "Angel." Both came back immediately with notifications that my information was entered incorrectly.

I figured I only had one more chance because Lani would return any second. And also because I wasn't sure how many mistakes AOL allowed you before it locked you out of the system. I'm not a subscriber to the McDonald's of on-line services.

Summoning up everything I knew about Inga was a brief exercise. But not entirely fruitless, because suddenly I recalled the luscious tattoo on her shoulder. For my final shot in the dark I typed in "Cherry," poised my finger over the Enter button, closed my eyes and pushed down.

Yahtzee! I was rewarded with those familiar chimes and that cheerful disembodied voice informing me I had mail. I quickly clicked on old mail and found an entry from 6:34 that morning. The sender was Platinum07.

The message read:

Hey Izzy,

By the time you read this I'll be gone. I can't stress this enough: It's really important that nobody tries to look for me!! Don't call either. I threw away my cell. Pls tell Lani and the crew I mean it. Just let me go.

I'll be in touch when I can. Guess it's time I go full Circle.

Wish you were here. LOL!

One from Pink Floyd (^) and one from the Who—can't explain.

Sorry, dollface.

Love,

A

The laptop wasn't hooked up to a printer, so I read the message again, committing it to memory, and then signed off.

Why would Inga say she had spoken on the phone with Angel when the communication had been by e-mail? The only possibilities I could think of were that she thought a phone call sounded more personal, thus validating her special relationship with Angel. Or else she didn't want the police confiscating her computer. But if that was the case, why hadn't she deleted Angel's message as soon as she read it?

The other thing I puzzled over was how Angel was able to send a message while she was on the lam. If it took a week of lessons for her to master her home entertainment system, I doubted she was carrying around a sophisticated handheld wireless device.

Before I could wrap my mind around either of these issues, Lani came back in the room, her eyes wet and red.

"What's wrong?" I asked.

"She cleaned out the safe," said Lani tearfully. "But she left me this." She held out a piece of paper. It was a green personalized stationery, crowned with angels reclining on a cloud. But these were no cherubs. They were curvaceous vixens from the church of Victoria's Secret.

On the sheet was scrawled:

AV,

Don't know how yet, but I'll be back. Counting on you to take care of things in the meantime, especially my crazy brother.

Love,
A

"What does AV mean?"

"That was her nickname for me. Aloe Vera. Because I could smooth over any situation." Lani began to weep. I plucked a couple of tissues from a box on the desk and offered them to her.

"Why are you upset?" I asked.

"Because this is when she needs me most and I feel like I can't do anything to help her."

I bent at the knee so I was eye to eye with her. I took hold of her arms just below the shoulders. "Look, Lani, for reasons we don't understand, Angel has gone into hiding. There's not much you can do until she resurfaces. For now, I think you need to just trust that she knows what she's doing."

Her head still slightly downcast, Lani looked up at me and nodded.

"Do you know how much money was in that safe?"

"I haven't looked in there in over a year. I would guess at least forty thousand dollars."

Enough for Angel to go underground for a long, long time.

The song titles were piling up. Undercover Angel. That made one from Pink Floyd, one from the Who and one from Alan O'Day.

CHAPTER

25

It was just after nine A.M. and I felt like I had already put in a full day.

During the ride back to the hotel, Stan didn't pry me with questions about what was going on inside the compound. Of course, he probably had better sources than me to rely on.

As I walked through the lobby, a young woman with frosted blond hair hailed me from behind the front desk.

"Mr. McNamara," she called. "There's a package for you."

It was a manila envelope inside of which was the picture of Mike Rouse left for me by Whitey.

I examined it on my way to my room. Mike Rouse had a very handsome Nordic face, framed by sandy blond locks. Rather like Brad Pitt circa *Thelma and Louise.* But the eyes were cold and cruel and there was an arrogant cast to his expression. No real distinguishing marks except for a hipster's soul patch of hair growing like an exclamation point under his lower lip. I don't remember seeing him in any films.

Even though I had been gone a few days, my room hadn't

been tossed again. Reasons to be cheerful. I drank a bottle of Calistoga water from the minibar. Then I called down to room service for a pot of coffee.

After the coffee arrived—tepid but flavorful—I booted up my computer. The thing that struck me about Angel's e-mail is that even though it had obviously been rushed, there weren't any typos. She was fairly precise at the keyboard. Perhaps the one beneficial residue of a strict Catholic education. I gathered her suspension for stomping that big jock in the boys' room wasn't invoked during the year she had typing class.

That made me think the capitalization of "full Circle" in her message was intentional and thus significant. Even without the punctuation, the phrase had set off a vague recollection in my mind. I started poring through sites of Angel's lyrics.

You have to love the Internet. It might prove arduous locating the speeches of Martin Luther King on-line, but there are a plethora of sources containing the words to every vapid pop song ever written. We live in a woolly-bully universe, baby.

I had to go all the way back to Angel's first and arguably best album, *Party Time,* to find what I was looking for. Believe me, that was a painful journey through some of the most trite, airheaded sentiments ever expressed in the English language. Compared to Angel, cheap greeting cards read like Gerard Manley Hopkins.

Seeing her lyrics starkly etched on the screen was a gruesome revelation. Even the naughty bits were boring. It made me shiver to think of the influence this airhead had on legions of young minds.

I don't expect pop lyrics to be intelligent or even original. Not everybody can be Tom Waits. But at the very least, they should be able to summon up a clear mental picture for the listener. Remarkably, as she moved from carnality and materialism on her early albums into what she fancied was the spiritual realm on her more recent work, Angel's lyrics were still all grubby appetite. I want, I want, I want. I wondered if her songs were ghoswritten by the Cookie Monster.

Anyway, there it was, a verse in a song entitled "City Girl": "I been round this island so many times/ I'm like the captain of the Circle Line." The record was as close to a concept album as Angel ever got. All the songs touched in some way on her crusade to vault from being an unknown to becoming a player on the big stage of New York City.

The Circle Line was the sightseeing boat that circumnavigated Manhattan several times a day. I took her statement that "it's time I went full Circle" to mean she was bound for New York.

That struck me as a smart strategy for Angel. She had lived for nearly a decade in the city, so she knew it well. And it was the perfect place to go unnoticed. Osama bin Laden could ride the subway all day and no one would recognize him. New Yorkers have their own problems to deal with.

If she was trying to signal her destination to Inga, I was convinced the message was far too subtle for Angel's dance partner to comprehend. But I got the elliptical reference and that's all I cared about. Ms. Saffron would have to fend for herself.

I sent an e-mail to Platinum07, noting the fact that while we hadn't gotten a chance to get to know one another, Lani would vouch for the fact that I was trustworthy. I asked her to please contact me and assured her I would do anything in my power to help her.

I felt like I was running on empty. A headache was trying to gain purchase in my skull—maybe from reading those atrocious lyrics. Whole clusters of brain cells had probably been wiped out in the process. Despite two cups of coffee, I fell asleep face down atop the mattress cover.

My first sensation when I awoke was the cold little reservoir of drool that had drained from my mouth as I slept. I opened my eyes and looked at the clock. Three-seventeen in the afternoon and I was groggy as hell. I considered calling down to room service for coffee reinforcements. But there are times when caffeine just won't do, when only rock 'n roll will rouse my soul.

When I travel, I always carry a few tracks for just such an occasion. Pretty much any selection from the Allman Brothers' *At Fillmore East* will do the trick. Another favorite is Muddy Waters's "Mannish Boy." I reached into the bottom of my bag for an old favorite that never fails to crank me up: "Fire in the Dry Grass" by Cry of Love. Moments later, I was bouncing on the bed, playing a wicked air guitar.

Thus enlivened, I tried calling Danny at the rehab to see how he was doing. A counselor told me Danny couldn't talk on the phone until he was out of detox in two more days. I asked if he could give me a progress report, explaining that I had brought Danny into the hospital.

"Hard to say," he said. "He seems pretty down, but I've seen a lot worse. Nobody walks around whistling the first couple of days."

I thanked him, hung up and then dialed my sponsor Chris at home in Sinking Springs.

"I can't believe that a couple of days ago I was bragging to you that this was going to be an easy case to crack. Maybe I should steer clear of the prediction business."

"What's going on?" Chris asked.

"Angel has left the building. She may have left the country. The police, the FBI and probably Interpol are looking for my client."

"Yeah, I heard something about that on the radio. But the details were pretty sketchy. What happened?"

I ran through the details of the previous night up through the discovery of Angel's abandoned Suburban.

"Her bodyguard—is that the same Cliff Johnson who was All-Pac 10?" Chris asked.

"You never cease to amaze me," I said. "You follow college football?"

"Only the West Coast teams. Not the whole BCS. Don't forget, a very long time ago, I went to Berkeley. Go, Bears," he said without the concomitant pep that phrase demanded.

I told him how helpful Whitey had been in throwing a spotlight on Mike Rouse as a suspect. I also filled him in on my conversation with Charlie, which raised the possibility that, given the right circumstances, Angel was capable of killing Gentry.

"I suppose," he said dubiously. "But then there's the whole question of motive. What possible reason would she have for killing him in cold blood?"

"I don't know," I admitted. "Maybe he insulted her voice."

"They were strangers. I doubt there's anything he could have said that would make her fly into a rage," Chris said. He was playing devil's advocate, a position he often adopted to help me knock around ideas on thorny cases. "Besides, where's the knife? She stabs Jones, hides the weapon, then comes back to stand over his body? Doesn't make sense."

"None of that matters, Chris," I said. "When she ran from the police today, she might as well have signed a confession. Game, set, match, buddy."

"That's one way to look at it. But it could also confirm what I suggested originally—that she's running from something that scares her worse than the police."

"Like what?"

"I don't know. I guess you're going to have to track her down and find out."

"That's just what I intend to do."

"I gotta tell you—assuming she's headed for New York because she hit the shift key—that's slim pickings, partner."

"Sometimes you have to go with your gut."

"Just make sure no one sticks something sharp in it."

CHAPTER
26

I spent the next hour debating with myself. Sometimes I spend whole days steeped in that noisome pursuit. But this time the committee in my head wasn't heatedly arguing about my intrinsic self-worth, but rather about what course to take.

The problem was, I wasn't sure how much of my future plans I should share with Lani. Ostensibly, since I was working for her, I should tell her everything. But I wasn't convinced all the members of Team Angel were playing for the same side. And nothing I relayed to Lani seemed to stay confidential for long. In fact, as far as I could see, the people around Angel gossiped more than a coked-up restaurant staff.

In the end, I had no choice. To make any progress in New York, I needed the names of Angel's friends in the city, the people she was most likely to contact. But no matter how I arranged my on-line Boolean search, I came up with the same roster of power eliteniks linked to Angel: famous fashion designer, well-connected magazine publisher, Wall

Street mogul, rowdy talk show hostess, former MTV honcha and the like.

That was no help. Angel would have to be crazy to reach out to such high-profile personalities while every cop and cameraman in the free world was hunting for her. And it gave me a headache just thinking about trying to track them down. These were the type of snobby, sheltered people who would never grant me an audience.

Celebrity, wealth and power all reside in the same gated community. The bigger they are, the harder to reach. You'd sooner get ten minutes with the Wizard of Oz than you would with Oprah.

But calling Lani was good because it reminded me of the urgency of the situation. "Have you heard anything?" she asked anxiously as soon as she came on the line.

"No. You?"

"No, and I'm worried to death, Jim. She's been gone all day."

"She said she was going into hiding, Lani," I reminded her. "I don't think you should count on her checking in regularly."

"Oh, Jesus," she sighed.

"But promise me you'll let me know immediately if she does."

"I will," she said. "What's your next move?"

"I'm going to check out of the hotel. There are a few leads I'd like to pursue."

"Like what?"

"For the moment, I'd rather not say. These people are kind of skittish," I lied, "and I don't want to take any chances on them bolting. But I'll be in touch with you every day."

"What if I need to reach you?"

"I'll call you when I land somewhere. Or you can e-mail me."

"How about I give you a cell phone?"

"No, thanks. Listen, Lani, I want to keep track of where

all the pieces on the board are, so will you let me know if Charlie or Inga or Cam leaves town?"

"I'll try, but it's kind of tough to keep tabs on Cam." She paused for a second, then said, "Come to think of it, all three of them are fairly unpredictable."

"I understand. Thanks."

"Anything else?"

"Umm, yeah," I said, trying to feather this request like it was a spur-of-the-moment thought. "Could you put together a list of Angel's friends in New York?"

"You're going to New York?" So much for disguising my intent.

"It's just one line of inquiry I'm considering," I soft-shoed. "I'm playing it by ear for now. But e-mail me those names as soon as you can."

"I'll get right on it."

"And I mean her real friends, Lani, not the people she goes to charity balls with."

"Angel doesn't believe in charity, Jim."

"Right," I said. "Okay, I'll be in touch."

"Please bring our girl back safely," she said before hanging up.

I packed with my usual deliberation. Open duffel bag, jam in possessions. Took less than two minutes. The basketball I left as a gift for the maid.

I considered having Stan drive me out to the airport. At least say goodbye to the guy. But I decided it was more important to keep my travel plans confidential. So I left his beeper with the concierge and hopped on a hotel jitney out to LAX.

I experienced a certain relief as we rolled toward the terminal, the way I used to feel as a teenager on the last afternoon of a summer job. I was glad to be rid of that dank hotel room, glad to be leaving this laminated city.

In my haste to depart, I hadn't made flight reservations,

instead planning on catching the first thing down the runway. That turned out to be an American flight with a layover in Denver. Two claustrophobic thrill rides for the price of one! Imagine my delight.

Passing the newsstand on my way to the gate, I saw that Angel now commanded the front page of every paper available. You could see her image peeking out from the hands of half the people passing by on the concourse. Every waiting lounge looked like an Angel collage as travelers leafed through their newspapers. They might as well have decked the halls with "Wanted" posters. This was going to make blending in rather difficult for our little fugitive.

Waiting for the plane to board, I booted up my computer. The wireless reception was surprisingly clear in the airport. I guess business travelers have clout.

Among the festering spam in my in-box, there was a message from Lani with what she assured me were Angel's "closest and dearest friends" in New York. It was a short list, containing the names of a famous fashion designer, a well-connected magazine publisher, a Wall Street mogul . . . et cetera, et cetera.

CHAPTER 27

All the way from Denver, the considerate soul in front of me had his seat fully reclined, making reading and, let's face it, life itself impossible.

When I hobbled off the plane at LaGuardia, I felt like I had been folded inside a footlocker for three days. After a $35 ride in a cab whose back seat looked like someone had recently undergone an organ transplant in it, I checked into a Sheraton in midtown. The small, stultifying room was generically appointed and the traffic noise seemed louder than it was on the street. Every night I stayed there, it sounded like a fleet of garbage trucks was holding a demolition derby right under my fourth floor window.

I never thought I would be nostalgic for Los Angeles.

Presumably I had beaten Angel to the city. I didn't believe she would take a chance on flying. If one passenger or flight attendant recognized her during the five-hour flight, there would be a posse of federal marshals waiting at the gate when she landed. Too chancy.

If she planned to hook up with one of her famous friends,

however, she would probably notify them she was on her way. So my head start gave me a chance to put some lines in the water.

It took me the better part of a consternating day to get through to the top five boldface names on my list, hours of wheedling and dissembling on the phone, pages of hotel stationery covered with names and numbers as I clawed my way toward my prey.

Not that I actually got to speak with any of them. But in three cases, I got through to their personal assistants. With the fashionista and the gabby TV hostess, there were layers within layers and the best I could do was an assistant to the assistant who promised to pass along the request. That apparently is the ultimate yardstick of success: when your personal assistant is too important to accept phone calls.

For all of them I left the same message: "Please call Jim McNamara. I'm a representative of Lani Ross and I need five minutes of your time." I felt that was vague but still insinuating enough to get my foot in the door.

I also sent another e-mail to Platinum07, telling her I had traveled to New York to find her, promising her the utmost confidentiality and asking her to please allow me to help.

That left me barely enough time to make it to the Happy Hour meeting at my old stomping grounds, the Perry Street AA clubhouse. As I exited the hotel elevator, I saw a device tucked into the phone alcove with a sign explaining that it would allow you to send or receive e-mail in exchange for a credit card or cash.

I had never seen one of these before, but it had all the hallmarks of a franchise. If these machines were installed everywhere—or at least in the L.A. bus terminal—it might explain how Angel had been able to contact Inga with her "full Circle" note.

Sure, Angel might have accomplished the same thing by ducking into a computer café or, for that matter, a public library, most of which offer internet access. Except that particular message had been sent at six-thirty in the morning.

But it got me thinking about how risky it is for a fugitive to log on to the Internet. I had no idea how cyber-savvy the police were or if they monitored e-mail traffic the same way they used to tap phones. A movie scene played out in my head, as the anxious police lieutenant barks, "Just keep him in the chat room for ten more seconds and we'll have his location!"

Jumping on the Seventh Avenue subway, I was surprised to find that tokens had become obsolete since my last trip on public transport. I had to buy a plastic Metro pass. The ground by the turnstiles was littered with dozens of these used-up orange cards. I was having a hard time understanding how this was an improvement on the old system.

When I walked out of the subway station in the West Village, I thought for a moment I had gotten off at the wrong stop. The neighborhood looked like it had been renovated by Martha Stewart. The funky chic atmosphere was gone, replaced by an affluent, prissy splendor that seemed chimerical. Unless you were a trust-fund baby, it was a pretty distressing transformation.

The clubhouse was a sanctuary of stability in a sea of change. It combined, as always, elements of an OTB parlor, a psych ward, an opium den and a Bowery soup kitchen. (Of course, I hadn't been to the Bowery in a while. It was probably wall-to-wall ritzy boutiques and limo towers by now.)

There were only a couple of faces I recognized. When this meeting had been a daily haunt for me, there were a handful of regulars who never missed Happy Hour. They were like the Mt. Rushmore of recovery to me and I assumed they would always be there.

Either they had moved on or I had picked an off day. Not that turnover should surprise me. It's one of the constants of the program. I have to keep reminding myself that change is good.

After the meeting I strolled over to Cooper Union, happily lost in the sidewalk throng. I caught a couple slices of pizza and a grape drink and then hopped the subway back uptown.

There were no FFOA messages waiting when I got back to my room. Nor was I expecting any Famous Friends of Angel to call that night. I had been thoroughly exposed to the rules of power phone when I worked at a record company a few blocks east of the hotel in which I was staying. So I was well aware that it is considered a sign of weakness to return a phone call to a nonsuperior on the same day you receive it. A twenty-four-hour moratorium must be observed. Don't ever forget that, Biff.

But I did have a message from Lani, which I returned. "So," she said, riding the word like she was sliding down a banister, "you're in New York."

"Hi, Lani," I replied, my biorhythm plunging. "How did you get my hotel number?"

"Because you left it with both Danny Falco and Anne Kasky. I had calls from both their offices this afternoon asking if you were legit." Falco and Kasky were, respectively, the publisher and the former MTV executive. "By the way, Jim, are these the people you were afraid would bolt? The 'skittish' ones?"

Okay, that ruse had come around to bite me in the ass. But at least Lani was being playful about it.

"Aww, I'm sorry, Lani," I groveled.

"I just don't see why you would think you have to hide anything from me. That concerns me to no end." Maybe not so playful.

"It won't happen again," I scraped.

"I should hope not. . . . So have you turned up anything?"

"Not yet. How about on your end?"

"We may have to turn the riot hoses on the press corps. They are completely out of control. Also I'm thinking of hiring translators. There are reporters from countries I've never heard of."

"You're at Angel's house?"

"I'm stuck here. The gate is under siege by the media. It's gridlock. The number of camera crews has tripled overnight. They're building a tent city out there. The neighbors are going nuts."

"Have you heard anything from the police?"

"About the tents?"

"No, about Angel."

"They're pulling their hair out, too. LAPD set up a tip line? And when I talked to them two hours ago, they had already received two hundred and thirty calls today with reported sightings of Angel."

"Any of them plausible?"

"Not unless she's hiding at the food court at the Sherman Oaks Galleria. And they told me FBI field offices have received nearly a hundred unsolicited calls. Angie has been spotted everywhere from New Hampshire to Hawaii."

"That girl gets around."

"Amen," said Lani. "So what made you think she's in New York?"

I hesitated. "A hunch," I said. I could hear Lani quietly seething on the other end. Clearly my avowed policy of keeping her informed was not off to a good start. I could tell Lani wanted to rip me. Instead, after a moment, she said with restraint, "I sure hope you're as good as they say you are. Call me tomorrow."

After we hung up, the room felt stuffy. The windows were permanently rigged so I couldn't open them. Everyone in Manhattan is on suicide watch.

But I wanted to get some air. So I left the hotel and walked down Broadway to the crossroads of the world at 42nd Street and then back up the other side of the broad and bustling street, just soaking up that special New York energy.

I didn't see Angel once.

CHAPTER
28

The dance of the diesel elephants outside my window made for a torturous night. I arose early and walked over to the East Side for the Wakeup meeting at Mustard Seed. A big crowd of people in business attire trying to salt away a little serenity before hitting the office.

The speaker was an attractive professional woman in her thirties who told an affecting and picaresque tale of tubing down the river of alcoholism. All these sagas begin differently but end the same way—with the plunge over the waterfall.

In general I don't like going to meetings above 14th Street. There's a little too much one-upsmanship in the rooms. But I love the speakers.

Afterward I stopped at a fancy bakery on Madison Avenue where they served me a blueberry muffin the size of an SUV. I wasn't sure if I should eat it or plant an American flag at its crest. I pictured a harried baker in a doughboy hat and white smock rolling this monstrosity out of the oven in a wheelbarrow.

When I got back to my room there were two messages.

Mr. Falco would like to see me in his office on Fifth Avenue at eleven A.M. and Ms. Kasky could fit me into her schedule at five P.M. RSVP.

I returned those calls and made a few others to fill out my dance card for the afternoon before heading out.

The building read "Falco Publishing," but for most of his career, Danny Falco had held dominion over a single property: *Rock On!* magazine. When he launched it out of a small office in San Francisco, the idea was simple: Treat rock music with the respect it was denied in the mainstream press.

Rock On! was an out-of-the-box hit, assuming the mantle of music industry bible. Because Falco essentially had the field to himself, he got great writers and extraordinary access to the musicians. Turned out he was only interested in the latter.

The magazine was Falco's platinum backstage pass. And once he had that, he ceased to care very much about the product. But he wasn't a groupie, he was a starfucker. At some point, he decided Hollywood was more glamorous than Woodstock. After that, the cover of *Rock On!* was more likely to feature an actor than it was a guitarist. In fact, the mission of the magazine got so lost, you couldn't find it with GPS. It read more like Ka-ching! than Kerrrang!

If rock 'n roll really was dead, I sometimes think *Rock On!* killed it with its careless, mercenary attitude. To no one's surprise, Falco moved the headquarters to New York. Curiously, in all those years no serious rival ever emerged with sufficient funding, even though Falco now seemed to spend all his time in Vail or East Hampton.

Maybe because they weren't willing to play hardball with publishing's bad boy. Magazine rackers, the people who control the placement and display of publications in every outlet across the country, are more mobbed up than any business except waste haulers. And Falco, as he proved over and over again, was willing to get in bed with anyone.

I didn't even read *Rock On!* anymore. Not since Falco hired one of the bright young British editors who flooded our shores a few years ago like the Marielita boat people. Happy Jack turned *Rock On!* into yet another risqué clone of the ubiquitous British lad magazine. Lots of pictures, aggressive T&A, a snarky tone and no writing longer than a caption. When did Benny Hill become tsar of the publishing business?

I was more than prompt for my appointment and I settled into Falco's imperial reception area for what I assumed would be a doctor's-office-length waiting ordeal. To my shock, I barely had time to sit down when Falco's haughty personal aide, a young man with the cheekbones and arrogance of a Ralph Lauren model, beckoned to me, ushering me into the great man's office.

It was like walking into a scene from *I, Claudius*. And that wasn't because of the splendor of Falco's office. Although the space was cathedrallike, with high, vaulted walls and a panoramic window that looked out over the spectacular promenade that was Fifth Avenue north of St. Patrick's Cathedral. The office was laid out on two levels. You entered on the top deck and descended three steps to the inner sanctum by the window.

What gave the room that decadent Roman aura was my welcoming committee. Falco was sitting hunched over on a plush white leather couch to my left. His hedgehog face was deeply tanned, his long hair very slightly, very fastidiously unkempt as if blown by a $1,000 wind. The sleeves on his Oxford shirt were rolled up and he wore cream-colored slacks and brown loafers without socks.

He was intently conferring with the guy to his left, a hatchet-faced man with tortoiseshell glasses and a bespoke suit and tie. Sitting in a high-backed chair, with one leg slung over the arm, was a man with thin, wispy brown hair in full retreat from a head that looked like a balloon with a slow leak. He had on a suit with a quasi-Edwardian cut that looked atrocious to me but I'm sure was the height of fashion. He affected an indifferent air, but he was listening closely to Falco's conversation.

Looking up, Falco said, "Jim, come in. Glad you could make it," in a voice that was both harsh and somewhat froggy. He introduced the spectacled man as his corporate lawyer and balloon-head as the managing editor of *Rock On!*.

No one stood up to greet me or shake my hand. But they all looked at me with the same expression: avaricious yet overfed. I felt like a giant Sloppy Joe sandwich walking into a doberman kennel.

Expecting an audience with Falco, I was surprised by the triple team. I sat in a chair across from the couch. "Let's cut right to the bone," Falco said. "We can offer complete secrecy. No leaks. We'll do a special issue, have it on newsstands three days after the interview.

"You name the terms and conditions, we'll make it happen. But we do want a photographer present. You can okay the pictures before they run. And my reporter says they can put him in a Turkish prison cell for life and he won't give up his First Amendment rights."

The lawyer and the editor laughed at this jibe. I stared blankly, without any idea of what he was talking about.

"So?" he said, spreading his hands and grinning like a dingo. "You don't have any demands? Or did I anticipate everything you walked in the door with?" Convinced that this was the case, he eased back on the couch, grandstanding for his flunkies. They applauded him with flattering smiles. I was speechless.

"What?" he said, sitting forward again. "Is it money? We don't pay for interviews." He held out his hand as if he were expecting me to object. "But . . . these are special circumstances." He winked at his editor, who nodded back. "I've written down a figure," he said, pushing a piece of paper across the glass coffee table between us, "that I think will help defray costs."

They all regarded me expectantly as I picked up the slip of paper. On it was written "$200,000."

I looked at Falco. He squinted at me. "What are you talking about?" I asked.

"What are *you* talking about?" he replied truculently. "That's a handsome offer. You think you can do better? . . . All right, three hundred thousand, and that's it. Only because she's a friend. Do we have a deal?"

"Look," I said, "I don't think we're on the same page. I came here—"

"You're representing Lani, right?" Falco interrupted.

"Yeah, but—"

"We're prepared to go anywhere and do anything to get exclusive access to Angel while she's in hiding. We can set it in motion right now—do the interview this afternoon."

"You don't understand."

Falco turned to the lawyer with a look of puzzlement. "Am I not being clear? I think I am."

"I came here to ask you if you've heard from Angel. I'm trying get in touch with her myself. I'm not negotiating an interview."

All three of them stared at me, dumbfounded. "You have *got* to be shitting me," Falco finally said. Then he began sputtering. "Does anyone . . . Did you . . . Ari!" His aide came buzzing into the office. "Get this guy out of here." he said without expression, his face buried in his hand.

Ari stood over me like a very stern mannequin. When I looked up at him, he widened his eyes, a look that said, *You better get your ass in gear, mister.*

On my way out the door, I heard Falco explode, "I can't believe I helicoptered in for this!"

CHAPTER
29

I don't know which city has more movie screens, New York or Los Angeles. It's probably pretty close. In New York, the projectionists who run these screens are all unionized. I know this because one of the first friends I made in AA was Tony S., who belongs to the union.

But Tony was in the elite arm of the sodality. He didn't set foot in the big cineplexes. He only worked the screening rooms that were sprinkled around midtown, small venues that existed so film critics could see the movies before they opened and write their reviews in advance. While most projectionists were responsible for four or five showings a day, Tony only had one, or at most two. Which left him plenty of time for meetings.

Tony was really generous about inviting friends to these private screenings. He never overdid it. Just one or two pals sitting in fifty-seat theaters that were rarely even a quarter full. The studio publicists who maintained the invitation lists and guarded the door never hassled Tony. At least not anymore.

Movie publicists have a reputation for being nasty and arrogant. I guess it goes to their head that they are entrusted with such important tasks as finding an egg-white omelette for Minnie Driver before *Access Hollywood* arrives. But the queen bitch of the breed was Toby Kahn.

One time she refused entrance to a couple of Tony's friends, launching into a salty diatribe that embarrassed them and embarrassed Tony, who could hear every word up in the booth. It was a crowded nighttime screening of *Patch Adams* and the most influential magazine and newspaper critics were in the house.

A nervous Robin Williams slipped into the back row just after the lights went down because it was an important film for him and he wanted to gauge the critics' reactions. Just before a pivotal scene, the film stopped. The screen went white. Equipment failure, Tony told a frantic Toby when she sprinted into the booth, spitting fire.

By the time the movie continued, twenty minutes later, the mood among the critics had grown mutinous. The guys from *Time* and *Rock On!* actually stormed out and Robin Williams was pacing and muttering to himself out by the coatroom.

No publicist ever turned away a friend of Tony's again.

During the first few months I was getting sober, I worked intermittently. So I went to a lot of afternoon screenings courtesy of Tony. Afterward we'd grab some coffee and then hit a meeting.

At nearly every screening I went to, Dotty Gilbride was in the house. Sometimes we were the only two people watching the film. Dotty was a show biz sensation. The hostess of a popular daytime talk show, she was hailed as the second coming of Mike Douglas. I don't know why that was considered a compliment, but it was.

And she was obviously a movie nut, hitting a screening, sometimes two, after her show taped. Then, as chronicled in the papers, she was at a Broadway opening or concert or some other high-profile Manhattan event every night. On her show and in interviews, the unmarried Dotty got a lot of sentimental mileage out of the baby boy she had just adopted, gushing about all the joy he had brought into her life and how hard it was to be a single mom. But with her schedule, it was hard to figure how she ever saw the kid.

Dotty had been buds with Angel for years, since they starred together in *Boat Gals*. The period comedy, often described as a distaff *Mr. Roberts*, was the only decent credit on either of their Hollywood résumés.

I had called Tony that morning from the hotel. After we caught up for a while, I asked him if by any chance he had a screening scheduled for that day with Ms. Gilbride in attendance.

"You kidding?" he asked. "Does a seal shit on ice?" I took that to be a yes. He gave the time and locale. "You gonna bust her chops?" he inquired. "Please, please, can I watch?"

"You have it in for Dotty?"

"Two-faced bitch. In public she's all kissy face. But as soon as the cameras are off, she terrorizes everyone within shouting distance. She's a mean-spirited bully. I'll like to rip her head off and use her lungs for an ashtray. So you wanna get some coffee after?"

Dotty was at the screening, as advertised. I didn't watch her TV show, but it looked to me like she had gained a lot of weight. She really was starting to resemble the reincarnation of Mike Douglas.

The film that day was a dreadful romantic comedy starring Hugh Grant, a fop who does all his acting with his teeth, his accent and his fretlock. I have seen Cary Grant, Mr. Grant. Cary Grant was an idol of mine. And you, Hugh, are no Cary Grant.

As the credits rolled, I shuffled across my aisle to approach Dotty. The film's mawkish, predictable ending obviously moved her. She was dabbing at tears with a tissue. Then she noisily and lengthily blew her nose.

"Excuse me, Ms. Gilbride?"

An odd crosscurrent of emotions swirled across her flushed face. The warm and open mood the film had fostered in her grappled with the resentment my addressing her had caused. "Jesus!" she exclaimed, holding the tissue a couple of inches from her face as if frozen. "Can't I get two freakin' minutes to myself? Is that too much to ask?" She turned her face toward me, now blank with mock shock.

"I'm sorry for intruding bu—"

"Then why do you do it? You can't wait until the credits end?" They had by now. The lights had come up in the room. I saw Tony's face peering through the window in the booth. "People like you are the reason I can't go out and enjoy a meal in a restaurant." She was angrily gathering up her things—jeroboam of Evian, canister of Cheez Doodles, teddy bear—and stuffing them in her carryall.

"I'm a detective, Ms. Gilbride, working for Lani Ross. We were hoping that Angel might have been in contact with you. We desperately need to find her."

"Yeah, well, I haven't heard from her," she said, rising with some difficulty and charging past me. She stopped a couple of steps up the stairs and scowled back at me. "And you can bet your ass I wouldn't tell you if I had."

"You self-involved cow!" I shouted at her back. She flipped me the bird over her shoulder as she exited. In truth, I wasn't all that upset at the way Dotty treated me. The parting shot was really for Tony's sake, a small repayment for the many hours of cinematic pleasure he had given me.

I looked up at the booth and, sure enough, he was beaming. He held a thumb up to the window.

One insult, two hand gestures. What a difference an index finger makes.

Tony and I chatted for a few minutes and made plans to hook up at a Saturday morning meeting we used to attend together. Outside the building, standing on a parcel of Seventh

Avenue that used to be known as Tin Pan Alley, I had the distinct feeling I was being watched.

Shaking it off, I headed downtown to meet Anne Kasky. She had become a legend in the TV business by "fixing" MTV. The channel was doing great at reaching its twelve-to-twenty-four-year-old demographic. The problem was the kids weren't sticking around long enough.

Kasky, who rose quickly through the MTV ranks after years in advertising, insisted that it was because MTV's programming staple, music videos, gave kids a convenient excuse to punch the remote every three minutes. Sick of the new Jay-Z video? Let's see what's on Comedy Central. Her solution was to gradually replace videos with more traditional and longer fare—half-hour series like *Road Rules* and *Cribs*

It worked. So what if she turned one of the only original outlets on cable into a tackier version of TBS? Average viewing time rose from seventeen minutes to twenty-four. Because of that slim but significant jump, Kasky was regarded as the Moses of broadcasting.

Unfortunately, she believed her press. A couple of years ago she tried to use her reputation to leverage a new contract out of the craggy and parsimonious head of MTV's parent company. His counteroffer? Clean out your desk.

So now Kasky hired herself out as a consultant. That's an executive euphemism for being unemployed. Her office was in Penn Tower, a couple of floors above CNN's New York bureau. Whatever time I had banked that morning with my immediate admittance to Falco's office, I squandered while waiting in Kasky's reception area. Judging by how quiet it was, I doubted she was too busy to see me. I think it was a standard freezing-out period to prove how important she was.

When she did come out to retrieve me, she was all smiles. Kasky had given up the hip, black outfits that were her trademark at MTV. She was wearing a blue pantsuit from the

Hillary Clinton collection. Her hair, once chopped and frosted, was now a brassy brown permed helmet.

"So how have you been?" she asked, pointing me to a chair in front of her desk, which was unblemished by any paper. We had had dealings about three years prior when one of the channel's most prominent on-air personalities vanished. Foul play was suspected. I tracked him down two days later in New Orleans in the middle of a week-long booze and coke bender.

It wasn't a difficult case. Turned out his new intern had also gone missing. No one at MTV really cared about her disappearance, but I had a talk with her roommate. She told me the missing girl, who had recently graduated from Tulane with a wild reputation as a party girl, had called her that morning from the Big Easy.

By the end of the day, I had found them, barricaded in a hotel room in the French Quarter. Your basic trace and retrieve. I have to say, though, that the matching panties and bra Mr. Cool was wearing when I came through the door were a bit of a surprise.

"I'm well, Anne. Thank you. How about you?"

"So this whole business with Angel is insane, huh?" she interjected, almost before I had finished speaking. "I'm counting on you to give me the inside dope."

"The thing is—"

"Did she really kill that guy? Of course not, right? I mean, it's ludicrous. But they charged her, so they must have something. How strong is their case? And why in the world did she run off like this? What is that girl *thinking*?"

When she took a breath, I tried to plow through some answers, roughly in order. But everything I told her resulted in a new torrent of questions. Finally I just stopped speaking and when she wound down, I said, "Look, Anne, the thing is we were hoping she might have contacted you, asked you to shelter her."

"Really? No, she didn't. Do you really think she might? Is

that what Lani thinks is going to happen? Did Angel mention me or something before she took off?"

Clearly this was a dead end. Kasky was pumping me for every shred of information she could extract. I didn't know if this came under the old knowledge-is-power heading or if she was just squeezing me for gossip that would make her the most popular dinner guest on Park Avenue that weekend. Maybe it amounted to the same thing.

As I excused myself, she was still winging questions at me. "What does Emmett make of all this? Do you know if Mordecai is in the country? There's a rumor he flew into Los Angeles the night she took off."

Waiting for the elevator, I decided to abort this line of inquiry. Although I had been looking forward to stalking Tomasa Galbana, the glitzy designer. But only because I wanted to see if she looked the same up close as she did in her pictures: like the missing sister of Johnny and Edgar Winter.

Questioning Angel's celebrity chums was a waste of time. These people lived in convex universes with themselves at the center. Nothing could enter their orbit unless it benefited them. They were no more capable of sacrificing for another than a jellyfish is of pole-vaulting.

Out on Eighth Avenue, I felt again as if someone were watching me. I stopped and scanned the sea of humanity surging around me. Might have never spotted him either, if it wasn't for that stupid hat that made him look like Weird Al Yankovic doing a spoof of *The Maltese Falcon*. There, across the street, the only person not moving in the taxi line behind Penn Station, was Bruno Volpe.

I started to stroll north and as soon as the traffic light on 33rd Street turned red, I sprinted across the street toward Volpe. He took off running into the massive train station behind him. I followed down a flight of stairs onto the main concourse.

Another person might have lost me in the crowd, but

Volpe's hat was like a beacon. I spotted him halfway across the room, passing under the electronic schedule board. The problem was the rush-hour mob was so thick I couldn't run through them. The Amtrak customers didn't scare me, but Amtrak shared the facility with the LIRR. And those battle-hardened Long Island commuters would stomp you without spilling a single kernel from their mounded popcorn bags.

Seeing that I couldn't make up ground while following him, I decided to outflank him, going left around the Metroliner waiting lounge while he went right. When he reached the stairs leading up to Madison Square Garden, still looking over his shoulder every few steps, I was waiting.

I considered yoking him as he passed, but ever since seeing Volpe in his furry birthday suit, I preferred to keep physical contact with him to a minimum. So I stepped into his path, forcing him to an abrupt halt.

"What the hell are you doing, Bruno?"

"My job." He nearly spat the words.

"Your job is following me?"

"Listen, shrimp boat, I've got the inside track on Angel. I'm just making sure you don't screw this up for me."

"Right. When did you fly into New York, Bruno?"

"Does Disney tell Dreamworks?"

Hadn't heard that one before. I looked at him, shaking my head. "Look, it's only fair we take turns. I'll shadow you tomorrow."

"Fuck you. We'll see who gets his hands on Angel first." With that, he turned around and waddled back toward Eighth Avenue.

At least we had another song title to throw on the barbie. This time it was Elvis Costello. "Watching the Detectives."

I was still smiling as he disappeared into the jostling tide of commuters. Turning back, my eye caught a striking-looking woman in a tight fur-trimmed red coat across the esplanade. It was Inga Saffron, avoiding my gaze and trying to act inconspicuous in front of a Krispy Kremes. The problem was not too many women with supermodel looks frequented that establishment.

About ten yards beyond her, a gigantic black man in a white arctic parka was attempting to hide his bulk behind an automatic ticketing machine. It was about as effective as a fig leaf. Oops had joined the party.

I laughed out loud. Why shouldn't I? I was obviously the most popular guy in Manhattan.

I waved them both over. Oops looked a little sheepish at being spotted. Inga was defiant.

"Well, well," I said when they were standing in front of me. "Is this it, or are you two just part of a charter flight from Los Angeles?"

Oops and Inga looked at each other. "I didn't know he was here until just now," she said.

"Ain't nobody following me," he said.

"All right, kids," I said. "Come with me."

I led them to a Starbucks on 34th Street. I ordered a red-eye, Oops got a vanilla steamer and two Rice Krispy bars and Inga demanded a "skinny decaf double latte." We settled into some easy chairs so I could debrief them.

"When did you fly in, Inga?"

"Last night on the red-eye."

"Oops?"

"Same."

"You weren't on my flight," said Inga.

"Yeah, I was," he responded. "You just never looked back in coach."

"How did you know where I was staying?" I asked.

"Lani told me," said Oops.

"I got the name of your hotel from Joanna," Inga said. "You know I can think of three much better hotels less than two blocks from that dump you're staying in."

"I bet. Why did you fly in, Oops?"

"'Cause I'm worried about her," he said, shaking his head. "Angel's tough, but I guess I'm used to keeping an eye on her."

"How about you, Inga?"

"I'm worried about her too."

Oops tilted down his chin and stared at Inga from under his eyebrows. He looked like a teacher listening to a career C student delivering her latest alibi for why her paper wasn't ready. Inga took in his expression.

"What?" she said, affronted. "I can't be concerned about a friend?"

Oops's chin dipped a little lower.

"Okay, I need to find her," she said. "Every cent I have is invested in the club Angel and I are opening in Miami in two months. And I want to make sure she doesn't skip out on the deal."

"It might be time for you to think about finding a new partner," I suggested.

"Maybe I will," she said, flashing her eyes. "Right after I get a check from Angel to cover the two payments she conveniently forgot."

"All right, guys, this is silly," I said. "I don't have a solid lead on Angel, just a feeling she's in the city somewhere. But I don't need you following me around while I look. It's boring as hell for you and it's only going to slow me down."

"Let me go with you," Oops pleaded. "I can help."

"Not yet, you can't. I promise I'll bring you in when I find something definite. But I don't need a posse right now. Just give me numbers where I can reach both of you and I'll call when I have something worth telling you."

They scowled at me, but I think they were both secretly relieved at being taken off surveillance duty. It wasn't a fit job for either one of them.

I passed them the spiral notebook I always carry and a Bic pen. "I'm staying with a lady friend in Brooklyn," Oops said as he jotted down his cell.

"I'm floating," said Inga, as she took the book from him. "But if she contacts anyone on the club scene, I'll find her before you will." She smirked at me.

"Listen, Inga, I've been meaning to ask you: Why did you tell everyone Angel called you the morning she disappeared?"

"Because she did."

"No, she e-mailed you. Why the lie?"

"How do you know that?" she asked accusingly.

I shrugged with what I hoped was an air of mystery.

She waited a moment to see if I'd answer, then said, "Fine. It's simple, really. I didn't want the police confiscating my computer. I do a lot of business on that thing."

I nodded at her explanation. "All right, thanks for chasing me around town. I'll be in touch."

We all got up to go our separate ways. I know because I lingered until I was sure they had both departed. Funniest thing, though. As I walked east on 34th Street, I had the most distinct feeling I was still being watched.

CHAPTER
30

One more rock to turn over. A luxurious one.

Back at the hotel, I called the L'Auberge, following the voice prompts to dial the guard shack. The L'Auberge was another of those magnificent old-money apartment buildings that loom over Central Park West like castles above the Rhine. It was three blocks south of the Dakota, where John Lennon lived and died. Angel was the building's most celebrated resident.

"Street entry," a man answered wearily.

I put a little subway gravel in my voice for this conversation. "Yeah, this is Tim Ryan over at Fleet Messenger. Who am I speaking with?"

"Rudy Pancoski."

"Hey, Rudy. Listen, I'm sorry to bug you, but my ass is in the wringer. One of my messengers just came back with a package from your building that he says was undeliverable."

"Who's it for?"

"It's just says 'Angel.' But it's from the Recording Industry Association, so I assume it's the singer."

"Yeah, she lives here."

"Damn! Why's it always happen quitting time on Friday?"

"No package came here and I been on since four."

"I think he went around to the service entrance. It says Angel, apartment 9A at the L'Auberge."

"Nah, she's in 1402."

"Aww, shit. Still, you'd think they'd sign for that even with the wrong apartment."

"Some people love to bust chops."

"Tell me about it. Fourteen-oh-two," I said slowly as if I were inscribing the number on a label. "I bet that's a hell of a view from up there."

"Actually the 01 units have the better view, 'cause you get the park and the skyline. That's why they sell for more. With the 02 units, you just get the park."

"Out of my price range. My main problem is finding someone to hustle this package back over there."

"For what it's worth, I don't think she's around."

"Guess she's got her hands full in California. You believe that shit?"

"My daughter is a fan. She says . . ." he paused. "I gotta go. There's a limo pulling up."

"All right, thanks for your help, bud."

After another noisy night of big-truck orchestra, I met Tony for our meeting in the basement of a church where Norman Vincent Peale once preached. We went to a Greek diner afterward and caught up. He did most of the talking because he had most of the drama. Tony had gotten married and divorced since I moved out of the city and an older brother had died of cancer. But he had gone through it all without drinking.

On a whim, I took a bus uptown, assuming correctly that on a weekend it wouldn't be an inch-by-inch crawl through traffic. The view was certainly better than on the subway. Hopping off at 57th Street, I provisioned myself first at Hammacher Schlemmer, (an expense account indulgence), then at a deli, before heading into Central Park.

Even though the day was raw, the sun was out and the park was alive with people strolling or exercising. After hiking around for a while, I found my vantage point and set up camp on a rocky rise about seven hundred yards in from Central Park West.

It offered an ideal sightline on the upper floors of the L'Auberge. I quickly calculated my target. Based on Rudy's information, Angel's apartment was thirteen floors up, on the north side of the building. As I set out my folding chair, telescoping spy glass and tripod, I reflected on what a bizarre and powerful superstition it is not to designate a thirteenth floor in buildings.

It would have been a pleasant enough way to wile away an afternoon—noshing on pastrami and practicing my J-J-J-Jimmy Stewart imitation as I pretended I was in *Rear Window*. But at least once an hour a female jogger would spot me and shout, "Pervert!" as she ran past on the path below. That was distinctly unpleasant.

How did they know I wasn't bird-watching? People just assume the worst these days. Of course, I couldn't get too self-righteous. I was a P-P-Peeping Tom. So I slipped on the earphones, cranked up my Aiwa and listened to a couple of Weezer CDs. They're my musical Prozac.

The view was uneventful. A heavyset Hispanic woman in a maid's uniform would occasionally cross through the rooms. There was a burst of activity when a guy in a serge maintenance outfit came in with a squeegee and began cleaning the five window casings facing the park. The maid stood nearby the whole time, peering at him suspiciously.

But no sign of Angel. I didn't really expect to see her parading around her apartment, but I wanted to rule it out. The sun was beginning to sink beyond the Hudson and Weezer's "Don't Let Go" was playing when I realized that everything I had done in New York so far was a waste of time.

Angel wasn't going to take sanctuary in her dee-luxe crib

or rely on her recently acquired upscale friends. "Full Circle" implied that she was going back to her roots—the haunts and pals she had when she first came to the city as a poor, scrabbling show biz hafta-be. She wasn't just going back East; she was, in effect, going back in time.

Packing in my surveillance, I headed back to my hotel. There are a bunch of things New York does better than anyplace else in the world. One of them is pizza. I dropped off my stuff and went for a couple of slices at Ray's Original.

Then, back in my room, I went on-line to leaf through the pop star's back pages.

Curious thing. Her first marriage, to a DJ named Frankie Flores, seemed to be recognized only retroactively. The first mentions I could find of it dated from her wedding to Cam Akers, when it was universally noted that this was Ms. Chiavone's second marriage.

Prior to that, there simply was no acknowledgment of her union with Flores. At least none that I could find. The chances of a coarse nineteen-year-old kid fresh from Michigan getting a wedding notice in the *New York Times* are pretty slim.

Back then, Frankie was more famous than she was, a dashing habitué of Manhattan nightlife. Her first album hadn't been released. The two were often mentioned together, usually as clubmates. The context wasn't even explicitly romantic.

The only reference I could find in clips from that era that hinted at a more serious relationship was a throwaway item in Cindy Adams's gossip column: "Little birdies are telling me that Manhattan's hottest DJ Frankie Flores and his favorite chanteuse Angel may be more than friends. Much more, children."

It was time to have a little chat with Angel's phantom husband.

CHAPTER 31

People in the music business don't keep banker's hours, so I waited until nearly lunch hour before walking over to the record label that had employed me during my worst drug abuses. I was still grateful to the company because they paid for my stay in rehab. But I don't imagine those warm feelings are mutual.

At least no alarms went off when I walked in the towering lobby. Most office buildings in Manhattan favor these awe-inspiring entry points to remind you that the corporation is far more powerful than any individual. At my request, the lobby receptionist called up to Steve Hicks's office and issued me a visitor's pass.

On the twenty-ninth floor, I was about to repeat my business to another receptionist when she said, "Steve said to go right back, Mr. McNamara. He said you know the way."

I certainly did. For more than two years, I had the office adjoining Steve's. He spent a lot more time in his, however.

Walking down the corridor, I was surprised at how little things had changed. I had expected to see a cavalcade of kids sitting behind those desks. Certainly there was turnover, but the median age of the label's executives was older than when I worked there. That's the problem with baby boomers: They don't know how to let go gracefully.

The maturing staff could also explain why the music business was going through such horrendous times. It wasn't Grokster and KaZaa and all those download services. The simple fact is you can't pick music for fifteen-year-olds with forty-five-year-old ears.

I wasn't about to mention any of this to Steve. Besides, when I stuck my head in his office and he rose from behind a desk piled high with a Lego-like stack of CDs, I could see he was basically the same—wiry body, fidgety energy and a boyish face topped off with a long, layered mane of hair.

"I can't *believe* you have the nerve to show your face around here again," he said, smiling broadly.

"I'm a little surprised they let me up."

Steve gave me a hug and gestured me to a chair. "It's great to see you, man. How long's it been?"

"Since that release party you invited me to for Primus."

Steve looked up at the ceiling and executed a toy sign of the cross. "Let us give thanks. That nasty band is putting my beautiful baby through preschool," he said.

"Whoa! You have a kid?"

"Oh yeah," he said, snatching a framed photo off his desk and bringing it over for me to admire. "Wife, kid, house in Jersey—as Zorba the Greek put it, 'the full catastrophe.'"

"She's beautiful, Steve."

He looked down at the picture and grinned. Then he said, "So I hear you're working for America's Most Wanted."

"Well, I'm on retainer. But I'm still not on speaking terms with Angel."

"Come on," he said dubiously. "You can tell your old pal Steve. Where are you hiding her?"

I looked around. "You promise not to tell?"

He made a fuller sign of the cross motion. I leaned in and spoke softly, "I have her stashed up at Grant's Tomb."

He gave me a slow wink and nod, to let me know this information would remain entre nous. "Seriously, you need some help with something?"

"I'm trying to track down an old-school DJ named Frankie Flores."

"Flores? Doesn't ring a bell with me, but I was never plugged into that scene. You should talk to Archie. Archie Pacheco. He's our urban guy. Maybe he can hook you up." He held up an index finger and reached for his phone, punching in a few numbers. "You're there. Cool. It's Steve." He listened and chuckled to the response. "Listen, I got a good friend in my office, Jim McNamara. He used to work here. He needs to tap into your expertise. Can I send him by?" He listened again. "Yeah, that's the guy." Archie's comment again made him laugh. "He's pretty well behaved these days. . . . All right. I'm sending him down now. Later." He hung up. "You are still a legend in this office, man. Archie said, 'Isn't that the guy who ripped the platinum records off Tommy's wall and hocked them for drugs?'" Tommy was the then head of the label. I had indeed paid a late-night visit to his corner office.

"Yeah, except I couldn't pry them off. I only succeeded in gouging a big hole in the wall."

"Your exploits have grown over time. Anyway, Archie is five doors down," he said, pointing south. "Maybe, when you're done, we could go out and get some lunch."

"I'd like that," I said, backing into the hall. "See you in a minute."

"Hey," Archie said, reaching to turn down his bouncing stereo as I leaned into his doorway. He was a squat, sharply dressed young guy with inky black hair on an ovoid head. "Come in." He held out his hand. "Nice to meet you."

"You too," I said shaking. "Look, I don't want to take up

your time. I'm trying to track down a DJ named Frankie Flores who was big several years ago."

"Wow," he said. "Frankie Champagne Flores. You are really taking me back. I haven't heard his name in ages."

"Know where I can find him?"

"No idea," he said. "The scene changes so rapidly in New York. Frankie is back in the Paleolithic era. I don't think he's worked anywhere in the past decade—at least nowhere respectable."

"You have any idea where I could find him?"

"Have you tried the gay clubs?"

"No, why?"

He slid his head away from me an inch, as if amazed at my stupidity. We stared at each other mutely for several seconds while the import of what he was saying sank in. "You should talk to Harvey French. He has a small record store on the East Side," Archie said, scribbling on a memo pad. "Harvey is a clearinghouse for all the old disco-dolly DJs."

"Thanks," I said, taking the directions from Archie. "Appreciate it." I sort of stumbled out of his office, still trying to digest his take on Frankie.

Lunch with Steve was a blast. Although I had been in a tailspin most of the time I worked there, we had still enjoyed some wild times in the company of some truly eccentric characters. I laughed really hard at some of the yarns because, even though I had been in on the jokes, I still didn't know the punch lines.

As Steve dredged up story after story of our escapades together, I was hearing several of them for the first time. I was so often in a blackout in those days. According to Steve, I was fairly functional through it all, fooling almost everyone until my physical deterioration became impossible to ignore.

It was late afternoon by the time I made it over to Harvey's record store. Technically it wasn't on the East Side; it was beneath it. About thirty yards from the platform for the subway shuttle that ran between Grand Central and Times Square. That meant I had to purchase another Metro card to get access.

The store was essentially a kiosk. Two long aisles running parallel through a space about as big as a subway car. In one section, CDs; in the other, vinyl. Harvey's selections ran toward dance remixes, rarities and truly vintage pop. The name of the store was a play on both the inventory and the location: Buried Treasures.

Incense burned, keeping the subway's more acrid aromas at bay. A few customers were seriously rifling through the stacks of music, but there were more pairs of men scattered in the aisles, chatting casually. Hanging speakers punched out a song with a heady, mincing beat. I think it was the Pet Shop Boys.

The atmosphere reminded me of an Algerian boîte. Of course, that might have had something to do with Harvey, who leaned over the counter by the far wall in an Arabesque robe and a red fez. With his dark, pocked complexion and piercing eyes, he reminded me of the actor F. Murray Abraham, with a bigger nose and a thicker girth.

"Is this your place?" I asked.

He gave me a slow, skeptical appraisal. "Yes, it is, sugarplum. What can I do for you?" His deep voice was like a fine-grained sandpaper.

"I come to you as a supplicant. I'm trying to find someone. I'm told that only you may know of his whereabouts."

"Hmm," he purred, closing his eyes and luxuriating in the flattery. Then his eyes snapped open and he shouted over my shoulder, "Take that record out of your bag this instant." A guy with long ragged hair in an Army jacket began to protest. Harvey lifted the flap on the counter and made as if to emerge from behind his partition. The man quickly reached into his canvas shoulder bag, pulled out an album and stuck it back in the rack. Then he skulked from the store, staring back angrily at Harvey.

"If you want to shoplift Streisand, for God's sake," he said rhetorically, "do it at Tower." Then he closed the flap and returned his attention to me. "Now whom did you say you were looking for?"

"Frankie Flores."

"Ah, Champagne," Harvey said langorously. "What a scrumptious man he was. And a great DJ. I can't tell you how alive this city was when he was spinning in the clubs. Oh, those were the days!" Harvey inhaled deeply through his nose as if he were in a field of flowers instead of a rancid subterranean pit.

I let him savor the moment before asking, "Do you know where I might find him?"

"Why are you looking for him?"

"I have a few questions regarding the disappearance of Angel."

Harvey's eyes rolled up. His disgust was palpable. "That brazen bitch. I warned him against getting involved with her. We all did."

"Did they really get married?"

"Oh, yes. Except for the slutty bride, it was a lovely ceremony. His friends made sure of that. She had no friends."

"Help me with this, Harvey. May I call you Harvey?" He twirled his head and blinked in assent. "Why would Frankie marry her?"

His brow flung up. "Good question. She obviously played on his sympathy."

"And why would she marry Frankie, knowing he was gay?"

"Every diva has to marry a gay man. It's a rite of passage. Although I think Liza has overdone it at this point." He shifted his attention to a customer, ringing up a sale, chatting with him about the Bobby Darin album he had chosen. When he turned back, he said, "Make no mistake, that little vixen Angel was a diva from the moment she stepped off the Greyhound. All she needed was fans to adore her."

"Why are divas attracted to gay men?" I asked, only because I found him to be a fascinating social theorist.

"Because we're the kindest creatures on earth. And because we understand and appreciate the temperament."

"Do you know where Frankie is?"

"I hear he's in Brooklyn. I haven't seen the boy in years and years. I don't do Brooklyn."

"Anything else that might help me find him?"

"No. But if I were you, I wouldn't put off your safari."

"Why is that?"

"The last I heard, Frankie was registered with God's Love We Deliver."

"What's that?"

"They bring food and company to late-stage AIDS patients."

CHAPTER
32

That afternoon I checked into a new hotel down by Battery Park. It was closer to Brooklyn. Plus I figured the maritime noise from the harbor couldn't be more intrusive than midtown traffic mayhem. I know it's the City That Never Sleeps, but I've never heard an insomniac make such a racket.

When I called Lani's office, she came on the line almost immediately.

"Any word?" she asked anxiously.

"Not yet."

"I need you to find Angel now, Jim. This whole thing has spun way out of control." I could hear the near-desperation in her voice.

"Understood."

"I need your cooperation."

"Got it."

"You report to me. You're not some free agent running around on your own."

"Right."

"So what are you pursuing now?"

"I can't say."

"You . . ." Lani dropped the phone, she was so flustered. But what was I going to tell her? My best lead was Frankie Flores, but I didn't want that going out on the Angel grapevine. I was determined to hold this card close to my chest. But at the same time, I didn't want to lie to Lani.

When she came back on, she was on the headset. "I hope you're not trying to be funny, Jim, because this is hardly the time for levity. The police have been embarrassed because of their ongoing inability to find one of the most famous women in America. Did you see *Saturday Night Live*? It was the opening skit. Letterman and Leno are teeing off on it every night.

"As a consequence, they are tightening the screws out here like crazy. They've virtually impounded Angel's house and I hear they're working on a warrant for this office. So I would appreciate getting a straight answer from you."

"I am being straight with you, Lani. I think I'm closing in, but for a variety of reasons I can't give you specifics right now. You're going to have to trust me. I'll give you a more detailed report as soon as I can."

"You better call Oops. He told me if you don't he will, quote, track your ass down and beat it like Rodney King."

"All right, I'll call him."

She fumed for a few more seconds and then I could almost hear her mood evanescing. "I meant to ask you," she said in a far more jovial tone, "what in the world did you do to Dotty Gilbride? She called here totally ballistic on Friday night."

"It didn't amount to much. I was just shaking some trees, seeing what fell out."

"Well, you definitely rattled hers. I have never heard her so pissed off—and believe me, that's saying something. Did you really call her a cow?"

"I meant it in the nicest way."

"Well, let's see," Lani said slyly. "I heard from Dotty, and Anne Kasky, and a very irate Danny Falco. So when you say you're closing in, that must mean either Tomasa Galbana or Philip Shiff. Am I right?"

"I can't say, Lani," I said glumly, as if she had foreseen my next move. If she wanted to believe I was pursuing the last two people on her list, the designer and the financier, that was fine with me. Maybe then Bruno Volpe and whoever else had been dogging me around could spend the next few days bouncing between the fashion district and Wall Street while I was over in Brooklyn.

She chuckled triumphantly. "By the way did you see the news? *Hot Chick* is on top of the best-seller list in its first week of release. And Emmett has decided to rush out a new greatest hits package."

"How many greatest hits collections does that woman already have?"

"Five. Early and late years. Love songs. And dance hits, volumes I and II. This one will collect all the number-one songs."

"How many of those are there?"

"Enough to make a very nice package. Oh, and I've heard from nearly two dozen producers who want to make quickie TV movies. Strike while the iron is molten."

"You sure you want me to find her?" I asked. "This murder-suspect thing is turning out to be a real shot in the arm for her career."

"Very funny, Jim."

Actually, I hadn't been kidding.

After hanging up, I called my sponsor Chris, leaving a message that said it was nothing important and I would try back another time. Then I dialed the administrative offices for God's Love We Deliver.

"Good evening," I said. "I'm trying to locate one of your clients."

"We don't use that word," a man said snippily. "And our records are confidential."

"I see," I said. "My name is Josh Hausman. I'm a legal aide with the law firm of Vogel Craddock and Stern here in New York. A gentleman named Frank Flores was a party in a class-action suit against a large insurance carrier that refused to compensate HIV patients. We recently won that suit. A check for Mr. Flores was sent to the address we had on file for him by certified mail. It was returned as 'Party Unknown. No Forwarding Address.'"

"How do you know he belongs to God's Love?"

"I don't. There's a note scribbled in the file that mentions your service. I don't even know who wrote it. But you're my last hope. If I can't get a valid address for Mr. Flores, his portion goes back in the settlement pool for the surviving plaintiffs. Three of the men who brought the suit are already deceased."

There was a pause. Then the man said grumpily, "Hold on." A moment later he was back. "It's 673 Bergen Street in Brooklyn. I don't have the zip."

"That's all right. I can get that. Thanks so much."

The weather had gotten cold when I walked outside. Maybe it was because the hotel was close to the water. But I didn't have far to walk. That's the great thing about New York. You can find a decent restaurant on just about every block—and an AA meeting. Later I tried to watch *Curb Your Enthusiasm* on HBO. Every one of those episodes looks like a rerun to me. I fell asleep as Larry was painting himself into yet another corner.

The next morning I took the subway out to Brooklyn. Frankie lived in the no-man's-land between Fort Greene and Park Slope. The address was a house in a row of brownstones that looked as soft and rounded as sand castles. An elderly woman with stringy hair, a knobby head and bad posture answered the bell. A smell like cooked cabbage pushed out the door behind her.

"Frankie Flores?"

She pointed down. "He lives in the garden apartment."

I walked back down the steps of the stoop. The entrance to the ground-floor lodgings was under the stairs. I couldn't get access to the door because it was recessed behind a slatted metal gate that was locked. So I knocked on the window.

I was considering my options—leave a note, stake the place out, have a chat with the landlady—when the curtain bunched and an eye peered out at me from a small opening. For a moment, I thought I had found the apartment of Gollum, the cave-dwelling creature from the *Lord of the Rings* movies. The pupil was milky and purblind, set in a sunken orb surrounded by skin that was rough and mottled. Then the curtain was released and the eye vanished.

Long seconds later, the front door opened. A hunched stick figure swayed in the shadows.

"Frankie Flores?"

"What do you want?" asked a voice, creaky with congestion.

"I'm Jim McNamara. I work for Lani Ross. Do you know her?"

"Yes," he said.

"I'm trying to find Angel to help her. I apologize for intruding, but I would really appreciate it if I could have five minutes of your time. I've come a long way."

There was a long pause. "Give me a minute." The door closed.

I needed the time to compose myself. Frankie's appearance had shaken me. His look went beyond gaunt, all the way to spectral. His skin, which sagged off his frame, was spotted with ugly purple lesions. His hair had grown patchy and hung off his skull like wilted lettuce. I've seen people ravaged by cancer, but this was worse. It was as if Death had already claimed him but neglected to collect him, leaving Flores as a wraith stuck between two worlds.

He reemerged a couple of minutes later, unlocked the deadbolt on the gate and said, "Come in." I followed him as he made his way with excruciating deliberateness down a short corridor and through another door that led into his low-ceilinged apartment. It was a three-room layout. There was a living room/kitchenette, a small den and, toward the front, what I assumed was the bedroom. I couldn't tell for sure because the door was closed.

The walls were decorated with posters of various art exhibits. There were pictures all around of Flores in his prime, a strikingly handsome Latino. I wouldn't have recognized him. One of the pictures on top of the credenza in the den was a wedding shot of Flores and a teenage Angel. She was dressed in rather plain, all-white bridal ware. Both the groom and the bride were smiling happily.

Out the back windows of the apartment, hemmed in on all sides by tall fencing, was a small rectangle of grass on which sat two rusting lawn chairs. A strip of tilled soil formed a perimeter around the grass.

Frankie lowered himself into an armchair and began coughing. If coughs can be wracking and feeble at the same time, his were. I sat on a stool by the Formica counter that formed the boundary to the kitchenette. On the counter was a frightening array of orange prescription bottles with white childproof caps. I didn't recognize most of the medications I was looking at, but Frankie's name was on all the labels.

"Sorry to keep you waiting," he said when he recovered. He jerked his chin at the closed bedroom door. "My roommate's real sick too. He's very self-conscious about his appearance."

"Don't worry about it. I don't want to disrupt your routine. I just have a few questions."

"I doubt I'll be much help. But fire away."

"Have you heard from Angel?"

"No."

"When was the last time you two spoke?"

"You know the police already asked me all these questions. Two detectives came over from the precinct."

"The police want to lock Angel up. I'm trying to help her."

"How?"

"How what?"

"What will you do for her? Help her flee the country? Get her plastic surgery? Seems to me she don't have many options."

"I don't believe she killed anyone. If I can talk to her and find out what happened, maybe I can make sure the right person gets arrested."

He nodded. "My birthday."

"What?"

"Last June. My birthday. That's the last time I think we spoke."

"What is your relationship like?"

"It's—what's the word?—cordial. We talk every few months. She helps me out with my medicine. Otherwise I couldn't make it. But I haven't heard from her since all the trouble started."

"You sure? I'm convinced this is where she was headed."

He visibly sagged. "Sorry," he murmured, "can't help you." Then he was swept up in another coughing jag that seemed to completely wipe him out.

"Okay, I'm going to leave you my card just in case Angel does get in touch," I said, reaching in my shirt pocket and writing down the number for the hotel. "Please have her call me. Or if you think of someone else from your mutual past that Angel would likely turn to, please let me know."

He flicked his hand at me, to indicate he had heard me.

"Thank you," I said. "God bless." I let myself out, closing the doors behind me and pulling the gate shut. Walking toward Flatbush Avenue, I felt terribly sad for Frankie.

I wondered why he struggled to hang on to such an agonizing existence. If I were in that position, I don't think I would bother with popping dozens of pills to squeeze out another day. I believe I would want it to be over.

But I wasn't in his position. Maybe when you get sick like that, the survival instinct gets more and more stubborn.

When life goes through your house flicking off the lights, maybe you start appreciating those rooms, however cramped, where the lamps are still on.

I stopped by a bodega on the corner of Bergen and looked back. A clear view of Frankie's stoop. Since I was in Brooklyn, I decided to call Oops.

He picked up on the third ring. "Yo," he growled in a lazy voice that reminded me of Shaq.

"Hey, Oops. It's Jim. You still want to help?"

CHAPTER
33

That afternoon I went running along the promenade by the harbor. A pair of round-trips thoroughly winded me, but I pushed myself to double the distance. I ran so hard I couldn't see straight and then I kept going. At the end, hunched over with my palms on my thighs, gasping for air, I looked up at the Statue of Liberty. The old girl looked pretty hot.

Okay, I thought, what is going on here? Exercising myself into a lather, totally inappropriate sexual response—maybe my own survival instinct had slipped its leash, desperate to prove that however sick others might be, my sap was still flowing.

After showering, I took a taxi over to the Perry Street clubhouse for Happy Hour. The guy sharing told a harrowing tale of violence and incarceration under the lash of alcohol. It reminded me that I have a terminal disease, just as surely as Frankie. But mine can be held in remission through the application of a few simple spiritual principles. I put a

lavish five bucks in the collection basket when it went
around and said a silent prayer of thanks.

I walked east to a Lebanese restaurant for dinner and then
all the way north to Union Square for a movie. From the
eight films playing, I chose a legal thriller only because it
had the closest starting time. Basically I was just trying to
distract myself. My recollection of the plot was that honest
attorney Morgan Freeman, after being dealt several indigni-
ties by Machiavellian millionaire Gene Hackman, was about
to get revenge. I left before the worm turned.

There were several messages when I got back to my hotel.
The one that grabbed my attention was from Oops. "You
were right," he said. "She was there. But I lost her."

I called him right back.

"You saw her?" I asked.

"Yeah, she came out the door under the stairs about an
hour and a half ago. Where you been, man? She had on some
funky-ass disguise, but I knew right away it was her, just
from the way she move . . . specially once she spotted me
and started running. No doubt it was Angel. I spent a lot of
time chasing behind her ass in Central Park."

I had given Oops the Bergen Street address, asking him to
watch the place from a safe distance.

"She got away?"

"Uh-huh. Ain't my fault. I'm in shape, but one thing that
girl could always do is run. She could keep up with Marion
Jones, man. Plus, she had about a fifty-yard head start. She
cut across a schoolyard, then through some apartment project. When I come out on Flatbush Avenue, huffing and puff-
ing, she was gone. I'm sorry, McNamara."

"I should have stayed with you, scoped out the place together."

"Not much point now that we flushed her. She ain't coming back there."

"Why do you say that?"

"She had a backpack on. Plus how upset she got when she spotted me."

I exhaled, fluttering my lips.

"What are we gonna do now?" he asked.

"I don't know yet," I said. "I'll call you, Oops."

"Make sure you do," he said. "I'm sorry, man."

"Not your fault."

I walked back over to the subway. Then had to wait nearly fifteen minutes for a Brooklyn-bound train. Rapid transit, my ass.

Arriving at the brownstone, I bounded up the stairs. Might as well start with management. The landlady answered the door clutching her housecoat to her throat.

"Sorry to bother you, ma'am." She just stared at me all goggle-eyed like a character from a William Booth cartoon. I suspect the landlady had taken a few snorts. "Does Frankie have a roommate?"

"Have you seen that apartment? Of course not. It's too small."

"I thought I heard someone in the other room when I was talking to him this morning."

"His sister's been visiting him. First time any of his family came around. I guess Frank isn't long for this world."

I was already on my way down the stairs. "Thanks," I said over my shoulder.

The curtain wasn't drawn in the front room. And that wasn't the only change. Frank came right to the door when I knocked on the window. He unlocked the gate, a smile on his cadaverous face. "Come on in," he said. "She said you'd be back."

His movements seemed more fluid too. Either he had sprung back in the last few hours or else he had been working me this morning. I guess if illness is the last card left in your hand, you play it as often as you can.

" 'She' meaning Angel?" I said.

"Yes." He sat in the same chair. I stood.

"She was in that bedroom the whole time?" I pointed toward the now-open door.

He nodded. I slapped my forehead. As Homer Simpson would say, "D'oh!"

"I'm sorry I misled you. But Angel doesn't want to be found."

"Where is she now?"

He shrugged. "She split. Wouldn't tell me where she was going. We cried in each other's arms before she said goodbye."

I groaned.

"Part of you knew she was here, right?"

"I suspected it, yeah."

"May I ask what tipped you off?"

"Your roommate story. If he was as sick as you, where was his cache of pills? They should be right on the counter. Like a pair of old newlyweds with their coffee mugs hanging by the cupboard together."

"I had to make up something. I couldn't say I had a roommate who wouldn't come out because he was shy."

"So how is she, Frankie?"

"Really good. More like the girl I knew than she's been in years. I mean, she got so ridiculously famous that I don't think even she could stand herself. Don't get me wrong. She's really scared. But she's alive in a way she hasn't been in a long time. She's living on nerve again, the way she did when she first came to New York."

"What is she scared of?"

"Of being caught. That terrifies her. She was really pissed when you turned up at the door. I won't tell you some of the names she called you."

"How long has she been here?"

"Three days."

"Shit. Why doesn't she turn herself in?"

"She says she has to stay hidden until she gets something worked out."

"Gets what worked out?"

"She wouldn't say."

I looked at him closely, trying to gauge his honesty. He returned my stare.

"How is she able to move around without being noticed by everyone?"

"She's always been good at disguise." He smiled at some private joke. "I bet you could pass her on the sidewalk and not know her." I thought of her video "Masks," where she morphed into about thirty different characters. They weren't exactly *Mission: Impossible*–caliber transformations. Every one of them looked like Angel playing dress-up to me. And now she didn't have the help of a battery of professional makeup artists.

"What's the disguise?"

He hesitated. "Look, I believe you're here to help Angel. But I need your promise that you won't tell any of this to the police."

"You have my word."

"Wig, glasses, fake teeth—it's good."

"What color wig?"

"Black. Shoulder-length."

I pictured Angel slinking around like the femme fatale in a Brian DePalma film.

"Did she tell you about the murder?"

"Very little," he said. "Could you pass me that water?" He gestured at a plastic bottle on the counter, which I handed to him. His hand was almost diaphanous. "She said talking about it is what got her in this mess to start with. So she was going to keep her mouth shut till she got it fixed."

"It?" I inquired.

He shrugged. "She said the less I know, the safer I'll be."

"Safe from what?"

"I don't know. But I don't think it's the police who are really scaring Angel."

"Has she been in touch with anyone, Frankie? Did she call Lani or her brother or anyone?"

"I think she'd like to wring her brother's neck at this point. But no, she didn't use the phone once the whole time she was here. I'm positive, because I never leave the house anymore."

"This is really important, Frankie. Do you know where she went? Did she give you any clue?"

"She said something about desperate times, desperate measures. And that this time, nobody was going to find her."

Not bad, I thought. I could work with that.

CHAPTER
34

By the time I got back to the hotel, it was after midnight. I stood at the window in my room, staring out over the hazy harbor. For a symbol of welcome, the Statue of Liberty looked awfully forbidding. I was just relieved she no longer resembled a green Heidi Klum.

I brushed my teeth, undressed, said my prayers and tucked myself in for a good night's sleep. I was in no hurry. I could even go back the next day and check out the end of that Morgan Freeman movie if I wanted to.

Sure, Angel had several hours' head start. But she couldn't use her driver's license, credit cards or any form of picture ID. That severely limited the travel options open to her. I felt reasonably certain that she was headed back to the town in Michigan where she had grown up.

I thought of Danny parked by his father's grave. For Angel, the last location anybody would think to look for her was her hometown, the place she had always been so desperate to distance herself from. It made the perfect sanctuary.

But I wasn't rushing because I knew I could get there a lot faster than she could.

My biggest challenge at the moment was how to deal with Lani. Having already stretched her patience to the snapping point, I couldn't very well take off again without accounting for my plans.

After wrestling with this problem for a few minutes, I decided the best approach might be the obvious one: Tell Lani the truth, that I didn't trust her to keep a secret. Honesty wasn't always the best policy, but it was certainly the simplest and cleanest.

It worried me that it always seemed to take me so long to embrace it. I guess the conniving junkie part of my brain was still very much alive. After seven years in recovery, I still sometimes lied even when I gained no advantage from doing so. Just out of some perverse reflex.

I got back on my knees for a supplementary prayer in the dark, petitioning God to make me honest in all my affairs. Boy, would that resolve be tested over the next few days.

That night I dreamed I was crashing through a forest when I came across a wounded deer with big brown eyes. I knew somehow that there were hunters in the vicinity wanting to finish the job. I tried to help the doe, but every time I approached her she limped away painfully. I felt distinctly powerless to protect her, but she kept looking at me imploringly with those eyes. It was anguishing.

Hours later, I awoke in a daze, like my head was full of Styrofoam. It's the same blank sensation you get when you sleep in a room with the heat turned up too high. I sat up in bed and scratched my head. That didn't help. I rumbled over to the bathroom and washed my face. Twice. Then I shaved. None of that helped either. It's the only time I can ever remember wishing I had some Aqua Velva to slap on my face.

I was going to need help just to get to the Starbucks around the corner. If ever a morning called for a musical wake-up siren, this was it. I pulled out an oldie and cranked it up: "Give Me Just a Little More Time" by the Chairmen of the Board. Now we were cooking with propane.

With that jump-start, I made it out to the elevators. Twenty minutes later, nearing the bottom of a Vente add-shot latte, I was starting to feel almost human. Close enough, anyway, to page my way backward through a *New York Post*. I always read the *Post* back to front, moving from TV features, to sports, to entertainment news, to gossip, to what passes for news in that shameless tabloid.

There were three stories on Angel, including one about an overweight psychic from New Jersey who claimed to have had a vision. Angel, she ventured, had been kidnapped by a Mideastern oil sheikh who had been hopelessly smitten with the pop star for years. Finally, unable to live without her, he had dispatched a team of ruthless thugees to abduct her. Gentry Jones had died in the first attempt, then they returned, spiriting Angel off to the sheikh's desert palace on his private jet. The *Post* illustrated this bulletin with a doctored photo of Angel in gauzy harem garb.

There wasn't enough latte in the world to get me through a copy of the *New York Times* that morning.

Back in my room, I booted up my computer and checked my in-box. Nothing from Platinum07, but there was a message from Chris:

Hey boss,

Sorry I missed you yesterday. Incredible as this may seem, your misanthropic sponsor was at a concert. Leon Redbone and Roy Book Binder. Two guys I've always wanted to see and here they were on a double bill right down the road in Reading. I figured it must be kismet, right? So I went with some friends from work. Great show.

I've been thinking about you. How could I not? I

heard a guy say once at a meeting, "I may not be much but I'm all I think about." That's the way the press is with Angel. She *is* the news. But at least I haven't read anything about the body count going up. So I assume you're safe.

Call me when you get a chance. And remember, wherever you go, whatever you do, ask yourself: WWJWD.

Peace out,
Chris

Those closing initials made me smile. They were a gag that went back to the beginning of my relationship with Chris. Soon after I asked him to be my sponsor, I pressed him into service as a career counselor. He asked that nefariously logical question: "What would you like to do?" Not having any answer for that, I tried a line of bullshit. "I would just like to make something in my lifetime as cool as 'Shotgun' by Junior Walker and the All-Stars."

From then on, whenever I was going to a job interview, Chris would remind me, "When in doubt, ask yourself: WWJWD."

It stood for What Would Junior Walker Do? That loosely translated as: Carry yourself with rectitude and soulfulness. Or maybe it meant shoot him fore he run. Either way, I didn't get many job offers.

With a smattering of keystrokes and a brace of mouse clicks, I soon took care of the rest of my business on-line. A search for "Angel AND hometown" yielded Grand Blanc, Michigan. A map search located it a few miles south of Flint. A travel service secured me an aisle seat on an afternoon flight to Detroit and a rented Ford Taurus. You don't want to drive a foreign car in Motor City.

I had a few phone calls to make before I left for La-

Guardia. First Lani. An assistant informed me that she wasn't in the office yet but that she would patch me through to her cell.

Lani came on the line, faint but bubbling. "I wish you could see this, Jim. Someone has put up a billboard on Sunset that says, 'Angel, please come home,' with that picture of her on a divan like Cleopatra. Everyone assumes the label paid for it, but we had nothing to do with it. And half the girls in the city are wearing these T-shirts that say 'To Forgive is Divine' on the front and 'Pardon Angel' on the back."

"That's great, Lani."

"Where are you, restless wanderer?"

"Still in New York. Listen, Lani, I wanted to clear the air with you. The reason I haven't been telling you stuff is because everything I say to you seems to leak."

"What are you talking about?" she asked affrontedly.

"The day after you found out I was in New York, Bruno Volpe was here, following me around town."

"Well, I sure didn't tell him."

"You're the only one who knew where I was. Maybe someone in your office?"

"On Volpe's payroll? No. No, I'm quite sure of it. My people are trustworthy."

"You told Oops where I was staying."

"Oops is family."

"How about Stan? He seemed pretty indiscriminate about who he sold information to."

"Stan the driver? He's not on staff. He's just a guy we use from time to time. And he hasn't been around the office since you left."

"Then maybe Volpe is tapping your phone."

"Are you serious? He works for *us*. He's not spying on our business."

"Do you know anything about this guy, Lani? He's tapped

more phones than J. Edgar Hoover. Reporters, lawyers, clients, you name it."

"Shit. I'm going to call Emmett and have the lines swept. If this is true, I'll have Volpe's ass."

"I just wanted you to know that's why I've hesitated to tell you things."

"I totally understand. What should we do?"

"I don't know. Get a secure line somehow, because I need to talk to you. I'll call you later today, okay?"

"Does that mean . . . Oh, Christ, never mind. Make sure you call me. I'll get this worked out. 'Bye."

Next I called Oops and told him my travel plans.

"Grand Blanc? Where the fuck's that at?"

"North and west of Detroit."

"What time is that flight?"

I told him.

"Shit. I can't make it. I promised the lady I'm staying with I'd meet her at her office for lunch. I think she want to prove to her friends that she didn't make me up. Where you gonna be staying?"

"I don't know. Some motel right in town. I doubt there are too many. I'll be driving a rented Taurus."

"All right, I'll catch up with you."

"Do you think I need to call Inga Saffron?"

"I don't think she's around anymore. I heard she flew down to Miami."

"Okay, see you soon, Oops."

"Right. In Grand Funk fucking Michigan," he said gruffly.

It was the usual joyride out to Detroit. I hadn't had lunch, so when the cart creaked by I ordered and paid for an execrable sandwich from the flight attendant.

I can't believe they charge for airline food. That's like a firing squad making you pay for the bullets.

We landed at Detroit Metro in what I think is the handsomest facility in the country and certainly the best named:

McNamara Terminal. Once I snagged my car, I got a little turned around on the highways, heading for Detroit when I should have been bearing toward Ann Arbor. But once I got settled on 23 North, it was a straight shot up to Grand Blanc.

As I drove, I hit the Scan button on the radio and after one rotation around the dial, I settled on a classical station, wishing there was a passenger with me to admire my sophisticated and mature taste. The signal was weak and as the miles dropped away, the precise interplay of a string quartet faded and a sound like water rushing through a cave bubbled out of the speakers, waxing and waning.

I considered changing the station, but for some reason the pattern of static intrigued me. It was as if a message were trying to break through from an unimaginable distance away. I thought of whales singing beneath the polar ice. Ever so gradually, the noise formed into notes. Even before the song was entirely distinct, I recognized it—or maybe I wished it into being. It was Jimi Hendrix's "Voodoo Child," the stormy apex of one of the greatest albums ever recorded, *Electric Ladyland*. This was a very good omen indeed.

I rolled into Grand Blanc and cruised around aimlessly, just getting the lay of the land. It was a sprawling blue-collar town with a dismal downtown, a Wal-Mart, some beat-looking supermarkets, and an equal serving of churches, donut shops and taverns. If there was a ritzy side of the tracks, I never saw it.

But I had found something more precious than gold—a good radio station. It was a listener-supported station broadcasting from the college campus in East Lansing. And a delightfully unpredictable mix of songs poured forth. After Hendrix, it was Adrian Belew, Chris Whitley, Bob Marley, Paul Brady, the Bodeans and Kings of Leon.

As I listened I pondered how to proceed. From my research I knew that Angel had three siblings: Charlie and two older sisters—Joan, who was a housewife and mother of four in Kalamazoo, and Susan, about whom nothing was ever written.

I wanted to see if the singer had any relatives left in Grand Blanc, but I didn't want to trigger anyone's radar by asking around town about the Chiavones. Used to be it was easy to find a phone directory. There was one in the phone booth on every other corner. But cell phones had changed that. I had to go into a twenty-four-hour convenience store and ask the sparsely mustachioed Indian gentleman behind the counter for a phone book.

There was one Chiavone listed: Charles at 1261 North Goodrich Lane. I jotted down the address and number and bought a local map. Goodrich was four blocks over, running roughly parallel to the main drag. All the streets in Grand Blanc were north or south depending on their relationship to Huron Avenue, the town's central thoroughfare.

Things got pretty sparse as you drove north on Goodrich. Near Huron, the houses were stacked one after the other and well kept. But several blocks down they began to spread out. The properties weren't bigger. There were just more vacant lots. Like the weed-filled, can-choked one I parked in front of to look across at 1261.

I'm not sure how to describe the architectural style: perhaps early appliance box. The structure was a squat un-adorned rectangle. The exterior was a particle-board veneer-tinted and striped to suggest hardwood. A fringe of tarpaper stuck out from under the roof that sloped slightly toward the building's rear in order to facilitate drainage. A rippled green plastic awning, supported by two poles, jutted out from the front door. Faded business flyers flapped in the aluminum molding of the screen. There was a cinder parking area, big enough only for one car. A couple of scraggly bushes flanked the entrance and a tall hedge ran about ten yards behind the building, marking the border of this half lot.

I don't know how Charlie could ever leave this behind for a mansion in California.

The other houses on the block were inhabited. Most were illuminated only by the lambent ghost light of a TV flickering on the ground floor. The lights were off at 1261 and nobody was home. In fact, considering the building's stale air of neglect, I would have been willing to wager that no one had been home in quite some time.

It's a long bus ride from Grand Blanc to Manhattan. And an even longer one back.

I could wait. I turned up the radio.

CHAPTER
35

At the end of a Rufus Wainwright song, I turned off the engine and walked down the street to a pay phone in front of a soft ice cream shed that had a sign out front promising it would reopen in the spring. Considering the lousy location, I didn't know why it would bother.

I called Lani's office collect.

"I'm glad you called," she said, "I've been waiting around to hear from you. I can't believe you were right. My phone lines were bugged!"

"Have you spoken to Volpe?"

"Not yet. I called his office and his assistant said he's 'in the field.' I'm going to get that asshole's license pulled. I guarantee you that."

Good luck, I thought. If Volpe was still in operation after all the unethical and downright illegal crap he had pulled, he had to be untouchable. Probably had some dirt on the state regulator.

"Anyway, the line has been swept so we can speak freely," she said.

"Actually, I'm outside at a pay phone. Let me check into a motel and call you back. Can you wait another half hour?"

"Sure."

I walked back to the car, drove to the corner and went left four blocks to Main Street. Another left and there were the welcoming lights of the Pioneer Motel. The rhomboid sign out front, bordered by light bulbs, reminded me of the old-style casino signboards from Vegas. It was probably the same vintage. But instead of Steve Lawrence and Eydie Gorme, it boasted HBO and Complimentary Breakfast.

Pulling in the lot, I saw only one car, a blue Chevy sedan, parked in front of the stacked rooms. When I walked into the office, a thin Indian man with a disproportionately large head was behind the counter beaming at me. "Hello, sir," he enthused. The smell of hot cooking oil emanated from the unit beyond the desk.

"Hello. I need a room."

"Of course. Are you traveling alone?"

"I am."

"Very good," he said, smiling more broadly. Either he preferred solo guests or he was trying to keep me from feeling lonely. "How long will you be staying with us?"

"I'm not sure. My plans are in flux."

"Not a problem. Let's see," he said, turning to the full rack of room keys behind him and, after some deliberation, choosing one from the second floor. I filled out a guest form while he took the imprint of my credit card. I had to go back outside to get the plate off my rental.

"We offer a continental breakfast in the lounge starting at six A.M. If there is anything I can do to make your stay more pleasant, please ask me."

I thanked him, grabbed my bags out of the car and headed up to my room. It was standard economy class: a standing-room-only bathroom with faded tiles, a steel bar to hang up clothes, a wall mirror, a counter with a TV atop it and two double beds with lumpy mattresses and threadbare coverlets.

A long window faced the balcony and parking lot, decked with a dusty orange curtain made out of a crinkly material found only in these motels. Under the window, a white plastic heating unit was built into the wall. I turned it on and called Lani.

"Are we cool to talk now?" she asked first thing.

"I hope so."

"All this secrecy has been driving me nuts," she said. "Where are you?"

"In the finest accommodations Grand Blanc, Michigan, has to offer."

"Oh, my God! That's the last place I would expect her to go. She hasn't set foot in that town in twenty years."

"I think that's the point."

"Is Angel there? Have you seen her?"

"Not yet. But I'm pretty sure this is where she's headed. Oops is joining me here. But I need some background information from you, Lani."

"Shoot."

"Does Angel have any relatives still here in Grand Blanc?"

She took a few seconds to consider that. "I don't think so. Since she brought Charlie out to live with her, I think her sister Joan is the only one still living in Michigan and she's . . ." Lani paused, her search engine whirring away.

"In Kalamazoo?"

"Right."

"How about her father? He's still alive, isn't he?"

"Angel bought him a condo down in St. Pete. You couldn't budge him out of there with dynamite."

"Does he maybe have family here in Grand Blanc?"

"No. If I recall right, Tony was an orphan. He has no family except the kids. And his new wife. He remarried a couple of years ago."

"How about Angel's mother? Was she from around here?"

"Indiana, I think. She died when Angel was so young, she never really got to know her mom's family."

"What about the other sister?"

"Susan? She and Angel are estranged. I think she's down in Florida somewhere too. But I'm not sure. They haven't talked in a long, long time."

"Is there anyone else you've heard her mention from her hometown? Anyone she stays in touch with—a girlfriend, a neighbor, a teacher?"

"No. She really sealed herself off from her past when she came to New York. Started over. Invented herself from the ground up."

That meant I would be concentrating my attention on Charlie's chicken shack.

"Have you been keeping an eye on the people I asked you about?"

"Uhh," she droned guiltily. "Inga took off without telling anyone. I think she went to Miami. Cam, I have no idea. He certainly hasn't been seen out in public recently. He could be out of town. Charlie is still here. He's in and out of Angel's house all day long. I think he enjoys the attention he gets at the gate. Katz too. He makes an appearance at Angel's house every day for no other reason than to get photographed."

"If you paid me a thousand dollars an hour to drive out to your house," I said, "I'd be a regular visitor too."

"So what's the plan?"

"I think I beat Angel here, so I'm going to sit on Charlie's house. I can't think of where else she might go. Why *does* he keep a house here?"

"It was on the market for a while, but there were no buyers. He had it priced at about five times what it was worth, figuring someone would pay a fortune for the onetime home of Angel's brother. He's not too good at gauging value. So he kept it. Still goes up there for a week every summer to show off his exalted Hollywood status."

"All right, Lani. For the time being, I need you to make sure you don't mention to *anyone* where I am, okay?"

"Mum's the word. But promise me you'll give me regular updates."

"I don't know if that's a good idea."

"Why not?"

"Volpe may not be the only one eavesdropping on you. The police might be monitoring your office phone logs. So I don't want to call you a lot from here. What I'd like to do is call you when I find her or if I leave town. I'll probably keep it vague. But you'll understand what I mean."

"I hope it's soon."

Looking around my dismal hotel room, I said, "Me too."

I walked down to the office with the idea of getting a restaurant recommendation. Though I interrupted his dinner, the owner was delighted to see me. I got the sense he was starving for company because with absolutely no prodding on my part, his life story came pouring out.

His name was Roger Napur. Actually, Roger was an Americanized approximation of the name he had been born with in Gujarat. Nine years ago, Roger had come over to live and work with his older brother in Chicago. He had bought this hotel two months before and was planning many improvements.

"So what brings you to Grand Blanc, Mr. McNamara?" he said with a friendly smile.

"Please call me Jim."

"All right. Jim."

"I'm looking for an old friend."

"Ahhh, I wish you luck."

"Thank you, Roger," I said, heading for the door.

"You want an alarm clock, Jim?" he called after me.

"No, thanks. You happen to have a coffeemaker for the room?" I figured I could hunt down some passable French Roast grind the next day.

Roger looked crestfallen at the request. "Free continental breakfast," he said, pointing with his thumb at the adjoining, now dark, lounge area.

"Right. Of course. Goodnight."

"Goodnight."

Very early in our conversation, I had decided that a guy new to town who cooked all his own meals in an alcove behind his office probably wasn't the most reliable guide to local cuisine. From the vending machine I got some crackers that were roughly the same color as the curtains in my room and ate them in bed, watching HBO. *The Divine Secrets of the Ya-Ya Sisterhood* was on. I dozed off wondering how Sandra Bullock ever became a movie star.

Breakfast wasn't a whole lot more exciting than dinner. The spread in the lounge consisted of four plain bagels, a smattering of donuts of questionable vintage and a plastic container that dispensed Froot Loops or cornflakes.

The only people in the room were an elderly couple at a far table who glared at me when I came in. Maybe they were just guilty because they had hoarded all the decent pastries. I settled for some watery OJ and a cup and a half of bitter coffee.

Hopping into my Taurus, I swung by Chez Chiavone. Still boarded up. I considered driving up to Saginaw, because it had once been mentioned in a Simon & Garfunkel song and I figured I would never be this close again.

But Michigan is a bigass state. I made it only as far as Flint, where I spent most of the day hanging around a mall I spotted from Dort Highway. Bought a pair of button-up jeans, CDs by Fountains of Wayne and the Tindersticks and a copy of Pete Dexter's latest novel. At the risk of offending my hosteler Roger, I also got some good coffee and a five-cup brewer.

Late in the afternoon, I drove back to the Pioneer. I took a short nap and walked over to Charlie's. Roger waved at me as I passed the office.

Turning onto North Goodrich Lane, I stopped in my tracks. No question about it. The lights were on in 1261.

Grand Blanc's most famous native daughter had finally come home.

CHAPTER 36

Charlie's abode was so ramshackle that from the door I could hear someone rattling around inside. I pulled open the screen and knocked. The interior instantly went quiet. After a long pause, a voice intoned, "Who's there?"

I had to laugh. It was so obviously a woman doing a gruff imitation of a man. "It's Jim McNamara," I said, careful not to announce her name on the street. "Could I please talk to you?"

There was some muffled cursing and then the sound of glass breaking. A few seconds later, something flitted past the opaque yellow porthole window set in the door. Whatever it was, was moving too fast for me to see. Perhaps Angel doing a flyby to confirm my identity.

Then the door slowly swung open. "God*damn*it," she said in a cadence like John Henry driving a railroad tie. I could hear her, but I couldn't see her. "Get inside," she demanded. I spotted her peering at me through the crack from behind the door.

I stepped inside and she slammed the door behind me.

She scowled at me as if deciding on the most painful possible way to end my worthless life. And I didn't like the look of that baseball bat she was gripping either. But at least I had been promoted to eye-contact status with her.

"What is your fucking deal, McNamara? I've had thongs that didn't stick to my ass as close as you."

I wasn't sure how to respond to that. Turning around and stepping over the broken remnants of a wall mirror whose wicker frame had fallen to the ground, she walked toward the kitchen.

She looked more like a demented battle-ax than the planet's best-selling female star. Her face was caked with dark powder. Her hair was matted to her head from days of being confined under a wig. She had on billowy black slacks with purple polka dots, a baggy gray hooded sweatshirt and hiking boots, all accessorized with a Louisville Slugger.

"You're really pissing me off. Do you know how long ago I got here?" she asked over her shoulder. "Twenty minutes ago. Jesus!"

"I like what you've done with the place."

The manse consisted of three and a half rooms: a super efficiency kitchen like the kind you see on a boat, the living room, which I was standing in, and at the other end a bedroom with one corner partitioned off as a bathroom. The facilities amounted to a coffin-sized shower and toilet. Suddenly my hotel room was looking pretty high-class.

The furnishings were minimal: a small table in the kitchen with a toaster-sized radio and Angel's wig flung on top and plastic upholstered chairs on either side, a spavined La-Z-Boy, a molting couch and a TV with foil-wrapped rabbit ears in the living room. The bed consisted of a plywood board on top of four cinder blocks. It was topped with an ultra-thin mattress and a sleeping bag. The pillows looked like used tea bags. I've seen Porta Pottis that were more comfortably appointed.

But the reason I made the disparaging crack is that since the last time anyone had been here, squirrels had apparently taken up residence—squirrels with an obvious vendetta against Charlie. Empty black walnut shells and small animal turds littered the floor. Any and all foodstuffs had been pulled out of the cabinet, their packaging shredded like chunky confetti.

"Yeah, well, Charlie isn't really my brother," she said, throwing herself in one of the kitchen chairs. "He was raised by bears."

"Messy bears," I muttered as I walked in and stood by the small stove. "Are you all right, Angel?"

"Do I look all right?" she asked. "I just spent nineteen hours on a bus that stopped at every buttfuck town in Ohio. I'm going to be smelling the disinfectant from that bathroom until the day I die and I couldn't sleep the whole time because I didn't want to wake up with state troopers standing over my seat. Then no sooner do I walk in the door than you show up. Did I mention you're really starting to annoy me?"

"You mentioned. But I'm here to protect you."

She looked up. "You? Protect me? That is so hilarious. Has it ever occurred to you that every time you track me down like this, you are leading the person I'm trying to get away from right to me?"

"You mean Mike Rouse? Why is he terrorizing you, Angel?"

The mention of Rouse's name coming out of my mouth palpably shocked her. It also confirmed for me that I had correctly pegged the killer.

Angel recovered quickly. "Oh, no! You don't get to ask the questions, buddy boy. Not until you've answered mine."

"Fine. After you."

"How did you trace me to Frankie's apartment in Brooklyn?"

"Lucky break. I saw your message to Inga on her laptop."

"My message to Inga? I didn't tell her where I was going."

"You said 'full Circle.' From that I deduced New York."

"You're kidding me! It never fails. Every time I try to be poetic, I get screwed."

No way was I going to touch that one.

"Based on *that* you flew three thousand miles? You really are a romantic."

I did my best Hugh Grant-bashful imitation.

"But how do you get from New York to Frankie's? It took me two days to find him and I was married to the guy."

"Frankie was sort of last-ditch. I tried your apartment, I checked with Dotty Gilbride and Anne Kasky and Danny . . ." I stopped because she was laughing. "What's so funny?"

"Those are people I might call if I was trying to get my picture in *Vanity Fair*. But the idea of someone hiding from the police going to that crowd for help . . ." She began laughing again. But instead of sharing her amusement I felt sad for her, because for the first time, I realized how alone Angel really was. I knew I could call anyone in my AA home group at three in the morning and they would put me up. No questions asked.

I guess you get the friends you don't pay for.

Collecting herself, Angel said, "Was it you who posted Oops outside Frankie's apartment?"

I nodded. "Yeah, he's on his way here—to Grand Blanc."

"Terrific. Did it ever occur to you that I'm trying to fly under the radar? Now there's going to be three people walking in and out of Charlie's shithole. You think the neighbors might notice that?"

"I'm staying over at the Pioneer Motel."

"Lucky you. That's where I lost my cherry, by the way. Fourteen years old. With the high school music teacher. Nothing but happy memories in this town." Her eyes floated up to the ceiling and she shook her head, exasperated. "But how did you know to come here?" A horrified look came over her face. "You didn't call Charlie and ask him about Grand Blanc, did you?"

I shook my head. "Haven't talked to him. It was something you said to Frankie."

"You went back to his apartment?" I nodded. "I knew you would," she said, pleased. "What was it I said?"

"Something about going where no one could find you."

She looked at me warily. "That got you here? You're starting to freak me out."

"I just try to think like you think," I said modestly.

"You don't even know me!"

"I admit that makes it more challenging. But," I said, making a theatrical flourish with my hands, "look at the results."

"How did you find Charlie's place?"

"He's in the book."

"That's the first thing you've said that makes sense. All right, last but certainly not least on the hit parade: What do you know about Mike Rouse?"

"You're the only one who knows everything, Angel. I'm still trying to put the pieces together. Now it's my turn to ask questions." She shrugged. "Let's start by ruling out the obvious: Did you kill Gentry Jones?"

"Yeah, right. I hacked up that kid, a complete stranger to me. That Ninja training just took over."

"Why are you running?"

She looked down at her hands. "Ask another question."

"Bullshit, Angel. I'm here and I'm not leaving. It's time for you to level with me."

She saw my level of anger and raised me a hundred. "Fuck you. I'm this close to walking out that door. And this time I guarantee you won't find me again."

"All right, you didn't do it but you know who did."

"Hell, yes," she said emphatically. "I was standing three feet away."

"It was Rouse, right? So why don't you turn him in?"

She turned to me with a look that would have been intimidating if it weren't vitiated by her weariness. She was like a fighting robot with her batteries running down. "We need to get something straight first. You work for me, right?"

"I do."

"That means you follow my directions. No cowboy shit because you think you know better. You do what I say, understood?"

"I won't take any actions without discussing them with you." We looked at each other. "So Rouse killed Gentry?"

"Yes," she said with flat resignation.

"Why? I don't get the connection. How do you know a lowlife like Rouse?"

"He's Cam's buddy."

"Why would your ex befriend a wackjob like Rouse?"

She blew out air like a surfacing whale. "Cam is an absolute fanatic about researching roles. He can't play a character; he has to be him. When he played a fishing captain in *Atlantic Drift,* he spent a month at sea on a trawler off Alaska before shooting started. When he was a disabled teacher in *Class Action*—"

"I know the wheelchair story," I interrupted. "I've read all about Cam's legendary preparation."

"Yeah, well, Mike has become an important resource for Cam. Cam thinks the guy gives him an inside line on psychos and convicts—which seems to be mostly the roles Cam gets lately. Apparently, Rouse had a particularly nasty childhood."

"Jesus," I said.

"Jesus got nothing to do with it, bud. It's just what Cam needs—hanging around with someone crazier and more violent than he already is."

"How did you get mixed up in this?"

"Believe it or not, Cam and I have been getting along pretty good the last few months. Then Rouse starts feeding him this caveman crap about the way I run around with other men, I'm making a fool of him. That a real man wouldn't let me step all over him like this."

"Did you point out you've been divorced for several years?"

"There's no talking sense to Cam at this point. The guy has no boundaries; that's why he's such a genius actor. He's become Rouse—with all his Neanderthal attitudes. All of a sudden, every time I run into him, if there's a guy with me, he's acting all macho and jealous. It's insane."

"Like that night at Momba."

She nodded. "That kid came over and started running his line of bullshit. I wasn't even paying attention and I look over and see Cam has gone into the vortex."

"Huh?"

"There's this V-shaped bone on his forehead that juts out when he gets out of control," she said, diagramming on her own brow. "It's a telltale sign he's gone over the edge. I call it going into the vortex.

"Anyway, he storms out of the club with that little TV chippy and calls Mouse—that's what his friends call him. The two of them start egging each other on and Mouse insists I have to be taught a lesson. He tells Cam to go back and do my new sex toy. What he means is he has to kill him. That poor fucking Jones kid. All he did was talk to me. He was just in the wrong place at the wrong time."

I flashed back on my encounter with Cam when he had referred to Gentry Jones as the murdered boyfriend. It should have set off alarms with me that he was the only person putting a sexual slant on Angel's contact with Gentry.

"Cam tells him he can't do that. Crazy as he gets, that's a line he won't cross. I've seen him kick, punch and bite people—throw shit at them—but I've never seen him try to seriously harm someone. Thank God. So Mouse tells him to go somewhere very public for the next few hours and he'll take care of it."

"Wait. How do you know the conversation between Cam and Mouse?"

"Because Mouse told me all about it. At the time he was in

my library, standing over Jones's body, using one of my curtains to wipe the blood off his huge blade. 'You run around like a whore,' he says, 'and this is what happens.'"

"He broke into your house?"

"I guess. But it was dumb luck too. That was the first time I had been alone with the kid all night, because he followed me out to the front of the house.

"Anyway, when Rouse first came at us, he stopped in his tracks and said to the kid, 'You're white?' All surprised-like. I guess when Cam told him he saw me with an NBA player, he must have assumed Gentry was black. God, it was awful to see the look on that boy's face when Rouse stuck his knife in him. Then, after he kills him, he warns me to keep my mouth shut. If I tell the police he was there, he says, I'm a dead woman."

Her account left me dizzy with questions. I clung to the most important one. "So why did you run away?"

"Because Mouse came back. Right after I got back from the club that night. Told me I better pack up my skanky ass and take it on the road. That's a quote."

"Did he tell you why?"

She nodded. "That stupid TV interview I did." Suddenly she grew incensed. "Did you see how much better they lit that airhead newswoman than they did me? She looked like a fairy godmother, all shiny and bright. I looked like a freaking troll doll!"

"Why would your *Primetime* appearance bother Mouse? You kept his secret."

"That's what I thought too. But when I told Carla that I was planning to plead innocent, Mouse considered that breaking our little pact. I still hadn't told anyone about him, but I guess in his twisted mind, he must have thought I was going to take the rap. Tell the police and the DA that I killed Gentry." She gave her head a quick cobweb-clearing shake as if to say, *You believe that shit?*

"Anyway, when he broke in my house the second time he

was really pissed," Angel said. "I don't know what crazy shit goes into his thought process, but he had somehow turned it around in his head that I had betrayed him."

"How did he keep getting in your house, Angel?"

"I really don't know. You have any idea how much I was paying that security firm to guard the house? And he still waltzed in there. He came from the kitchen side both times."

"I still don't get it, Angel."

"I would think you'd be used to that," she said snidely.

"I'm serious. This guy breaks into your house and stabs someone to death in front of you. Then he warns you not to tell anyone and you agree to this? Why didn't you tell the first cop who walked in the door? Mouse would have been arrested the same day."

She didn't respond, merely closed her eyes and began twirling her head to work the kinks out of her neck. Fatigue was evident on her face.

"Then this same guy comes back and says it's not enough you got arrested for murder, he wants you to run and hide. And you do that too. Tell me, Angel, is he hypnotizing you? Because I can't think of another reason you might even consider listening to Mouse."

She stared at me with what I took at the time to be annoyance. I later realized it was deliberation.

"This is absurd," I insisted. "We can call the LAPD right now. Tell them you'll need protective custody until this guy has been arrested. They'll lock his Mousy ass up for eternity."

Angel scrunched up her face as she scratched the back of her head. "I'm fucking famished," she said. "Do you think you could get me something to eat?"

"Sure. What do you want?" I said, leaping into people-pleasing mode.

"I'd adore one of the seafood salads they serve at La Parnaise on Beverly," she said, handing me the key. "But right now I'd settle for a turkey sandwich."

"What do you want on it?"

"Lettuce, tomato and a dab of saffron-infused mayo."

I thought she was overestimating her hometown, but I nodded and headed for the door. "I left my car back at the hotel," I said. "So this could take a few minutes. By the way, how did you get the key to this joint?"

"It was under the mat. Charlie is nothing if not predictable."

I turned to go. "Get some Doritos," she called at my back. "And some pomegranate juice." As the door shut, I faintly heard her shout, "And some Evian if they have it."

It was colder out than I expected and as I walked, a dusting of just-fallen snow blew around by my feet in patterns that resembled stylized Japanese paintings of cresting waves. About halfway down Main toward Huron, I found a small market. It was small and aseptic-smelling, but it was open.

The hefty woman behind the counter had red cheeks and arms like a butcher. I decided not to even mention the spice infusion. But I got a few sandwiches, a bag of Doritos, some Welch's grape juice, Dasani water and a box of Fig Newtons. They were the closest things I could find to Angel's wish list.

When I let myself back into Charlie's, Angel was no longer in the kitchen. I put down the bag of groceries and walked to the other end of the house. Still dressed, she was sound asleep on the bed. With her muddy makeup and oppressed hair, she looked like a character in a Bertolt Brecht play, like some refugee matriarch.

Leaving the key on the kitchen counter, I walked back to the hotel. The reason I was a pedestrian was because I had wanted to leave the car at the motel as a marker for Oops.

It worked. When I strolled in the driveway, he was leaning on the second-floor railing outside my room.

"You on an expense account and this is where you register?" he said as I walked along the balcony toward him. "I'd hate to see what kind of dump you stay in when you on your own dime."

"Yeah, well, I picked it for its location, not the amenities. How'd you find it?"

"Had a taxi drive me around till I spotted your car. Then I checked with the proprietor. He said you were here, asked if I was the friend you were hoping to meet. I told him I thought you were looking for a lady friend. You find her?"

"Yeah, she's tucked away at her brother's house. About five blocks from here."

"She all right?"

I shrugged. "A little worse for wear. But she's sleeping peacefully now."

He nodded. "You take me over there first thing tomorrow?"

"Sure."

"All right," he said, opening the door adjacent to mine. "Goodnight, neighbor."

"Night."

I got into bed a short time later, but I didn't sleep much, thinking about what Angel had told me. And what she hadn't.

CHAPTER
37

At some point I must have drifted off, because when I awoke the sun was trying to break through my Halloween curtains and someone was knocking on my door.

I opened it to Oops. Fully dressed and ready to go. "Aren't you the early bird," I said, squinting at my wristwatch.

"All I'm getting lying in that bed is a backache," he said. "And I want to see she's all right."

"I'm not going anywhere until I have a cup of coffee," I said stubbornly.

"Come get me when you ready," he said.

Fifteen minutes later, after I had prayed, showered, shaved and savored that all-important first cup, we started walking over to Charlie's.

Roger came out of his office as we passed. "Good morning, gentlemen," he said cheerily. We responded in kind as we continued toward the street.

"You're not partaking of the breakfast?" he asked as if this concept thoroughly puzzled him.

"Not today, Roger," I said. When I glanced back at him,

he was staring at us, his mouth open in disbelief.

"You didn't tell anyone you were coming here, did you Oops?" I asked.

"Course not," he said. "Who you think you dealing with?"

"Not even family?"

"I called my moms," he said. "That a problem?"

"It could be. I think someone is tapping the phones of the people around Angel."

"I never mentioned Angel's name. I just told my mom I was going to some backass town in Michigan for a few days on business. Otherwise she worries 'bout me."

It wouldn't be too hard for someone to decipher his destination, I thought. Of course, it was equally possible someone had trailed one or the other of us from New York.

When I turned down the driveway at 1261, Oops stopped in his tracks, taking in the house warily. "This the place?"

"Yeah."

"Man, that Charlie a class act, ain't he?" he asked, shaking his head in wonderment.

We knocked and Angel answered immediately. She looked right past me and beamed at Oops. "Heeey," she said softly, opening the door so we could come in.

"Hey, girl," Oops said. They hugged and then he held her at arm's distance. "Let me look at you." After a brief inventory, he shook his head disapprovingly.

She flicked her hand at him dismissively and walked back to the kitchen.

I don't know what he was objecting to. She looked a lot better than she had the night before. The whole house did.

Angel had put away the groceries and swept the floor. Her hair was brushed out and pulled into a ponytail, the dark makeup was gone and she was wearing jeans and a black long-sleeved blouse.

I followed her into the kitchen, where she had resumed wiping the shelves in the cupboard with a sponge. Oops stayed in the living room. Guarding the door, I assumed.

"Don't I know you?" I said.

She smirked. "Ain't this a bitch?" she said. "I spend my life trying to get out of this shithole and here I am again, cleaning some dingy house in Grand Blanc."

"Could be worse."

"How do you figure?"

"I don't know," I said, flustered at having my cliché questioned. "It could always be worse."

"Thanks for cheering me up."

"I'm not fully awake yet. I need another cup of coffee. You want me to bring you back some?"

"I'll go with you."

"You really think that's wise?"

"I've covered like five thousand miles in my disguise and no one has recognized me yet. Give me five minutes," she said, grabbing her wig and heading for the bedroom. I wanted to point out that her chances of being detected were slightly higher in Grand Blanc. She was an icon everywhere else on the globe. Here, as the town's only native celebrity, she was a deity. But in our brief time together, I had learned that arguing with Angel wasn't productive.

When she emerged, I got the full effect: the black wig, which looked like rayon, the impasto makeup, a mouth fitting that made her seem bucktoothed, frumpy clothes and industrial-rimmed eyeglasses.

I wasn't impressed. Yes, she looked like the lead in a Lifetime movie about a Hasidic wife undergoing chemotherapy. But it was a Lifetime movie starring Angel. Were people really that unobservant that she could walk among them in this gaudy but transparent getup without incident?

"Let's go," she said, her dental cap making her sound thick-tongued and addled. I smiled and gestured to the door. This I very much wanted to see.

Oops lumbered up off the BarcaLounger.

"You coming too?" I asked.

"You going to eat breakfast?" he asked.

I nodded.

"Then what you think?"

Another two inches of snow had fallen overnight. The sidewalks on Goodrich weren't shoveled, so we walked in the street until we got to Main. Oops trailed behind us by a yard or so.

The night before at the market, I had spotted the peaked roof of an International House of Pancakes farther down the street. We headed there.

As we walked, I asked her how she had made her escape from L.A.

"As soon as I drove out the gate, I put on a floppy hat someone left at the house and I stuffed up my hair underneath. I wore the biggest, ugliest sunglasses I have and I threw my cell phone out the window so I wouldn't be tempted to use it. I drove the Suburban straight downtown to the bus station, double-parked it, walked into the station and right out the other side. Took a taxi to an intersection about three blocks from a theatrical outfitting store we use for my tours.

"That left me a couple of hours to kill, so I went to a twenty-four-hour pharmacy and bought this horrible makeup. Then I walked to a Catholic church and sat through early Mass in one of the back pews. I lit a votive candle and said a few prayers, asking my mom to watch over me. Then I wrote a list of the stuff I wanted—the wig, the fake teeth, the nonprescription glasses—with instructions to charge it to my stage designer's account. I gave the list to a wino I saw on the street with half of a fifty-dollar bill. When he came out of the store, I put on all that stuff in the bathroom of a coffee shop. And when I emerged, voilà! The new me.

"I made a quick stop at a chintzy clothing outlet and took a taxi to Union Station. Figuring they might be watching the coast-to-coast trains, I took a whole bunch of short routes—L.A. to San Diego, San Diego to Phoenix, Phoenix to Denver, Denver to Chicago—working my way east. You know the rest. I took a bus back to Detroit. I totally forgot how the other half lives," she concluded the account of her odd odyssey. "It sucks."

There were about four other occupied tables, and none of those customers found us worthy of attention when we walked in. A couple of them looked right past us at Oops. The waitress seated us without a second glance. This was blowing my mind. *Come on, people,* I felt like shouting. *Could this be any more obvious?*

Without anything being said, Oops had taken a seat at the counter.

"You don't eat with the help?" I asked.

"His choice," she said. "He likes to keep an eye on the door."

I focused on working my way through a carafe of weak coffee. By the time I got to the bottom, I was grinning broadly. It struck me that I was in the middle of the most surreal scenario I was ever likely to experience: Here I was sitting across from the modern era's biggest pop star and the country's most notorious fugitive—my own personal amalgam of Diana Ross and Patty Hearst. In a booth at an IHOP. I thought of the title of a song I'd like to write someday: "Waffles with Elvis." The fact that Angel was dressed to look like Ruth Buzzi made it all the more bizarre.

This was a situation that called for one thing: silver-dollar pancakes.

"What's so funny?" she asked after our orders came.

"Being here. With you. Like this."

She looked around and smiled. Or rather, her lip rose above the tangled choppers of her oral implant. "I have to admit, I don't get out for breakfast much these days," she said, spearing a sliced triangle of pancakes. "I remember how bad I used to want my father to take us here, like after Mass on Sunday. Never happened." She chewed for a few seconds. "So where'd you grow up, Mac?"

I nearly spit coffee out my nose, I was so shocked.

"What's wrong?" she asked.

"Nothing. You took me by surprise is all."

"It's not a tricky question."

"I know. It's just that you don't usually seem all that interested—"

"In other people?" she said, accurately completing my thought. "You're saying I'm self-involved?" With mock indignation, she flung a wadded-up sugar packet at me. "You have no idea what it's like to be me. The expectations, the constant overwhelming attention."

The couple at the table nearest us had paid up and left, so we could speak with relative impunity. "Actually this is kind of liberating," she said, slurping up some orange juice. Drinking with her false teeth necessitated suctioning fluids into her mouth. "You have no idea how relaxing it is to be incognito, to walk down the street without everyone staring at you. I may keep it up after I get my life back."

"Like the princess and the pauper," I suggested. "Venture out among the common people."

She thought about this for a moment. "Who am I kidding? Pigs in a blanket are tasty. But breakfast in bed beats this all to hell."

We finished the meal without incident and walked back to Charlie's in our triangle formation, passing several shoppers and pedestrians. No one batted an eye at my companion. She must have been exercising some kind of Jedi mind control on them, because I swear, a pirate's bandanna and an eye patch would have been a more persuasive makeover.

As soon as we got in the door, she went to peel off her camouflage. Oops dropped into the BarcaLounger again, and I sat at the kitchen table, tuning the radio to that station from East Lansing I liked. It didn't disappoint. The first two songs were by Jules Shear and by Buddy and Julie Miller.

As I stared out the grimy window at Goodrich Lane, I thought I had died and gone to Valhalla. The opening notes to Emmylou Harris's "Heaven Only Knows" started to play.

I reached to turn up the volume just as Angel walked in the room, brushing her hair.

"You like this country crap?" she asked.

The question pissed me off for a number of reasons, not the least of which was her hypocrisy. On the cover of her latest CD, *Dream Catcher,* and in the video for the title track, Angel had caused a fashion sensation by sporting a cowgirl hat and posing as the sweetheart of the rodeo.

I hated people who publicly appropriated the symbols of a style and privately disrespected its substance. That stern disapproval must have shown on my face.

"What?" she demanded. "Oh, I should have known. You're one of those music snobs who thinks this hootenanny shit is noble and genuine, but you can't stand my music. Right?" She was leaning on the table, the brush still gripped in one hand, her face close to mine, her tone taunting. "Come on. Admit it."

"You in trouble now, son," Oops called from the other room.

I tried to restrain myself. Really I did. But the open dare in her eyes incited me. "You or Emmylou," I said pointing my thumb at the radio. "That's not even a contest."

She smirked and nodded her head like she had my number all along. "And why is that?" she asked, and resumed stroking her hair.

"Because her music is beautiful and artistic and honest and yours is plastic and commercial and fake."

She smacked me on the side of the head with the brush. Hard. "Well, meanwhile I've sold over sixty million albums. How many has Ma Kettle sold?"

"Uh, Angel. That's kind of my point."

"Right, because it's popular it can't possibly be good."

"No, it isn't good because it's shrill and soulless."

"You know what? It's stupid to argue taste with elitists like you. You just don't get it. But I'm all about showman-

ship anyway. Until one of these farm girls can put on a stadium show like mine, they're really not in my league."

"Are you serious? I'd rather see a Dixie Chicks concert
than one of yours any day."

She chuckled scornfully. "Is that so? Why?"

"Because they play their own instruments. And because
your voice sucks." I flinched as I said it, but she still caught
me a good shot off the top of my head.

"Fuck you," she said irately. "All right, hotshot, if I'm not
a good singer, then who is?"

I stood up and got behind her. I wasn't going down this
path until I was out of range of that brush. She sat in the seat
I had just vacated. "Wow," I said. "Where to start? Okay,
there's Al Green, Otis Redding, Marvin Gaye, Aaron
Neville, Stevie Wonder, Little Anthony—"

"Whoa, whoa, whoa," she said, throwing up her hands.
"Apples and oranges. I'm a pop singer."

"Okay, how about Paul Carrack, Frankie Miller, Paul
Rodgers, Terry Reid, uh, Robert Palmer, Michael McDonald, Pat Monahan, Daryl Hall . . ."

"I haven't heard of half those people," she protested. "But
I notice they're all guys, you misogynist bastard."

"Fine. Let's talk women. Aretha, Chaka, Anita Baker, Ali-
cia Keys—"

She interrupted me with a loud sigh. "Back on the soul
tip."

"Okay, Bonnie Bramlett, Bonnie Raitt, Allison Moyet,
Wynonna Judd, Chrissie Hynde, Martha Davis, Mariah . . .
Look, we can keep shaving this down until we're only com-
paring you to singers from Grand Blanc with a last name
that starts with C. And there will still be five who are better
than you."

"Asshole!" she shouted, winging the brush at my head.
She had a pretty good arm.

Maybe I had been a little too harsh. But there was no

question my comments had been a conversation killer. After a long awkward silence, she turned to look at me, her eyes narrowed, her expression all smoky and knowing. "So," she said. "You want to have sex? I'm horny as hell."

Boy, that invitation popped me out of gear. Where did it come from? I never thought insulting a woman would make her want to take me to bed. Of course, I had never met a woman like Angel.

But I didn't want her. Never had. The truth was the only time I ever thought of Angel in a sexual context was when I was making love to a woman and wanted to delay coming. Some guys thought of old women they had seen riding the bus with opaque support hose on. I thought of Angel's crass mouth and predatory eyes.

I wasn't about to tell her that she was my orgasm anchor. A snub like that was likely to hit her like a Spanish fly. And she was entirely capable of trying to rape me on the kitchen table. So I settled for the obvious objection.

"With Oops sitting right in there?" I whispered.

"Are you kidding?" she asked loudly. "He's seen me have more sex than any man except my first husband. Isn't that right, Oops?"

"Is that what you was doing? Having sex?" came the voice from the other room.

She laughed and then looked at me with hooded eyes. "So?" she asked suggestively.

Squirreling up my face as if I were deciding this with the greatest reluctance, I said, "Maybe some other time, huh?"

The sharp smile she directed at me said, *Now I've seen everything.* Her hand shot out, grabbed my shirt just below the collar and pulled me down toward her. I wasn't sure if she was going to ream me out or kiss me.

I never found out because just then there was a sharp knock at the door. We had company.

Bad company and I won't deny.

CHAPTER 38

Oops got up and peered through the tinted porthole on
the door.

"Someone from the gas company," he said, looking to Angel for instructions.

She had released me and now stood with her fists on her
waist, laughing mirthlessly. "Isn't that something?" she said.
"How long have I been here? Less than twenty-four hours.
And MichCon is at the door. My father always used to say,
'The shortest unit of time in the universe is the period between when you turn on a stove for the first time in a new
house and when the gas company sends someone out to take
a reading.' You deal with him, Oops."

As I chuckled at Tony Chiavone's observation, I glanced
out the window at the threshold. A young man was standing
with his back to the door, looking off at the street. He was
dressed in a green service uniform, holding a metal folder
full of papers with a harmless pronged instrument dangling
from his belt.

As Oops threw open the door, the man on the stoop

turned. I noticed the smile on his face and the way that smile stretched the soul patch under his lip.

"Oops, don't—" I shouted. But I already saw the muzzle flash and heard the blast from the .45 the man had held cradled against his thigh. Oops crashed against the wall behind him and slid heavily to the floor, his eyes open wide.

Mouse stepped into the corridor and turned to face me and Angel, still smiling.

"I was beginning to think I'd never find you, darlin'," he said with what sounded like a phony Southern accent.

"What do you want? I already did everything you asked," Angel said. She sounded more annoyed than frightened.

"I've given some thought to our arrangement," he said. "Decided that when push comes to shove it won't work. I don't know why I ever thought I could trust a whore like you."

Angel backed away toward the sink, trying to get out of his direct firing range. Mouse shook his head. "Now, let's not make this any harder than it has to be," he said.

I stepped into the entryway to the kitchen. He appraised me, then smiled again, raising the gun. "You think you're gonna protect her, huh?" he said. "You know what a hero is, don't you? He's the fool who dies in the movie's first reel."

Pleased with his kernel of wisdom, he stepped toward me, aiming at my chest. I glanced down, where a large hand had just encircled Mouse's ankle. From the ground, Oops grabbed him and yanked him backward. Mouse went down like a rug had been pulled out from underneath him.

I heard a crash behind me. Angel was using the baseball bat she had brandished the day before to smash out the last pane of glass in the kitchen window. She backed up and, taking two quick steps, dove outside through the casement like a vanishing mermaid. The last thing I saw were the soles of her sneakers.

As I was putting these events together in my mind, I heard two gun blasts and then the sound of Oops moaning. I didn't need any time to process that. I dove out the window after Angel—although not as gracefully. I brought some shards and part of the frame with me onto the permafrosted grass of the backyard.

Angel was already sprinting for the slumping wooden fence behind the hedge at the back of the lot, still clutching the bat in her right hand. Let me tell you, she was a far better athlete than she was a singer. I caught up with her as she was tearing aside a second weathered slat off the cross beams.

"Was that Mouse?" I asked.

"Who the hell do you think it was?" she responded.

"I thought you said he only used a knife."

Turning sideways to fit through the opening she had created, she muttered, "Yeah, well, I guess he's branching out."

As I squeezed through the hole behind her, I heard the sound of Charlie's front door being battered open.

I caught up to Angel as she was tearing into the yard across the road. "We have to stay off the streets," she said, without breaking stride. And then an angry afterthought. "Shit! I left my disguise back there."

"Head for the Pioneer," I said, keeping pace. "We can re-group there." She led me on a merry chase, a full-tilt obstacle course, as we ran along driveways, past garbage cans, over fences and through foliage. She didn't look behind her once.

Finally we emerged from the alley by a consignment shop onto Main, sprinting the final forty yards to the motel. Roger was working on one of the door handles on the ground floor with a screwdriver as we ran into the lot and up the stairs. "Ah, Jim," he called out, backing into the parking lot so he could see us on the balcony. His tool belt clattering, he smiled broadly and said, "I see you have located your friend. I'm glad for you."

I gave him a rushed salute as I unlocked the door and we piled inside, heaving it closed behind us. Angel threw herself on the nearest bed. I flicked on the light, fit the chain into its slot on the door and sat down in the room's only chair. I gave us both a minute to catch our breaths.

"Okay," I said. "I think it's time you told me what's going on."

"Pretty obvious, I think," said Angel, scooching back to sit against the headboard. "You led Mouse right to me and you got Oops killed."

"Bullshit. Nobody was following me."

"He followed either you or Oops. How else do you think he found me?"

"I don't know," I said with vexation. "But we can argue about that later. I want you to tell me what the deal is here. Why haven't you gone right to the police?"

She glared at me murderously, like a momma grizzly at a wayward hiker. "Because," she said, practically spitting out the words, "he said he would kill my daughter."

I'm not sure what the literal meaning of dumbfounded is, but I'm sure I was the picture of it sitting there. "Y-your daughter?" I finally stuttered.

"Fuck me," she said sourly. Taking a deep breath, she folded her arms across her chest and poured out her soul.

"When I got to Manhattan, I was still a teenager and naive as hell. I was living in a cold-water flat in Alphabet City with two other girls, working at a secondhand clothing store in the Village and stealing them blind. I needed clothes because I was out clubbing every night. And begging everyone I met with any juice to give me a chance to sing. Back then I only needed about an hour of sleep a night.

"Anyway, I fell for this bartender, Tony Funari. God, he was a stud. The most gorgeous creature I had ever seen. Too bad he turned out to be a total cretin. When I told him I was pregnant, he was like, 'So? Get it fixed.' I told him, 'No way, honey. We're getting married.' I wasn't exactly thrilled about it either, but I wouldn't consider any other scenario. I just figured that was the way it was supposed to happen."

She shook her head. "God, I was a baby myself. Tony

strung me along for a few months and then one day he just disappeared. I got a little frantic. I didn't know what to do because no matter what, I wasn't coming back here pregnant, with my tail between my legs. So I badgered Frankie into marrying me. That man is a saint, putting up with what I put him through.

"And everything was cool through the pregnancy. We were pretty happy, really, playing house together. Then the baby arrived and that was incredible too. Until I realized what it actually meant to be a full-time mother. I couldn't go to shows or auditions. I couldn't even make it down to the corner to buy a magazine. All my dreams—singing onstage, getting a record contract—I saw them flying out the window. And that's when I realized I had made a big mistake.

"So I swallowed my pride and called my older sister Susan. Toughest phone call I ever made. Me and her never got along. She was going for her master's down in Tallahassee. I asked if she could take the baby, just until I was settled in my music career. After she got done telling me what a selfish, immature, stupid brat I had always been, she said she would take her on one condition: that I never contact her or my daughter again. No phone calls. No letters. She made me swear to it on our mother's grave.

"Frankie drove us down to Florida in a van he borrowed from a friend. And that's the last time I was ever with Ariel. Susan legally adopted her and later changed her name to Amanda Stewart. My sister changed her own name from Chiavone years ago so she wouldn't be bugged by reporters.

"When I hit it big, I offered her money, a lot of money. No strings attached. Susan was furious. Reminded me that we had a sacred pact. Stubborn bitch. Every couple of years I hire a private detective to check on my baby and have him take some pictures with a zoom lens. You should see her. She's so beautiful. A sophomore now in college. Has a nice boyfriend. Wants to be a teacher." Angel rubbed her eye with the back of her hand. "You have any tissues?" I pulled a couple out of the wall dispenser in the bathroom and handed them to her.

"And you kept this a secret all these years?"

She nodded. "Not even Lani knows."

"But I assume Cam does?"

"Yes, I told him."

"How the hell could he share that information with Mouse?"

"I told you—they're practically inseparable."

"So what happened?"

"After Mouse killed that poor kid, he told me he knew all about Ariel. He said he had a buddy down in Florida who just loved college girls. That he's keeping an eye on a special one right now. He told me if I breathed a single word to the police, his psychotic friend would snatch up Ariel two minutes later and that she would die, but only after his friend taught her things they don't learn in college."

"Jesus, Angel, that's terrible!"

"Tell me about it," she said. "I've never been so scared. And so furious. I couldn't call Susan with news like that—not after all these years. So I sent my brother Charlie over to talk to Cam."

"I hope he smacked some sense into him."

She laughed mordantly. "Charlie's not big on family loyalty. Besides which, he worships the ground Cam walks on. But he can carry a message. I told him to tell Cam that of all the fucked-up things he's ever done—and believe me, that's a long fucking list—this is without question the most heinous. I told him this is all on him. That he's got to rein in his crazy pal and I don't want to see him or talk to him until he's done that."

"What was his response?"

"And I quote, 'Tell her she don't understand.' Nobody ever understands poor Cam. That's why I divorced him. I got tired of being his translator to the rest of the big, bad universe."

"But he came over to your house."

"Yeah, and tried to call me like ten times. But I wouldn't listen to his bullshit. The only words I wanted to hear out of his mouth were: 'I took care of Mouse. He won't bother you or Ariel.' Once I knew help wasn't coming from that direction, I decided to just wait it out. I figured no one could actually believe I killed that kid even if I refused to talk about it."

"That must have been rough."

"It got a whole lot rougher after that psycho came back and told me to bolt. If I'm not out the door in ten minutes, he says, I die and Ariel gets tortured. Now I really don't know what to do. I know what running is going to look like. But I can't risk Ariel's safety. So I took off and hid. It was going pretty good too, except this idiotic detective kept turning up, blowing my cover."

"You can't run forever, Angel."

"I didn't have to. Just until I figured out how to fix this whole mess."

"It's not as bad as you think," I said encouragingly. "First of all, this phantom friend down in Florida is a bluff. He's a bogeyman Mouse made up to terrify you."

"Well, it worked."

"Forget it. I guarantee he doesn't exist."

"I'm not willing to take that chance," she said angrily.

"Okay, not a problem. You tell the cops the same story you just told me. You ask for protective custody for yourself and for Ariel until Mouse is behind bars."

Jaw clenched, she shook her head. "First of all, Susan would never forgive me if Ariel suddenly needed a twenty-four-hour police escort because of me."

"So what? At least she'd be safe."

"No," she said. "I gave my word. And second of all, I know you said this creep in Florida doesn't exist, but what if he does? Even if Mouse is arrested, the other guy could still be out there. Is Ariel going to get a permanent police guard? I can't do it."

We looked at each other for a moment. "All right," I said. "Give me a minute and I'll work out a solution."

She circled her palms over the bedspread as if she were making a mattress angel and looked around the room. "And I thought Charlie's crib was seedy. You're living in the lap of crusty here."

"Yeah, but look what I have," I boasted, reaching into the shopping bag by the TV, pulling out the packet of ground French Roast coffee and tossing it to her.

She unlatched it and gave it a sniff. "Mmmmm, that smells great. God, I miss my coffee at home. I have my own barista, you know."

I took back the satchel and set about making a pot of coffee. "What else do you miss?" I asked.

"Yoga, massages, the woman who does my nails. And my bathroom. Definitely. And it's not that I'm spoiled. But for more than a week, I've been using public toilets in trains, buses and gas stations. That will make you miss the comforts of home in a hurry."

As the coffee began to brew, it gave off an earthy, tangy aroma that was delightful. Picking up the motel's thin Styrofoam in-room cups, I began to regret that I hadn't invested in a couple of decent mugs when I was at the store.

Didn't really matter, though.

We never got to taste it anyway.

CHAPTER 39

There was a pounding on the door and a high, querulous voice shouted, "If that's your Taurus out in the lot, somebody set it on fire."

Angel and I looked at each other, neither of us sure what to make of this development. After our narrow escape at Charlie's house, I wasn't about to make myself a sitting target in the window by pulling back my orange curtain. So I opened the door to the limit of the chain and peered cautiously out the opening.

All I saw was the ridged sole of a boot smashing into the door just above the handle. The chain's anchor tore loose. The door flew open, knocking me backward. And a smiling Mike Rouse walked in, closing the door behind him.

He looked just like his casting photo—the good looks marred by an aura of deprivation. He had the pinched face of someone who had missed a few meals and more than a few hugs. Another feature cinched his identity: the vicious knife he dangled by his side. Broad and sadistically rococo with a variety of cutting surfaces, it was a warrior's blade, like the kind you see in Conan the Barbarian fantasies.

Mouse looked down at me on the floor. The door had bashed my nose and my eyes were filled with tears.

He looked over at Angel standing between the beds. "Well, lookee here," he said, his voice strangely excited. "You just collect men like a dog does fleas, don't ya? I flush you out of your little love shack and you end up here in a no-tell motel. Is it your smell? Is that how you do it? Come over here. I wanna check you out."

I'm sure Angel was terrified but she hid it well, gazing at him evenly and disdainfully as she walked over. He began sniffing at her noisily, first her hair, then her armpits, her chest and finally her crotch. "Naw, I ain't catchin' it, but it must be some kind of musk. Like a bitch in heat. But you know what?" He took her chin and pinched it between the thumb and forefinger of his free hand. "I bet I can cut that right out of you. Clean as a whistle." His voice took on an accusatory tone. "You shouldn't have made me chase you all over the goddamn map." He gave her face a twist. She kept her eyes on his. "It raises all kinds of hell with my parole officer."

"Hey, asshole, you're the one who told me to run."

I could tell the logic of her observation didn't sit well with him. He was preparing to show his displeasure by hurting her, so I sat up, mostly to divide his attention.

"Don't you even think about getting up, pardner," he said, moving her a few steps away from me on the narrow stretch of carpet between the window and the front bed.

"Can I ask you a question?" I said.

He considered it. "Yeah, I'll give you one. Seeing as how I'm about to gut you like a smallmouth bass, I suggest you make a meal of it." His comment seemed to amuse him.

"Did you find Angel here in Michigan by following me?"

"No, but I did trail you around New York for a while. Never been there before. Man, that is a crazy city." His manner was decidedly voluble, like he was charming the hell out of us. "But you vanished on me." He faced Angel. "No, I came here because your brother got a call from one of his neighbors, said somebody had taken up residence in his house."

"Great," said Angel.

He pinched her face hard. "You keep that sweet mouth shut until I stick something in it," he said, moving his eyes so close to hers, they could have exchanged butterfly kisses.

"Do you really have an accomplice in Florida, Mouse? Or did you just make that up?" I asked, to break up their not-so-tender moment.

"You see? Now, that just chaffs my ass," he said bringing the blade up by his face for emphasis. "I think I was pretty clear I was giving you one question. I hate people who don't listen when you tell 'em something." The fake Dixie accent was still there. But all trace of his false goodwill was gone. I knew he was through toying with us. "I think it's time you learned yourself a lesson."

I was tensing myself to spring up from my position on the floor, but before he could advance on me, a voice called from outside, "Jim, are you okay?"

"You better come in here, Roger," I shouted. I hated to put the motel owner in danger, but I was stuck for options. We heard the passkey inserted and the handle began to dip. Mouse turned, holding the knife across his chest, poised to deliver a devastating backhand stab to whomever walked in that door.

At the precise moment that Mouse shifted his attention, Angel deftly slammed her knee into his nuts. If she had been punting him, he would have traveled about sixty yards in the air. Gasping in pain, he slid to the ground.

She vaulted over the bed to get out of knife range and grabbed me under the arm, pulling me to my feet.

"Come on," she said, yanking me toward the door. A befuddled Roger, his tool belt jangling, backed out onto the cement balcony to let us pass.

We went left, down the stairs and across the lot to my Taurus, which thankfully was not on fire. The only other car in the lot was a white Mustang, mottled with road splotch and salt. As I cranked the engine on my rental to life, I looked up through the tinted strip at the top of the windshield to the second floor. Mouse came weaving out the door and up to the rail, looking down at us with outrage and determination.

From my angle, I never saw Roger striding up behind him. All I saw was a crescent wrench, landing a resounding blow right on Mouse's temple. And down he went again, screaming so loud, it sounded like he was in the back seat.

Just before I peeled out of the lot, I caught sight of Roger scurrying down the balcony toward the far end of the hotel. May you have no vacancies, my plucky friend.

I drove north, following the same route I had taken a couple of days before, trying to put some distance between us and Mouse. Maybe I'd get to see Saginaw after all. It started to snow again. If this was early April, I'd hate to spend January in Michigan.

Angel didn't seem too rattled. She had commandeered the rearview mirror and was giving her face a meticulous thrice-over from every conceivable angle.

"How do you think he found us the second time?" I asked.

"Not too many hotels in Grand Blanc to check," she said, eyes locked on the mirror, examining her cheek. "Pulls in, sees the rental car and goes to the only room with lights on."

"Listen, you handled yourself really well back there. Not just at the motel but at Charlie's too."

Having completed the inspection of her pores, she slapped the mirror back to an approximation of its original position and shrugged.

"No, I mean it. You were like freaking Wonder Woman."

She slouched down so her head was resting on the top of the front seat. "When I was going out with Efraim," she said, referring to Efraim Barnes, Hollywood's most notorious Casanova, an actor who was twice her age, "we were at a party at Nicholson's house one night and someone complimented my new video. She said there was better acting in that three minutes than in most feature films. And Efraim said that the only real talent I had that was worth discussing was as a survivor. He said, 'When nuclear winter comes, the only things left on the planet will be ten million cockroaches and Angel. And she'll still have the best-selling album.' "

I responded with the requisite laugh, although Efraim's witticism had been repeated in the press often.

"But there's some truth to that," she continued. "Pop tastes change faster than the weather in St. Barts. Christ, when I came up my biggest competition was Annie Lennox and the Eurythmics. Now it's Beyonce, who's young enough to be Annie's daughter." Or your own, I reflected.

"You don't get on top and stay on top in this business unless your survival instincts are a lot sharper than that knife Mouse carries around."

"That is one nasty weapon," I said. "Scared the hell out of me just looking at it."

"You're very fortunate you didn't get to see him use it. That's a total horror show. Fucker enjoys his work too."

"I told you he didn't trail me here."

"I'm still working out the appropriate punishment for Charlie," she said grimly. "But believe me, he will pay, the douche bag."

"You don't seem as angry with Cam."

"Cam is who he is. He can't help himself. He gets lost in his shit, abandons himself to his art," she said. I guess in her crowd, talent was the ultimate get-out-of-jail-free card. I didn't live in that rarified set. When this was all over, I was going to make sure Cam Akers was prosecuted for his active collusion in all of Mouse's activities.

"First thing we have to do," she said, "is get me a new disguise. I can't travel like this without getting arrested. Or mobbed."

"Or both," I said. "I know a place. You make a list of what you want."

Sometime later, I pulled into the same mall on Dort Avenue in Flint that I had patronized a few days before. I parked in the garage, sliding the Taurus between two SUVs so that Angel would be minimally exposed to scrutiny. She slumped in the front seat and I went shopping.

Obviously this would have gone a lot faster if she had made the purchases. I had never bought a wig before. I filled a bag with makeup at a discount drugstore and went into a ladies' clothing chain to purchase an ensemble. I was getting a headache looking at the tables stacked with blouses. I didn't see why she couldn't just pull up the hood on a sweatshirt and go as the Unabomber.

I was sizing some ugly slacks on a clearance display when out of the corner of my eye I saw Angel running past the store. About three seconds later, Mouse hustled after her. Shit, and I had just found something that would fit her.

When I came out, Angel was darting through the crowd by the food court with Mouse about twenty yards behind her. Heads were turning, but it was the alarm evident in their rapid movement, not Angel's celebrity, that was drawing attention.

As I followed, I saw that Angel was running out of the room as she approached the far end of the mall. The final and largest retail space was boarded up, with signs announcing that an Old Navy store was opening soon. The only egress was the sluggish escalator to the upper level, which was jammed with shoppers.

But the cockroaches' favorite chanteuse had one more trick up her sleeve. She leaped up on the chrome balustrade between the up and down escalators and began belting out the opening lines to "Cheap Date Girl," her biggest hit and signature song: "I don't need no candy/ No sweet-smelling flowers/ Wine me, dine me, I don't care/ Let's go park your car somewhere."

The mall, in my opinion, was a pretty dreary shopping environment. But the acoustics were fantastic. Angel's voice rang out as if amplified. Her tone, as always, was flat and lacking in melisma, but it got the job done.

A mob gathered with astonishing speed, buzzing excitedly as they realized who was in their midst. People came running over; the procession from the down escalator spilled out and stalled; those headed up stopped in their tracks.

Angel had created pedestrian gridlock, with Mouse trapped on the periphery. As he began to shove into their midst, making slow, antagonistic progress, Angel concluded her brief performance by gracefully leaping onto the vacant rising escalator and quick-stepping to the second-floor concourse.

An excited contingent of the crowd hurried onto the escalator to follow her, the way drivers will quickly zoom into a vacant lane after an ambulance has gone by with its siren blaring.

Knocking people aside like bowling pins, Mouse tried to claw his way through and over them. A supersized teenager on the escalator dressed in a black and orange high school letter jacket objected to the shoving. He grabbed Mouse's shoulder as he went by and began to berate him.

From where I stood, I caught a flash—the light gleaming on Mouse's knife as he pulled it out and stabbed the kid three times quickly below his rib cage. People began screaming. The kid toppled backward, setting off a domino effect on the escalator. Security guards emerged from various stores, gripping walkie-talkies, their eyes anxiously surveying the crowd. They began sprinting toward the escalators. This was going to get ugly.

I looked up and saw Angel running along the upper level. People had recognized her by now and she had to feint and duck around fans who wanted to engage her. She looked like a baseball player who has just hit a World Series–winning home run and is trying to circle the bases after the exultant crowd has spilled on the field. She spotted me marking her progress and mimed steering a car as she passed overhead.

I ran for the garage and started the car. I noticed a white Mustang with its front door hanging open parked across two spaces just down the ramp as I backed out. I was idling by the exit sign when Angel came hurtling down the garage steps and flung herself neatly in the front seat. I only wish it had been a convertible so she could have jumped in while I was accelerating, like one of those cowboy heroes leaping onto his galloping steed.

We spiraled down to street level, where a line of cars waited at each of the payment booths. "Go around! Go around," Angel exhorted. I spun the wheel to the left, sending orange parking cones flying as I pulled into the opposing lane. If the driver of a Chevy Tahoe hadn't alertly stood on his brakes, we would have met head-on. I continued left around him and then pulled the wheel hard right to smash through the striped traffic arm by the ticket-dispensing machine. Tires squealing, I narrowly averted a minivan. The horrified face of the woman behind the wheel was framed by the windshield like a vintage horror movie poster. Run for your lives; it's the Blob!

It had started to snow harder while we were inside and I nearly lost control as I fishtailed out onto the street. I was all jacked up on adrenaline as we sped away, a chorus of angry horns blaring behind us.

"What the hell happened?" I demanded.

"How do I know?" she yelled back. Two days together and already we were bickering like a married couple. "I was looking in the mirror, fixing my eyelashes, when I see Mouse storming toward the car. I had to jump out and scramble over the hoods of three cars to get some running room." She grabbed the front of her blouse and twisted it, peering at her left side. "And I still think he got a piece of me as I ran in the mall." There was in fact a three-inch rip in the material.

"Where do we go now?" I asked as we pulled up to a ma-

jor intersection bedecked with stacks of directional arrows.
Angel looked around and pointed at one of the blue and red
placards for the interstate. "Jump on highway 69 and head
east," she said decisively.

We wobbled a little on the steep entrance ramp. Condi-
tions were getting treacherous. "You want to tell me how
Mouse found us? Because I know that's not the only mall in
Michigan."

"I don't know. Cam must have outfitted him."

"With what?"

"One of those high-tech tracing bugs. He's got a garage
full of that shit. When we were married he did that film
Fetch? And those crazy bounty hunters he was hanging with
just loaded him down with all these gadgets. I can't believe
any of them are legal, but Cam claimed—"

"Hold on. Are you saying he has us LoJacked?"

"You have another explanation?"

"Then we should pull off and try to find the device," I
said, looking for the next exit.

"No," she said. "Keep driving. If he catches up to us, I'll
fix his ass when we get to Port Huron."

That sounded ominous enough to me. I drove along,
slightly faster than the conditions warranted but not taking
any wild chances. As the sun started to dive for the flat hori-
zon behind us, she asked me about various stars I had worked
for, showing a surprising familiarity with my résumé.

Twenty miles outside of Flint, just as my nerves were settling down, I spotted a cloud approaching through the storm.
The Mustang was gaining on us rapidly, plunging ahead so
fast it looked like a comet in the snow.

"Buckle up, sweetheart," I said. "This ride's about to get
bumpy." I figured if Angel was going to handle all the physical stunts in our partnership, at least I could chip in the
hard-boiled dialogue. She looked back and frowned. "Now
we know he's got us tagged."

Leaning on his horn, Mouse roared up on my left. I could

see his face in the mirror, set with maniacal resolve. He tried to pull abreast of us, two tires on the road, two tires on the snowy shoulder. I waited until his front tire was parallel with my rear and then drifted into him.

When my tail tapped his front quarter, the Mustang wavered once and then flew off into the four-lane's depressed median. Mouse tried to steer it back onto the road but couldn't get purchase. The car spun around and then slid sideways to a stop, spraying snow like a skater slamming on the brakes.

Five miles later and he was back, pulling up behind me with his brights on. Now, that was rude driving etiquette. This time, he faked to the left and whipped over to the right to pass. I didn't have to do a thing. His maneuver caused his wheels to lock. The Mustang drifted up on the shoulder, tipped and slid down the embankment.

It took him a little longer to get back on track this time, but he did. I think he was beginning to understand that we had a couple of advantages. His Mustang may have had more horsepower, so he could always catch us. But the Taurus had a wider wheel base and was more stable in the snow. That made it hard for him to pass us. Then too, Mouse clearly wasn't a really good driver. He was probably locked up when the rest of us were taking Driver's Ed. And as a California boy, he probably had negligible experience in the snow.

So the rest of the way into Port Huron, he contented himself with sitting about five car lengths back, waiting us out. Personally, I would have hung back out of visual range, relying on the bug, pulling up only when we stopped. But it was nerve-wracking to have him over my shoulder mile after mile. It kept me glancing nervously at the mirror but it didn't seem to effect Angel. She looked like we were on a Sunday drive.

"This is it," she said finally, sitting up in her seat. "Head for the Blue Water Bridge." She glanced over her shoulder, making sure Mouse was still there. Then she slouched down again with a satisfied smirk on her face.

We passed several signs with increasingly large lettering informing drivers that they were approaching the last exit in the United States. "Canadian border?" I ventured. She wiggled her eyebrows by way of response.

The Canadian officials weren't conducting very rigorous checks. Mostly it was a glance inside the car, a simple question and you were waved on in. More like a tollbooth than an international border. But it was enough to bring traffic to a crawl halfway over the bridge.

"The first time you come to a complete stop," she said, "I'm going to jump out."

"You sure about this?" I said as I braked.

"Trust me," she said. Then she threw open the door and circled around the front of the car, running to my left. Jumping up on the guardrail, she shimmied up a cable and scaled the partition dividing the north and south lanes. Up and over.

On the door-mounted mirror, I saw Snake jump out of his car to pursue her. He cleared the partition too, with the same easy alacrity Angel had. I waited until he had one leg over the top to follow myself. As I ran for the divider, a few drivers stuck behind us called out to me, questioning my sanity. But nobody cursed or blew their horns. Those Canadians sure are polite.

When I dropped down, it took me a second to locate the runners. That's because Angel was circling back in the direction of traffic toward the American side. The traffic was really stacked up on this side of the bridge, as the guards conducted more thorough inspections. Angel was running along the center-lane marker between the idling cars, Mouse loping behind her. I took the same route.

As she ran, Angel was waving her arms above her head. A guard looking in the back of a conversion van spotted her first. He spoke rapidly into a microphone rigged to his uniform coat. This was a relatively sleepy crossing, but those boys scrambled fast. In a matter of seconds, a mix of INS agents and military personnel were converging on her.

You could see the looks of astonishment on their faces as they realized whom they had just captured. Their game faces turned to smiles. You'd have to go back to John Dillinger or Bonnie & Clyde to find an American fugitive this celebrated. And those old bank robbers didn't have a single Grammy between them.

Mouse had come to an abrupt stop about fifteen yards from the scrum around Angel. No one was even paying attention to him, even though Angel was gesturing at him repeatedly. I don't care how professional you are, when you've just bagged an international sex symbol, it's hard to get excited about some garden-variety psychopath.

I stood in the shadows about ten yards from Mouse using a Ford Explorer as a shield. Still unnoticed, Mouse began to back into the shadows. I didn't want him running around loose anymore.

So I shouted as loud as I could, "That guy's a terrorist! Right over there!" I pointed dramatically at Mouse. Every head in that uniformed crowd turned to check out the threat to national security. They looked at me, and then followed my pointing finger to Mouse, who had frozen when I started yelling. He took a hesitant step backward and a handful of men immediately fanned out to cut off his escape.

As they neared him, he drew his knife from inside his coat, dropping down in a crouch, his back to an overnight delivery truck. I think it was some atavistic posture, the trapped-rat defense.

It didn't do him much good. Three pistols and two automatic rifles were immediately raised and aimed at his chest from close range.

A furious scowl molded his face, and for a second I thought he was going to try to take them on. But he dropped the knife. They ordered him to turn and put his hands on the truck. When he complied, a soldier scurried over and kicked the knife away. Then he roughly searched him as the other men closed in.

Mouse was handcuffed and trundled off.

Me? I surrendered to a cute blond agent right outside the administration building. Nothing like a woman in uniform.

CHAPTER
40

It took a while to sort things out. They were burning up the wires between Port Huron and Los Angeles. Meanwhile, Angel was getting more autograph requests than any murder suspect I've ever met.

She cooperated fully. The only request she made from the time they brought us inside was that they contact the police department in Tallahassee to request protective measures for one Amanda Stewart.

Finally the station chief for immigration took us up in his office. I could tell from the shocked looks on his staff's faces when he entered the building that seeing him here after dark was practically unheard of. His office was a glassed-in enclosure above the main floor. From there you could see everyone in the room working. And they, of course, could see you.

Heads were craning up all over the room, as if they couldn't believe their famous visitor was really there.

"Well, Ms. Chiavone, despite what your friend here implied, Mr. Rouse does not seem to have a political agenda."

Here he gave both of us an indulgent smile. "But I can assure you he will spend the rest of his days in prison.

"As for you, you're not out of the woods yet. There remains the sticky matter of fleeing jurisdiction. But I suspect that too may be dropped eventually. The important thing is that the Los Angeles authorities have confirmed the substance of your account. They have agreed to allow you to return under your own recognizance."

"I don't care about that. Have you spoken to Tallahassee?"

"Yes, it's all taken care of. They have confirmed that Ms. Stewart is safe. The police and campus security are maintaining an unobtrusive safety cordon around her.

"Mr. Rouse has been interrogated on this point. He has said there is no accomplice in Florida, that he invented him to get you to do his bidding. But we're not taking his word for anything. LAPD has impounded his cell and home phone records and there are no calls to the 805 area code—or anywhere else in Florida, for that matter. So it looks like that threat was a fabrication. But we'll keep watch over Ms. Stewart until we're certain. Is that sufficient?" he asked, clearly expecting to be showered with thanks.

But Angel had stopped listening to him about halfway through his peroration. Instead she was standing over by the glass, waving happily to Oops, who had just been walked into the building by a pair of paramedics. Oops wasn't waving back. His chest was heavily bandaged and he was having trouble just keeping his head up, but he smiled when he spotted Angel.

"I just got off the phone with Mr. Langdon from your record label," the station chief droned on. "He and Ms. Ross are flying out here in a private jet to take you home. Now, if you'll excuse me, I have to see to the transfer of Mr. Rouse."

I watched as he walked across the floor, where a delegation of state and local police brass waited by the front desk. All of their eyes were trained on the office, trying to get a glimpse of Angel.

I turned to face my client. She was leaning back languidly against the chief's desk, looking at me with the sleepy, smoky bedroom eyes I had first seen in Charlie's kitchen. There were probably posters of her posed just like that on ten thousand teenage boys' bedroom walls. But I had never seen them.

"So," she said, patting the top of the desk, "*now* do you want to have sex?"

LET *NEW YORK TIMES* BESTSELLING AUTHOR

DENNIS LEHANE

TAKE YOU TO THE EDGE OF DARKNESS

Sacred
0-380-72629-7
$7.99/$10.99 Can.

Mystic River
0-380-73185-1
$7.99/10.99 Can.

Darkness, Take My Hand
0-380-72628-9
$7.99/$10.99 Can.

Prayers for Rain
0-380-73036-7
$7.99/$10.99 Can.

A Drink Before the War
0-380-72623-8
$7.99/$10.99 Can.

Gone, Baby, Gone
0-380-73035-9
$7.99/$10.99 Can.

Shutter Island
0-380-73186-X
$7.99/$10.99 Can

Available wherever books are sold or call 1-800-331-3761 to order.

HarperAudio
An Imprint of HarperCollinsPublishers
www.harpercollins.com

AuthorTracker
www.AuthorTracker.com

DL 0204

HarperTorch *An Imprint of HarperCollinsPublishers* www.harpercollins.com

Felonious fun with *New York Times* bestselling grand master

LAWRENCE

BLOCK

The Bernie Rhodenbarr Mysteries

THE BURGLAR WHO
LIKED TO QUOTE KIPLING
0-06-073125-7 ■ $7.50 US ■ $9.99 Can
Things don't go according to plan when Bernie
wakes up in the apartment of his client's female
go-between to find the book he has stolen gone,
the lady dead, a smoking gun in his hand and the
cops at the door.

THE BURGLAR ON THE PROWL
0-06-103098-8 ■ $7.50 US ■ $9.99 Can
Bernie's up to his burgling neck in big trouble.
Again. And this time it includes his arrest, no less
than four murders, and more outrageous coinci-
dences than any self-preserving felon should ever
be required to tie together.

BURGLARS CAN'T BE CHOOSERS
The First Burglar Book
0-06-058255-3 ■ $6.99 US ■ $9.99 Can
Bernie has made his share of mistakes. Like
accepting a burglary assignment from a stranger
to retrieve an item from a rich man's apartment.
Like still being there when the cops arrive. Like
having a freshly slain corpse in the next room, and
no proof that Bernie isn't the killer.

Available wherever books are sold
or please call 1-800-331-3761 to order.

AuthorTracker
www.AuthorTracker.com   LBB 030

GRIPPING SUSPENSE FROM AWARD-WINNING AUTHOR

G.M.FORD

BLACK RIVER
0-380-81621-0 • $6.99 US • $9.99 Can

The river of lies, corruption, and murder surrounding the trial of a crime boss as well as his dearest friend Meg's near-fatal "accident" runs much deeper and more dangerous than even rogue journalist Frank Corso anticipated.

FURY
0-380-80421-2 • $6.99 US • $9.99 Can

Slow, sheltered Leanne Samples trusts no one but Frank Corso to tell the world that her courtroom testimony that put Walter Leroy "Trashman" Himes on Death Row was a lie.

A BLIND EYE
0-380-81622-9 • $6.99 US • $9.99 Can

Beneath the rotting floorboards of an abandoned shed are human bones—lots of them—the last thing Frank Corso and Meg Dougherty expected to find when they took shelter from a vicious Wisconsin blizzard.

AND NEW IN HARDCOVER

RED TIDE
0-06-055480-0 • $23.95 US • $36.95 Can

The further Frank Corso investigates, the closer he comes to unraveling the chilling truth—that an apparent simple murder is actually a prelude to a terrorist act of mass destruction.

Available wherever books are sold or please call 1-800-331-3761 to order.

www.AuthorTracker.com

GMF1 0704

PERENNIAL DARK ALLEY

First Cut: Award-winning author Peter Robinson probes the darkest regions of the human mind and soul in this clever, twisting tale of crime and revenge.   0-06-073535-X

Night Visions: A young lawyer's shocking dreams become terribly real in this chilling, beautifully written debut thriller by Thomas Fahy.   0-06-059462-4

Get Shorty: Elmore Leonard takes a mobster to Hollywood—where the women are gorgeous, the men are corrupt, and making it big isn't all that different from making your bones.   0-06-077709-5

Be Cool: Elmore Leonard takes Chili Palmer into the world of rock stars, pop divas, and hip-hop gangsters—all the stuff that makes big box office. 0-06-077706-0

Eye of the Needle: For the first time in trade paperback, comes one of legendary suspense author Ken Follett's most compelling classics. 0-06-074815-X

More Than They Could Chew: Rob Roberge tells the story of Nick Ray, a man whose addictions (alcohol, kinky sex, questionable friends) might only be cured by weaning him from oxygen. 0-06-074280-1

Coming soon!
Men from Boys: A short story collection featuring some of the true masters of crime fiction, including Dennis Lehane, Lawrence Block, and Michael Connelly. These stories examine what it means to be a man amid cardsharks, revolvers, and shallow graves.
0-06-076285-3 • On Sale April 2005

(📱 AuthorTracker)

Don't miss the next book by your favorite author.
Sign up now for AuthorTracker by visiting
www.AuthorTracker.com

An Imprint of HarperCollins*Publishers*
www.harpercollins.com

DKA 010

NOVELS of SUSPENSE featuring
CHIEF INSPECTOR ALAN BANKS from
INTERNATIONALLY BESTSELLING AUTHOR

PETER
ROBINSON

A DEDICATED MAN
0-380-71645-3 • $7.50 US

A NECESSARY END
0-380-71946-0 • $7.50 US

BLOOD AT THE ROOT
0-380-79476-4 • $7.50 US

PAST REASON HATED
0-380-73328-5 • $7.50 US

GALLOWS VIEW
0-380-71400-0 • $7.50 US

COLD IS THE GRAVE
0-380-80935-4 • $6.99 US

WEDNESDAY'S CHILD
0-380-82049-8 • $7.50 US

And new in trade paperback
THE FIRST CUT
0-06-073535-X • $13.95 US

Available wherever books are sold
or please call 1-800-331-3761 to order.

AuthorTracker
www.AuthorTracker.com

ROB1 1004

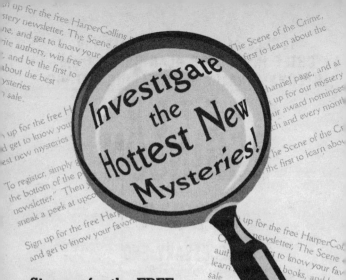

Investigate the Hottest New Mysteries!

Sign up for the FREE HarperCollins monthly mystery newsletter,

The Scene of the Crime,

and get to know your favorite authors, win free books, and be the first to learn about the best new mysteries going on sale.

To register, simply go to www.HarperCollins.com, visit our mystery channel page, and at the bottom of the page, enter your email address where it states "Sign up for our mystery newsletter." Then you can tap into monthly Hot Reads, check out our award nominees, sneak a peek at upcoming titles, and discover the best whodunits each and every month.

Get to know the magnificent mystery authors of HarperCollins and sign up today!

MYN 020